NOT FAR FROM DREAMLAND

VAL HENNESSY

First published in 2015 by Quartet Books Limited
A member of the Namara Group
27 Goodge Street, London W1T 2LD
Copyright © Val Hennessy 2015
The right of Val Hennessy to be identified
as the author of this work has been asserted
by her in accordance with the
Copyright, Designs and Patents Act, 1988
A catalogue record for this book
is available from the British Library
ISBN 978 0 7043 7387 7
Typeset by Josh Bryson
Printed and bound in Great Britain by
T J International Ltd, Padstow, Cornwall

The author and publisher are grateful for permission to quote the following:

'Oh, I Wish I'd Looked After Me Teeth' from *The Works: The Classic
Collection* by Pam Ayres, published by BBC Books, reproduced by
permission of Sheil Land Associates

'Worry', by Roger McGough, which appears in *It Never Rains* (Penguin)

To the memory of the woods and hop-fields of Cobham,
Kent now buried beneath tarmac and the Hi-Speed rail track.

JANUARY 2012

I do like a nice sausage sandwich. I like it with all the burnt scrapings from the pan plus a dollop of brown sauce. In fact I'm enjoying a sausage sandwich as I write this. Tonks is the name. Ronald Tonks. Worrier by nature, up khaki creek by circumstance. And here I am writing my Anxiety Management journal as suggested by my Anxiety Management counsellor, Andy Bean. More about him later. What I need is a good laugh. Matter of fact I had a little chuckle yesterday over a birthday card that arrived (three months late) from my vintage book-seller friend. It had an illustration of a droopy-looking dog sitting by a post box, tongue hanging out, and the words *SORRY I'M LATE* in red glitter. Inside was scrawled:

TO RONALD:
You're seventy-one today
A year beyond the barrier
and what was once a magic flute
is now a water-carrier.

Too true! Don't remind me. I've enough worries as it is without getting into a state about my lack of action in the magic flute department. I worry too much, that's a fact. The last time I visited my GP – Doctor Ng – who looks more like a Bangkok lap-dancer than a GP – she told me that I'm one of the 'worried well'. So, as I told her, what's NOT to worry about as you approach the final curtain? Things can only go downhill - cardiac arrest, cancer, Alzheimer's, Parkinson's, stroke, incontinence, prostate problems... you name it. If that's not enough to worry about there's also hypothermia, emphysema, losing your keys, breaking your specs, gas bills, sorting out income tax, too much salt, not being able to get the hang of on-line banking, not being able to get the hang of computers, full stop. I can't tell the Internet from a mosquito net. When I do stop worrying for five minutes and settle down with a fag and a can of Scrumpy Jack, some radio or TV doom-monger starts sounding off about fags and booze which cause untold havoc to the brain, heart, lungs, oesophagus, colon and what have you.

So, yes, I'm a worrier. My prostate has been hanging over my head for the last year. It keeps me awake at night. I'd never given my blasted prostate a thought until I read about it in one of Doc Ng's hand-outs. Good grief! When I asked Doc Ng for some happy pills to take my mind off my worries she wagged her finger at me and, with her beady eyes dancing about behind her rimless specs, warned me that tranquilisers are the start of the slippery slope. Stone me. The way she started carrying on, anyone would think I was pleading for some crystal meth. She insisted that there's nothing much wrong with me apart from my flat feet which, I might add, are not to be sniffed at. With any luck, and the odd corn-plaster, they should keep right on to the end of the road. She then dished out a Quit Kit to discourage smoking and advised me to do physical jerks, eat vegetables, look on the bright side and count my blessings.

Blessings? All right. I'm lucky to have a roof over my head. I own my bungalow, The Shack, inherited from an aunt. The Shack faces the sea at Saltmarsh on the Thames estuary. For six months of the year it is hell here with The Shack shuddering as the north-east wind whips across the Kent marshes and howls through the gaps in my rotting window frames. The sea comes slapping up the shingle and sleet, pebbles and horizontal rain rattle against the windows, strips of roofing felt peel off and land all over the sparse clumps of dead grass aka the garden. My two-bar coal-effect heater (St Mildred's Hospice, £4) fights a losing battle against the icy Siberian draughts. I've lived alone for twelve years, since my wife aka The Nutcracker, skedaddled. She slammed out of The Shack after twenty years of marriage, shrieking: 'What did you ever do for ME? Leave the toilet seat up? Cut your toenails all over the carpet? Ruddy men! Wake up and smell the soddin' coffee, Tonks! We're finished. Good riddance!'

What did I ever do for HER? I worked my fingers to the bone that's what. I was proprietor of Saltmarsh's second-hand and vintage bookshop TONKS BOOKS. Admittedly the takings could have been better, but I did once find a first edition – signed – of John Lennon's 1965 *Spaniard in the Works* and a number of Captain W.E. Johns 1932 *Biggles* books which I sold via my vintage bookseller friend for a pretty penny. You have to keep up to speed in the second-hand book trade.

'Bloody books all over the place, collecting dust... I'm out of here Tonks, you hopeless bastard,' the Nutcracker had bawled. A rock came through the window as she disappeared into the sunset. Once she gets the bit between her teeth there's no stopping her. That woman never appreciated my finer points. She never took to books. What I say is thank the Lord (or some unfathomable higher source incomprehensible to the human brain) for books. Books are my escape and inspiration. And the good news is that here in Saltmarsh it's bonanza time for bookworms. The charity shops are snowed under, stacked floor to ceiling with fantastic books, often brand new, five for a pound. What with the arrival of poncy hi-tech gadgets – e-books, tablets, computers et cetera – no one these days apart from us old-timers, wants real, old-fashioned books cluttering up their homes. The shelves at The Shack sag and sometimes fall off the wall under the weight of my extensive book collection.

So here I am, huddled in front of my two-bar, coal effect, playing my Leonard Cohen album. Whew! There's a voice that tells a life story. Let's hear it for Leonard Cohen, bard of the bedsit. What a genius. Now going on eighty, his croaking, doom-laden vocals can still make me cavort across the lino and jiggle my geriatric hips. Leonard Cohen's songs have been the backing track of my life. Yeah! 'Looks – like – freedom – but – it – feels – like – death / It's – something – in – between – I – guess / It's – Closing - Time…' to quote from one of the bard's great LPs (RSPCA, 50p) Whew! Yeah again! Whoever said it better? Leonard Cohen looks old age in the face, offers it a fag and croaks out consolation for us old codgers hanging in there with a song in our hearts and a booster seat in our armchairs.

For company I have my dog, Bingo, a wire-haired dachshund with very sparse hair. He develops bald patches down his back and along his sides. Not a good look for a dog. You don't feel much like patting a bald dog. The vet diagnosed Seasonal Alopecia Disorder in dogs (SADD). This information cost me £40. Vets don't come cheap. The diagnosis was followed up by two blood tests and a skin biopsy. Another £85. All of which merely confirmed the vet's original opinion. This took a hefty chunk from my state pension. I never gave private pensions a thought during the golden Tonks Books years. Mad fool.

I worry about Bingo going bald all over. I worry about myself going bald all over. Apart from baldness worries plus my previously mentioned long list of worries, I worry about my wobbly teeth. Or choking to death on a sausage sandwich. Or breaking a hip and winding up in a mixed-sex geriatric ward where none of the nurses speak English. Or dropping dead at The Shack and no one noticing my absence for weeks during which time Bingo will have gnawed through my extremities.

As the poet Roger McGough wrote – hitting the nail on the head as always:

Where would we be without the worry?
It helps keep the brain occupied,
DOING doesn't take your mind of things.
I've tried.

It was Doc Ng who suggested I get myself assessed for Anxiety Management sessions.

'The trouble with you, Mr Tonks, is that you have chronic hypochondria,' she said.

'Oh no! Not that as well?' I groaned. Yet one more thing to worry about…

As for the Anxiety Management assessment – well, what a farce. The assessor handed me a form to fill in. This included a section headed SEXUAL ORIENTATION. The assessee (Yours Truly) had to tick one of five option boxes which were headed HETROSEXUAL, HOMOSEXUAL, BISEXUAL, OTHER, DON'T KNOW. There were also 'further comment' boxes next to the option boxes. What is OTHER I wondered? Paedophile? Zoo-ophile? Necrophile? Vampire? What idiot is going to own up to that on an official form? I debated briefly whether to tick the DON'T KNOW box and put 'can't remember it's been so long' in the comment box. Or whether to tick the OTHER box and put 'Celibate, due to force of circumstances' in the further comment box. But then I started worrying that the assessor might think I'm being frivolous and not taking Anxiety

Management seriously so I ticked the HETROSEXUAL box and further commented 'if given the chance'.

The Anxiety Management counsellor, Andy Bean, recommended that I write this journal, detailing my worries, activities (what activities?), literary observations, philosophical musings, lines of poetry that may have caught my imagination and everyday concerns. He told me that seventy is the new fifty. Ha! If this is so, then I've been missing out. According to Andy, Britain is heaving with old-timers jumping out of helicopters, running with bulls, trekking across Antarctica, bungee jumping, paragliding, marathon running, abseiling down Big Ben, jogging to John O'Groats, canoeing across the Atlantic, white-water rafting, roller-blading, motorbike riding on the Wall of Death and so forth. All I can say is that you don't find any of these dare devil veterans in Saltmarsh, where a toddle to the doctor's or a coffee and cake at Age Concern is a big adventure.

Oops! The phone is ringing. Bingo starts barking. Sure to be my mum. Heart sinks.

'Hello, Mum? How are you getting on with—'

'Ronald? Can you hear me, Son? Thought you should know that an article in my paper says ONE sausage a day can cause cancer. ONE A DAY! Are you listening? Two rashers of bacon are even worse. Highly carcinogenic. Don't ever eat bacon again, son. Deadly! And watch out for pancreatic cancer, "the silent killer". Must go. Milk's boiling over. Ta-ta.'

We all have our crosses to bear. My mother is mine. Ninety-four and still roaring around on her mobility scooter. A slave to her *Daily Mail*. Rather hard of hearing these days, but not soft of voice.

But back to my anxiety problems. My new-year horoscope hasn't filled me with optimism. But it certainly hits the nail on the head by magnifying the limitations of my solitary existence. Here are my horoscope predictions for 2012 in a *Daily Mail* TV guide I found at Doc Ng's surgery. My own comments in brackets:

LIBRA

Still sitting in the same room? (Yes. And it's still ruddy damp and freezing.)

Still thinking about the same situation? (Yes. 'Looks like freedom and it feels like death,' to quote Leonard Cohen.)

Still eating the same kind of food? (Yes. Porridge. Sausage sandwiches.)

Still getting phone-calls from the same folk? (No one ever calls except my nonagenarian mum.)

Still wrestling with the same problems? (Yes you could say that, though 'wrestling' is putting it a bit strong.)

Still up against the same challenges? (Yes. Can't make ends meet, dog bald, prostate getting bigger.)

Still looking forward to the same bright ray of hope on the horizon? (Have almost given up to be honest.)

Well, enjoy all that consistency and familiarity while it lasts. 2012 has just begun. You will soon have to start getting used to a lot of positive changes. Things really are about to get significantly different.

Really? I blinkin' well hope so. What do you do when you're too young to act old and too old to act young? *Positive changes* would be very welcome, no two ways.

Oh no! My toenails need trimming again. What a palaver. Can't bend down due to bad back, need my reading specs to focus, I lean forward, specs fall off, worry I might miss the toenail and slice off my ruddy toe… just one more thing to worry about. That's one of the drawbacks of living alone.

No one to cut your toenails. Such an everyday undertaking could turn out to be fatal if your specs fall off every time you bend down. Speaking of which, that great writer, Kingsley Amis, tackled the topic in *The Old Devils* (War on Want, 50p). His character, Peter, is forbidden to cut his toenails in the house by his Nutcracker-like wife, Muriel. She makes him go outside to cut them, sitting well away from the house on a distant garden seat. So, there is poor old Peter, out on the back lawn, trimming away in peace, where 'his clippings can fly free and fly they bloody well did, especially the ones that came crunching off his big toe – massive enough to have brought down a sparrow on the wing.' Brilliant! Blinkin' hilarious, eh? Good old Kingsley Amis. Always makes me laugh.

But toenails apart – what a turn up! My stars were right. The horoscope said things are about to get 'significantly different' and they suddenly have.I found a *Shell Guide to Kent* in fairly good nick (War on Want, £2) and flogged it to my vintage book seller friend for £50, FIFTY quid! Straightaway I called in on Jinxie Wicks, my friend (strictly platonic) who lives on the caravan site along the road, to tell her the good tidings. She suggested I treat myself to a dental check-up with my windfall. DENTAL CHECK-UP? What a party-pooper! No, I said, you and me, Jinxie Wicks, are going on the razzle. Matter of fact due to a minor mishap it's a wonder I'm still alive and able to record these events. When I arrived at Jinxie Wicks' static caravan, she handed me a bottle before disappearing into her kitchenette. I unscrewed the cap, took a swig, choked, spluttered, my tongue turned black. Jinxie Wicks rushed in, banged me on the back, shouting: 'You stupid git, it's for the dog. It's a hair restorer remedy for male baldness. It was advertised on the telly and I thought it might solve Bingo's hair-loss problem. You're supposed to rub it on and massage it into the skin twice a day.'

Well, we had a good laugh about it once I'd got my breath back. I've been rubbing the hair restorer on Bingo twice daily for a fortnight but no hair has started sprouting as yet. I live in hope. Hope the palms of my hands don't start turning hairy.

Anyway, instead of a dental check-up I booked a table for lunch at the Plucked Duck where they do a two-course pensioners' special for £10. Jinxie Wicks wanted her friend, Daphne, to come too, so we made a merry little trio, Daphne being a great girl, a widow, and a bit on the posh side.

The three of us entered the Plucked Duck to find a lunch-time celebration of some sort in full swing. Tables pushed together, pink helium balloons tugging on strings towards the ceiling, paper hats and so forth. A bevvy of beauties – glamour girl types with very profuse heads of hair, spider-leg eyelashes, too much lipstick, blue stuff on their eyelids, fancy frocks, well boosted chests – were enjoying a right raucous knees-up. Turns out they were celebrating a transgender group reunion. The waiter told us, sotto voce, that they were from a Kent male genital realignment group. Talk about knocking back the booze. At one point they all stood up, arms linked, stamping on the floor and singing, 'Sometimes it's hard to be a woman' – like a Welsh male voice choir wearing high heels. Hats off to them. Say it proud, say it loud and so forth.

Not that everyone shares my liberal attitude. I read in the paper recently about a pub landlord who is being sued by a group of male to female transsexuals. He upset them by ordering them out of his pub after one of them used the ladies loos. The transsexuals claim that they were victims of sexual discrimination. In his defence the landlord said, (and I'm quoting from the paper): 'Four of them still have their male parts, which I would say is highly inappropriate in the ladies loo.' Though HOW he knew this fact is not explained. The mind boggles.

But back to lunch. We tucked into Thai fish-cakes, and sesame pak choi. What happened to good old-fashioned steak and kidney pie and Brussels sprouts? For afters we had something called Banana Surprise, the surprise being that mine had no banana in it. As we nibbled our cheese-and-biscuits one of the genital re-alignment group stood waving a newspaper.

'Listen up, girls,' she announced. Then, in a booming bass voice, read out the results of a recent poll that's discovered that one in five men don't change their underpants every day.

'Oh no, not while I'm eating my lunch,' said Daphne. Everyone (except me and Daphne) roared. The genital re-alignment group whooped and drummed their high heels on the floorboards. It was like being in a Ken Russell orgy sequence.

'Knickers worn twice are not very nice,' shouted Jinxie Wicks, entering into the spirit of things.More whoops and high-heeled stamping. The ringleader, whose impressive head of hair had become a bit skew-whiff, shouted that the same poll found that 16 per cent of men do not wash their clothes until they are noticeably dirty.

'Too much information!' murmured Daphne who, as I mentioned, is a bit posh, then she treated our trio to an Irish coffee.

'Call me the last of the Big Spenders,' she joked. I'd call her a bit of all-right. She looks like the Queen Mother looked in her heyday, with varifocal specs. A man would happily change his Y-fronts every day for Daphne.

After lunch I said 'Cheerio' to the girls and it was back to The Shack. And here I am trying to keep warm, Bingo on my lap in front of the coal-effect, a can of Scrumpy Jack to hand and having a bit of a Leonard Cohen moment. 'Like a bird on a wire...' et cetera, et cetera.

Speaking of birds on a wire the blasted seagulls are restless today flapping about and screaming. It's like a Hitchcock movie out there. Pesky things have become almost human. I met this chap from Torquay who once had a seagull in his garden, called Percy, who became a family favourite and arrived every day for eighteen years to be fed. Then one day Percy saw a For Sale sign in the front garden and dropped dead with shock. Do I hear you say that seagulls don't live that long? Oh yes they do. The longest living herring gull on record reached a remarkable 32 years and one month. They have also learnt to aim their droppings on target. I saw, with my own eyes, a seagull deliberately score a direct hit on Bingo who was outside guarding his food bowl. The thieving scavenger flapped away with a fiendish glint in its eyes, screeching in triumph like a footballer who has just scored a goal. Bingo was in shock, splattered and trembling.

Blimey it's cold. People in this sort of weather drop dead of hypothermia. The thought of which has started me worrying about my funeral arrangements. Where to have my ashes scattered and what have you. The Kent of my youth, the woods and bosky by-ways where I once went bird-nesting, hop-picking, bike riding and rolling over in the clover, if you get my meaning, would be my first choice but it's now buried under the High-Speed rail link to London. A relevant news item about funeral arrangements recently caught my attention. A Kent woman had left instructions in her will to be buried in the back garden of her semi-detached bungalow. The neighbours are up in arms.

One neighbour said that she was trying not to be a wimp about it, that she had in fact got along fine with her late neighbour, but drew the line at having her decomposing a few yards away from her decking and barbecue station. Talk about a classic case of not in my backyard! Her complaints to

11

the council met with the response that the deceased's choice of burial site is perfectly legal and there is nothing she can do about it. Apart from move I suppose. Incidentally, I learnt from a magazine in Doc Ng's waiting-room, that TV star Larry Hagman, whose four-bottle-a-day champagne habit has resulted in a liver transplant, has announced that when he kicks the bucket he wants to be fed through a wood chipper and spread as fertiliser over a wheat field. Then he wants a cake to be baked from the fertilised wheat crop and shared amongst his pals. Way to go, as the youngsters say.

The phone just rang. First time for a fortnight. The dentist's receptionist informs me that my annual check-up is overdue. Three years overdue in fact. I remember the days when check-ups were free. Nowadays they cost half my weekly stipend. No wonder us senior Saltmarshians can't bite a banana without our gums bleeding. We all walk about flashing grey teeth with botched fillings that slant at crazy angles like mini-Stonehenges. Even the Queen Mother – expense being no object in her case – wound up with dingy teeth. It happens to the best of us, despite all that wealth.

Which reminds me of a Spike Milligan poem:

English teeth, hero's teeth
Hear them click and clack
Let's sing a song of praise to them
Three cheers for the brown, grey and black

Spike must have got his inspiration after a visit to Saltmarsh.

Whoops! Just knocked my Scrumpy Jack over and Bingo is licking it up. Meanwhile my social life is hotting up. Thanks to Doc Ng's intervention I am now a member of Saltmarsh Pensioners' Anxiety Management (SPAM) group.

Fortnightly meetings take place at the Portakabin opposite the car park, aka, the Saltmarsh Community Hall.

There are eight or so SPAM regulars, including Jinxie Wicks. SPAM leader, Andy, has shiny teeth too big for his face, tinted horn-rims, vertical ginger hair and many years to go before dodgy water-works and bungalow-knees start making his life a misery. SPAM members sit in a circle on hard chairs that do my back in.

Yesterday's session went with a swing.

'Hi everyone! Greetings!' says Andy hearty, fresh-faced, well-meaning, 'What has three hundred legs and seven teeth? The front row at a Rolling Stones concert. Boom boom.'

A few wheezy laughs. Someone yells out, 'You're being a bit ageist there, Andy…'

And Andy says, 'Aw, come on, lighten up… Is anyone ready to share? Len! Len? Welcome! Good to see you again, how about you starting the ball rolling?'

So Len – grog-blossoms all over his nose, and clearly a man who exceeds his 25 units a week if ever I saw one, says that he's had a bad fortnight. Very bad. His overwhelming fear of flying is ruining his life. It stops him from visiting his daughter in Australia. Andy pulls his intensely caring face, makes a tube of his lips so that his mouth looks like a cat's bottom and slowly, ponderously nods the vertical ginger hair – nod, nod, nod. He asks Len to identify exactly what he is frightened of.

Len takes a deep, shuddering breath and replies, 'Well, the plane bloody crashing for a start. Or the wings dropping off. Or a bomb exploding on board. Or the engines cutting out. Or a bunch of nutcase hijackers storming the cockpit… things like that, Andy.'

Andy tells Len to consider carefully and analyse each of his fears one at a time. He reminds us all that statistically it is a thousand times safer to travel by plane than to travel by car.

Someone shouts, 'Not when my wife is driving it ain't'.

A muted chuckle or two reverberates around the Portakabin.

Len reaches into his trouser pocket and produces a crumpled newspaper cutting headed 'TERROR ALERT'. This is a report about a pilot getting locked in the WC on board a Chatauqua Airlines plane as it approached New York. By bad luck the passenger who went to find help for the pilot had a strong middle-eastern appearance and accent. As he tried to enter the cockpit, the co-pilot, fearing a terror attack, raised the alarm.

With the jet in a holding pattern above La Guardia Airport the co-pilot informed air control, 'the Captain disappeared in the back and, uh, someone with a thick foreign accent is trying to access the cockpit.'

You couldn't make it up, could you? At this point the helpful passenger, still outside the cockpit door, again tried to explain that the pilot was locked in the lavatory. The co-pilot, fearing that this was a terrorist ploy, didn't dare let him in. By the time the pilot managed to force the lavatory door and make his way back to the cockpit, fighter jets had been put on alert in case of a terrorist attack. FBI agents and police met the jet when it landed at La Guardia.

Len says, 'Knowing my luck, I'd be sure to get locked in the toilet if ever I went on a plane. Or the toilet would fall through the floor with me sitting on it and plummet into the sea.'

We SPAM members all go, 'Whew! Blimey.'

Andy says, 'We hear what you say, Len.'

Len says, 'Fact is, Andy, to me fear of flying is logical. What I can't understand is why all plane passengers don't start screaming and go into melt-down the minute the engines start revving and they fasten their seat belts.'

Good point, Len. How these massive metal items stay up there is beyond me. Then a female SPAM member tells us about a Fear of Flying course she attended at Gatwick. It was cancelled on week three because the tutor, a handsome young pilot, according to the female SPAM member, was killed in a crash when the plane he was piloting fell out of the air during a freak storm.

This little anecdote has Len rushing into the Portakabin WC muttering, 'Trouble with the waterworks, folks.' He returns a few minutes later exuding a powerful whiff of alcohol. We all start rabbiting on about plane crashes, bird strikes, Lockerbie, turbulence, the Concorde disaster, the Twin Towers, volcanic ash clogging up the engines…

Andy holds up his hands and shouts, 'Wooah! Calm down folks – remember, you can get killed crossing the road.' He then tells the group to take on board the fact that most human beings go through life looking on the bright side. This is known as the Optimist Bias – the *It won't happen to me* syndrome. Andy says that the human brain is hard-wired to look on the bright side. He says that most of us (but not me and Len) live in a state of denial about planes crashing, the inevitability of death, global warming, and so forth.

Jinxie Wicks chips in that she wishes she could live in a state of denial about losing her looks. 'Looking like your grandmother is bad enough, even worse is when you start looking like your grandfather.'

She tells the group – or 'shares' as Andy would say – that yesterday morning she walked into the shower, caught sight of herself in the mirror and started screaming. She was holding her head between her hands with her mouth hanging open just like Munch's *The Scream*.

Her neighbour rushed in and said, 'What's up Jinx?'

And Jinxie Wicks moaned, 'I look like an old age pensioner.'

Her neighbour replied, 'Well you ARE an old age pensioner, so what?'

Since then Jinxie Wicks says that she's been worrying non-stop about her looks.

To be honest I can't help thinking that the old girl has left it a bit late in the day to START worrying – darn fine woman that she is, and a great cook, her pork faggots in onion gravy being one of her triumphs. Then Andy says it's time to put the kettle on and to hand round the mince-pies left over from Christmas. Len tells us about a 92 year old neighbour who has been refused a bus pass because he has no documents to prove his eligibility. Bureaucracy gone mad.

Bad start to the day. Get up, go into the kitchen, padding about in bare feet and – well – Bingo has done what a dog has to do. Brown stuff squelching between my toes. I hop across the lino, skid, land flat, arms and legs flailing like a beetle on its back. It doesn't help my ongoing lower lumbar problems. Bloody hell. Ouch! Damn dog. Stagger through to the bathroom. No hot water. Wash my feet. Perishing cold. Apply disinfectant, then go back to tackle the kitchen floor. Bingo gets a wallop with a rolled up newspaper. He skulks under the table. I shove him out the back. Almost puts me off my porridge and sausage sandwich.

One hour later I've recovered somewhat, Bingo is looking sheepish, whining in his basket. I'm just about to put my sausages in the pan. Phone rings. It's my mum. Heart sinks.

'Morning Mum, better make it brief because I'm shortly setting off to the gym for my Pulmonary Exercise session – '

'Wha-a-a-t?! Did you say "gym"?—'

'Along at the gym, down by the—'

'Gawd almighty Son, you're taking your life in your hands, going to the gym, only this morning I was reading that—'

'The exercises are intended to keep me fit, Mum, and improve my—'

'—at one London gym a world famous microbiologist found 132 million bugs in "an area the size of a 2p coin"!—'

'Blimey, Mum, how can one man count 132 million bugs on—'

'—they also found that the average pair of trainers has 76 times more fungi on them than a toilet seat! AND they found billions – yes, BILLIONS of bacteria lurking on towels! Even worse – the sweat-soaked exercise mats were crawling with the herpes virus and worse—'

'Well, Mum, you're certainly making me think twice, but—'

'—listen to this, son – one teaspoon of warm whirlpool water contains 2.17 million bugs, which can cause hot-tub lung—'

'Point taken, Mum, but—'

'—it is caused by the bugs that live in slime found in water-pipes! So steer clear, my boy, avoid going anywhere near the gym if you want to stay in the land of the living…'

Hot-tub lung? Slime in water pipes? Ye Gods. No way could I tackle my porridge and a sausage sandwich after that.

So here we are at the end of the month, and the Charles Dickens's bicentenary has kicked off on TV and Radio. No doubt we are in for a year of top hats, cobbled streets, urchins, mutton-chop whiskers, timber frame cottages and cockney characters who can't pronounce their 'V's, who say 'werry' 'wicious' 'wittle' and 'wolcano'. I'm all for it myself. Now there was a man – a genius – who knew how to put pen to paper and I speak as someone who studied English literature for two years at the SnodlandTech evening classes (long defunct). In flights of sentimental fancy I picture Dickens popping a cork or two and hitting it off with Lionel Bart (RIP) in the hereafter. There are many people, Jinxie Wicks for one, who are of the opinion that Lionel Bart's musical is better than the book - more pacey and easier to follow. The same could be said for the *Jesus Christ Superstar* musical – heavy-going book, but toe-tapping musical.

Not many people know that Dickens was a great dog lover. This week I attended a talk (free) – Dickens and Dogs – at the SPAM Portakabin where a university professor filled the audience (all five of us) in on Dickens' canine companions. These included a white Pomeranian, Mrs Bouncer, a bloodhound, Turk, and a St Bernard, Linda. In 1865 Turk was run over by a train. Dickens' Newfoundlands, Don and Bumble, enjoyed regular swims in the River Medway. His Irish bloodhound, Sultan was so aggressive that he had to be constantly muzzled. Sultan was the scourge of the Kent countryside around Gad's Hill. He tried to eat Mrs Bouncer. He did actually eat one of Dickens' favourite cats. He savaged a local child, and had to be put down (a single shot to the head) by Dickens' gardener. Dickens' cook (and note how well Dickens had done for himself from humble beginnings, what with his gardeners, cooks, housemaids, etc.) would prepare all the dogs' dinners once a day, dishing them out on separate plates, lining them up in a row. One day Bumble sneaked in just as they'd been lined up and wolfed the lot. His stomach swelled up, and distended to such an extent that he became unconscious – rather how I felt after a recent blow-out at the Saltmarsh Golden Chapatti – and had to be revived by being held under the Gad's Hill water pump. It's amazing the stuff these intellectual academics come up with. Quite amazing.

And speaking of dogs, an interesting item in the newspaper headed 'How Fido Causes Three Rows a Week' caught my eye. Only three? Not in my experience! According to research, man's best friend is responsible for plenty of household friction. Canine conflict causes 2,000 family arguments during a dog's lifetime. 17% of dog owners questioned admitted that one family member had slept in the spare bed, or on the floor following a dog dispute. Speaking for myself I believe that the behaviour of one particular dog, a spaniel, was the final nail in the coffin of my marriage.

Her name is Bubbles. The Nutcracker has booked us a 'weekend break' at a bijou country hotel. Bubbles comes too. While the Nutcracker and I are downstairs in the dining-room stuffing ourselves on 'locally sourced cuisine' Bubbles, alone in the en-suite, chomps her way through two toilet rolls and a box of cotton wool balls. At about midnight, when all is silent, Bubbles starts being sick, spewing up in a very explosive, full-volume way. Her loud retchings, which sound like the air-locked blasts you hear when Dyno-Rod unblock the drains, and her prolonged vomiting noises reverberate through the night.

'It's YOUR fault,' squawks the Nutcracker. 'If you had left Bubbles in the car she wouldn't be suffering as she is now.'

MY fault? Bubbles eats two toilet rolls and a box of cotton wool balls and it's MY fault? Meanwhile Bubbles' stereo-effects are getting louder.

'And I'M not cleaning it up' adds the Nutcracker. Someone in the room next door bangs on the wall. Someone in the room on the other side does the same.

'Good grief! Talk about embarrassing! I hope the other guests aren't thinking it's ME,' I say, mopping up as best I can.

'You'd better take Bubbles outside to sort herself out' snaps the Nutcracker.

Out I go, hen-pecked idiot like Joe Gargery in *Great Expectations*, in my pyjamas, in the pitch dark, freezing cold. Bubbles starts wagging her tail, rolling on her back with her legs kicking and lolloping around the grounds emitting playful little barks. I go to take her back inside and – oh no! Calamity! – I'm locked out. The Nutcracker meanwhile has put her ear plugs in (precaution against my snoring) and fallen asleep. Snoring herself, I might add. As the old adage goes, 'laugh and the world laughs with you, snore and you sleep alone…' Anyway, it's four a.m. and I'm stuck outside in my flimsy jim-jams and a pair of those fluffy white flip-flops they provide in posh hotels. No car keys, no door key, no room key. I take shelter in a lean-to shed and huddle up with Bubbles until six a.m. (no wonder I've succumbed to a wheezy chest in my senior years) when a porter appears in the reception area, and switches on the light.

'Dearie me! Good gracious, Mr Tonks! With your delightful doggy!' he says, aghast to see me standing at the front entrance, lips blue, pyjamas sopping wet, covered in dew and condensation.

'But WHY, Mr Tonks didn't you ring the Night Porter's bell?'

I couldn't actually SEE the blasted night porter's bell, could I, hidden behind a hanging basket, in the dark, without my specs.

And what does the Nutcracker say when I finally return to the room?

'Poor old Bubbles, she looks frozen'.

And whose idea had it been to bring Bubbles on our weekend break in the first place? The Nutcracker's. Believe me, compared to Bubbles, Bingo is a paragon. We received many dirty looks from other guests when we ventured downstairs for breakfast. Everyone stared and glared and gave us the cold shoulder. I could tell that they were all thinking that Yours Truly had provided the night time sound effects.

Anyway, the big event this week has been the arrival of a new SPAM member. Andy had arranged us in our 'sharing' circle, tucking in to more left-over mince-pies and told us one of his jokes:

'Have you heard the one about the dyslexic Irish man who walked into a bra?' No one got it. He then said, 'Now folks, let us welcome our new friend, Tex Tozer'. A tormented-looking chap wearing a scuffed leather bomber jacket that would have been too young for him twenty years ago and a baggy pair of cargo pants showing an expanse of white, hairy ankle, was sprawled in a chair cracking his knuckles. We all waited. He banged his forehead with his fist. He stared across the room.

'The group welcomes you, Tex,' prompted Andy, turning his cat's bottom lips towards Tex.

'Hi. My name is Tex Tozer. I am an alcoholic,' announced Tozer, in a fifty-fags a day rasp, with a strong Welsh lilt.

'No. No, Tex. Wrong routine. SPAM is an Anxiety Management Group, not Alcoholics Anonymous,' said Andy.

'Oh. Right. Point taken. My name is Tex Tozer. I am a poet. Yes, a poet working in *the foul rag-and-bone shop of the heart* as W.B. Yeats once said. Ha! And I am in shock. Indeed I am. Imagine if you will, the shock of arriving home one day to discover that your wife – did I say WIFE? Ha! Some wife… has walked out on you. Buggered off. Emptied our joint bank account, cashed in the joint ISA's by forging my signature…'

Here Tex Tozer paused, coughed productively as Doc Ng would say, banged his chest and cracked his knuckles,

'… she took my signed copy of Ted Hughes's *Hawk in the Rain* – a first edition, I might add, ditto my first edition signed copy of the Liverpool poets' *Mersey Sound*.'

'Women, they're nothing but trouble' interrupted Len, 'and, you know what? They can even become airline pilots these days, hogging the cockpit, flying jumbo jets.'

Ignoring the interruption Tex Tozer continued, '...just about the only thing she didn't take was the cat. Without that creature's feline devotion I fear I might have cracked up, gone down, gone under...'

'Oh my Gawd! I thought you said "down under"!' interjected Len, interrupting Tex Tozer's flow again. 'Never mention the words "down under" when I'm within earshot. For me "down under" means twenty-four hellish hours, travelling at 500 miles per hour at 35,000 feet, crammed into a metal tube, with solar radiation bouncing off the walls AND the terrible possibility that it's being piloted by a woman.'

Tex Tozer, in full flood, continued, '...I am completely stunned, my certainties shattered, my mind fragmented. In fact I am in hell. I stayed in bed for two weeks – apart from letting the cat out. I was hitting the bottle. Swallowing pills. Shaking with anxiety. The only food that passed my lips was Tesco TV dinners and boil-in-the-bag kippers until the microwave exploded. I've got writers' block. Can't FEEL. Can't sleep. And I can't stand boil-in-the-bag kippers. Ah me! We are all sons and daughters of catastrophe.'

Speak for yourself, old boy! Melodramatic sod. All the SPAM regulars were beginning to fidget. Then Tozer lifted his nicotine-stained hands to his head and started tugging at his matted black hair, looking like Heathcliff when Cathy kicked the bucket. He was wearing filthy, mud-clogged trainers. (Tozer, I mean, not Heathcliff).

Andy thanked Tozer for 'sharing'. 'We hear what you say, Tex. We acknowledge that you are in a dark place.'

Someone farted rather loudly. It might have been Tozer. Andy opened a window and said, 'We welcome you Tex...

now, Len, how's about putting the kettle on, and passing round the mince-pies?'

I noticed that Daphne was up and out of her chair in a flash offering the plate to Tozer who muttered 'ANYTHING is preferable to boil-in-the-bag kippers'.

I was wondering how my worries compared to Tozer's. I mean, how does a bald dog, unpaid gas bills, toenail tribulations, prostate panic, where to scatter my ashes… compare to Tozer's shattered certainties, writer's block and fragmented mind? Okay, I can sympathise with his fury on discovering that his wife had skedaddled with his copy of a signed first edition of Ted Hughes' *Hawk in the Rain* and ditto the Liverpool poets' *Mersey Sound*. But on the other hand, was the whingeing, windbag over-egging the pudding? Was he playing to the audience for a bit of sympathy? Take me – when MY wife legged it from the marital home I breathed a sigh of relief, opened up a can of Scrumpy Jack and dusted off my Leonard Cohen CDs. No shattered certainties or fragmented mind there.

Following Tozer's outburst we had an informal group debate about new government proposals for the nation to buy HM The Queen a new 80 million pound, six-hundred and-fifty-foot-long royal yacht to celebrate her Diamond Jubilee. We all agreed that if ANYONE can afford to buy HERSELF a royal yacht it is Her Majesty. Len and Jinxie Wicks were against the idea. They said that Her Majesty is too old to go cavorting about on yachts. And they were worried that old 'Jug Ears', as Len calls the Prince of Wales, would be swanning around the Mediterranean with Camilla aboard the 80 million pound yacht at the tax-payers' expense.

Tozer said 'Don't get me started on that poncy prat. He even has a flunky to squeeze the paste onto his toothbrush. And another flunky to slice the top off his boiled egg each morning.'

Daphne piped up, 'As far as I'm concerned Her Majesty never puts a foot wrong.'

Royal Yacht or no Royal Yacht Len said that he, personally, would never travel anywhere by boat. He's been watching TV reports about the 400 million Costa Concordia cruise ship that came to grief after crashing into rocks off the Isla of Giglio in Tuscany. The Captain abandoned ship and jumped into a lifeboat, leaving behind thousands of terrified passengers. He then defied orders to get back on board.

'Do we want to put Her Majesty in that sort of peril?' asked Daphne.

Most of us couldn't give a damn. Tozer remarked 'The Royals? A bunch of parasites! Privileged layabouts!' While he had our full attention, he recited a poetic verse – not one of his own, as I immediately recognised thanks to my time at the Snodland Tech evening classes – with a look of puffy self-importance:

The boast of heraldry, the pomp of power,
And all that beauty, all that wealth e'er gave,
Awaits alike the inevitable hour
The paths of glory lead but to the grave.

At which point, I bit down on a Fisherman's Friend lozenge (for my wheezy chest), felt a twinge and spat out bits of tooth. Definitely time to see the dentist. Mind you, my teeth may be a worry, but my dental problems are minor ones compared to those of Louis XIV. In her book, *The Sun King* (The Red Cross, 50p), which I have been enjoying, Nancy Mitford writes: The King... *suffered from his teeth; part of his jaw bone had been removed while one of them was being torn out so that he had difficulty in masticating his food, bits of which came down his nose.*

Not nice. But teeth? What a load of grief. These days I am getting very 'long in the tooth'. I used to think the phrase means that your teeth grow longer with age. If this was the case, by the time you reach eighty they would be dangling down your chin, wouldn't they?

FEBRUARY 2012

Way-hey! Thanks to free 'computers for ninnies' sessions at our so-called library – yet another Portakabin overlooking the car park – I'm beginning to explore the murky mysteries of computer technology and the Internet. Distracted as I am by hordes of infants in the junior section clomping about, clapping and warbling 'If you're happy and you know it stamp your feet' (What happened to the libraries 'silence' rule?) the web is beginning to make sense. Twenty-first century words like google, dongle, yahoo, download, gigabytes, app, router, subwoofer, megapixel, scrolling, cookies, blog, log-on, browser, cyberspace, maxapixel, toolbar are entering my vocabulary. Mind you, using computers can be risky. People who over use them can get something called 'Digital Dementia' that affects the short-term memory by bombarding the brain with electronic information. Or they can get HOLS (Hunched Over Laptop Syndrome) and a chronic stiff neck. More worries to think about.

'To switch OFF, you click on the START icon. Just accept that it's all a bit bonkers, and off you go,' explained the Age UK volunteer who was showing me the ropes. I could see Jinxie Wicks bashing away in her corner, clicking, googling and going like the clappers.

So what's behind this new enthusiasm? Well, last week, on a sudden impulse, I found myself perusing the Soul Mates pages of the *Saltmarsh Gazette*. What a revelation. Talk about spoilt for choice. Dozens of females – *blonde, slender, bubbly, loving, youthful, bouncy* – proclaiming their attractions and preferences in very small typeface, which, incidentally, got me worrying about my eyesight. Must remind myself to get my reading specs tested, may need stronger lenses, eye-tests being free for the over-sixties.

How to make a selection? (Females, I mean not reading specs). Do I go for:

'*CAN YOU DING MY BELL?* – *Wendy enjoys most things in life* (except Morris dancing) *and is up for anything, whatever you fancy, I'm willing to give it a go.*'

Or '*FED UP TALKING TO THE DOG* – *Fun-loving red-head, G.S.O.H, young 70's WLTM tall gent 65/75 for in-and-out evening.*'

Or '*DING DONG MERRILY Wanna spend Chrimbo with a big, busty bimbo? Tracey, separated and looking for fun! Likes bowling and line-dancing. Come on, you have nothing to lose. Any age/looks.*' (As this appeared in February, it shows that Tracy is a person who plans ahead).

Would my type be '*BODYWORK GOOD, SOME RE-SPRAYING* – *recently, retired Kentish lass, 1940 vintage, very young-looking, youthful outlook, WLTM fun guy, non-snorer, likes wining and dining.*'

Or '*SPORTY NURSE (50) own camper-van, stylish widow, likes birdwatching, camping* – *let's get in tents.*'

I phoned the *Saltmarsh Gazette* information desk to find out how to decipher the abbreviations. For future reference *WLTM* – *would like to meet. GSOH* – *good sense of humour. OHAC* – *own house and car. LTR Long Term Relationship. CDC* – *Company Director. VGL* – *Very Good Looking. NS* – *Non Snorer. NFR* – *Non Sexual Relationship.* (Hmm. Party-pooper.) *DFC* – *Desperate For Company. TBN* – *Total Bloody Nutcase.* Joke! I made the last two up.

Which reminds me, a SPAM member, who is something of a Lonely Hearts expert, knows of a woman who put an ad in the L.H. column saying: 'HUSBAND WANTED'. Next day she received one hundred replies all saying: 'You can have mine.' He also told me about a couple who had divorced amicably and were still good friends. The husband, on the lookout for a new partner, began to scour the ads. He drew red circles round the names of three women that he liked the sound of, but was too timid to make the phone call. Days later his ex-wife left a message on his answerphone to say 'popped over to take the dog for a walk, saw the adverts you've ringed. Don't contact the second one. It's me.'

So after much humming and haa-ing I decided on *BODYWORK GOOD – SOME RE-SPRAYING*, and phoned a *Saltmarsh Gazette* number to leave a message. And here's the twenty-first century bit, in the message I left for *BODYWORK GOOD* I detailed my newly set-up email address. However – and this shows what a canny old codger I've become – I set up the email in a false name! Just in case! I was advised to do so by the aforementioned SPAM member who urged caution. He warned that if you don't watch out you can find yourself being stalked by some sex fiend or homicidal maniac. Just like Clint Eastwood in *Play Misty for Me*. He suggested that a good way to invent a nom de plume is to take the name of your first pet, and the road you first lived in. So, on my email, I am Tommy Churchill (Tommy tortoise, Church Hill –a steep Kent terrace, rather on the skids in the 1940s). Crafty eh?

So there I was, fingers crossed and eagerly anticipating a potentially amorous encounter. And before you could say 'dongle' things started hotting up. I was in the library everyday emailing *BODYWORK GOOD*. She turned out to be a sixty-something divorcee, Mrs Minnie London. We were *emailing* back and forth for a week. Here's a sample of our electronic communications undertaken as we exchanged simple, friendly, getting-to-know-you sort of messages, nothing too deep or personal:

T.C. I would describe myself as the strong, silent type, but am witty and able to hold my own in company when put to the test.

M.L. Hold your own? No need for that with me around, Tommy. Ha ha. Friends describe me as very bubbly and young-looking for my years. I always say that the way to a man's heart is through his stomach.

T.C. Home cooking is something much appreciated and sought after by Yours Truly.

M.L. Home cooking, eh? Are you being cheeky, Tommy? Take my word for it, chaps go mad for my Lancashire Hotpot.

T.C. What a happy coincidence. I am a great fan of Lancashire Hotpot.

M.L. In that case you should also go mad for my toad-in-the-hole.

T.C. Will do. Will do eventually I hope... I haven't yet described where I live. My modest house over-looks the sea and the Thames estuary, a wonderful spot for bird-watching.

M.L. Bird-watching hmmm. My small detached residence overlooks the boggy end of the Kent marshes – plenty of birds to watch there if that's what tickles your fancy, not that I'm much of a watcher myself, more a do-er, Tommy, if you get my drift.

T.C. Watching can certainly be a slow pastime - by the way I forget to mention that I have a large extension. Very useful!

M.L. Lucky you! I'm rather partial to large extensions. No garden as such chez moi but I do have a large bush of vigorous habit near the entrance.

T.C. Also I have been attempting to smarten things up al fresco, one day it would be an honour to show you my water-feature.

M.L. Does your water feature go on and off unexpectedly?

T.C. As a matter of fact it does, being solar-powered and rather unpredictable. A bit like Yours Truly in fact.

And so forth…

We decided not to exchange home addresses or photographs, as Mrs Minnie London maintained that 'the camera always lies' and 'it's unwise to swap addresses and phone numbers with strangers'. This was a relief to me because the only recent snap I have of myself was taken for my bus-pass in one of the booths at the Post Office. Six pounds it cost. Scandalous price. It makes me look like Bob Dylan (circa 2005) with a comb-over.

Did I say hotting up? Not half! Minnie London emails to suggest we meet up. Asks me to name a venue. So I email back suggesting The Plucked Duck. A date! A blind date! Good grief, what am I letting myself in for? She emails that she will be wearing a smiley badge pinned to her coat for identification purposes. I email by return that I'll be wearing my fur-trapper's hat with ear flaps.

When the day arrives I go a bit overboard with my Lynx Temptation body spray (black pepper fragrance). Lynx for MEN! You said it! I get myself togged up. Best bib and tucker. Clean socks. Clean Y-fronts. A quick can of Scrumpy Jack to give myself Dutch courage. With my knees knocking like a young girl's arriving at the honeymoon hotel, I arrive at The Plucked Duck. Walk in. Place is packed. Here's where the lights go on, I'm thinking to myself.

I look around, and – oh no! – there, over by the ingle-nook, is Jinxie Wicks. All done up like a dog's dinner. And she's wearing a smiley badge pinned to her red coat. The penny drops. Minnie (mouse) London (Road). No wonder she's always been in the library punching the computer keys each time I've availed myself of the Internet facilities. We've been sitting in the same room emailing each other! Has she spotted me? Beat a retreat, Tonks! I quickly whip off my fur-trapper's hat and stuff it into my coat pocket. What a fiasco. I turn around and leg it – racing home with the speed of a marathon winner. Call me a cad. Call me a bounder. Call me a silly old sod with a dream.

Phew! Narrow escape. That'll teach me. I must never mention this unfortunate episode to a living being. My lips are sealed. Not to say chapped by exposure to the freezing cold wind during my full-speed escape. Must see Doc Ng for some chapped lips ointment. Worse is to follow. Later, that afternoon I'm walking past the library and cannot resist logging on in order to delete my email address. And, there's an email for me. It reads:

LISTEN YOU SILLY OLD GIT, I SAW YOU SCUTTLING OUT OF THE PLUCKED DUCK. CONSIDER OUR LONG FRIENDSHIP FINISHED. END OF. AND DON'T EVER COME ROUND CADGING DOUBLE HELPINGS OF MY PORK FAGGOTS IN ONION GRAVY AGAIN.

This week she's ignoring me. She blanked me in the butcher's. She cold-shouldered me at SPAM. Bumped into her in Help the Aged and she barged past me, getting me all tangled up in Bingo's lead. Next, she'll be heaving a brick through my window. I need to get back into her good books. I must devise some sort of damage limitation plan.

Hell hath no fury like a woman scorned. Lesson learnt. No more Soul Mates shenanigans for Yours Truly. Once bitten et cetera... Meanwhile life goes on. It was with great trepidation and fear of coming face-to-face with Jinxie Wicks that I attended the SPAM meeting, but her friend Daphne was there with her. Andy was recovering from 'flu', puffy eyes, red-rimmed round the nostrils, and all his 'm' sounds, sounding like 'b's.

'Cub on folks the beetings about to start… Daphne? Is Daphne present? Ah, Daphne, how's about you getting our SPAB beeting off to a start?' Tozer, looking increasingly gaunt and tragic, no doubt due to his booze and boil-in-the-bag kippers diet, announced that he was raring to kick off, but Andy was nodding in Daphne's direction.

'No bonopolising the beeting, Tex, if you don't bind. This week it's Daphne's tibe to share'.

Daphne looked worried. But then, that's why we attend, because all of us are worried. She also looked rather eye-catching, I don't mind saying, wearing a pink polo-neck, new bifocals with red frames. When she started up it was as if Vanessa Redgrave was in the room, performing Chekhov. Talk about tugging at the heart strings. Daphne told us that to be a widow is like a punishment. Two years on she said and she's still coming to terms with living alone after thirty-five years of marriage.

'I'm not saying my hubby was a saint,' said Daphne. 'He could be rather irritating, never lifted a finger round the house, but—'

'Christ sakes, Daf' chipped in Jinxie Wicks. 'Look on the bright side! You know, in your heart, what a miserable old bugger he could be. All that booze. All those fags. His black teeth. Moaning about his bad knee all the time. Playing his Conway Twitty album. Putting up the kitchen cupboards that fell off the wall…'

Daphne agreed that her late husband was no saint. 'Too right. Too right, Jinx, he was no saint but he was good company. But, nowadays I'm lonely. It's taboo to admit to being lonely. I have conversations with him in my head. Then I tell myself, 'Get a grip', Daf - you're too old to have an imaginary friend.'

We SPAM members were all close to getting out our hankies and dabbing our eyes.

Tozer chimed in with a gloomy literary allusion, 'The great Aldous Huxley once remarked that 'our life is a sentence of perpetual solitary confinement'.' Pompous prat. Tozer, I mean, not Aldous Huxley.

Daphne 'shared' that having someone to do things with is what she misses most. And someone to do things for.

'Come and do things with me, Daphne,' I was thinking.

'Come and do things with me, Daphne,' shouted Tozer.

'Now, now, Tex be bore sensitive during SPAB beetings,' said Andy.

Speaking as a single person myself, I have Bingo to do things for, although, unlike Daphne, I'd rather have someone to do things for me. I was just about to suggest that Daphne ought to get herself a dog, when she started 'sharing' again, saying that she's sick of people telling her that she ought to get a dog. And that although her daughter and grandchildren are a comfort, they live fifty miles away.

'At least they don't live in Australia' grumbled Len. 'At least you don't have to get on a bloody jumbo jet if you want to visit them.'

Everyone went, 'Shhhh. Shaddup.'

'Share sub bore, please Daphne,' said Andy. Daphne said that the word 'widow' has 'negative connotations'. That it conjures up an image of a drab old lady. That she worries about how she ought to be fitting in. Should she think of herself as a merry widow, out there searching websites for a 'soul mate'? Or should she think of herself as an old granny, busy knitting and playing her Max Bygraves' L.P.s?

'You are certainly not a berry widow type Daphne, bake no bistake,' said Andy.

Daphne took off her red specs, mopped her eyes and continued, 'Everything is geared towards couples. I'm always alone! Alone! Who wants to go on holiday alone? Or to the pictures alone? Who wants to be a sad old biddy eating in a restaurant alone?'

'Drab old lady? Sad old biddy? No way!' I was thinking.

'Drab old lady? Sad old biddy? No way!' shouted Tozer.

Andy's vertical hair was nodding overtime as he brought the session to a close. 'Bany of us in this roob know where you are cubbing from, Daphne. By goodness, by dear, you have made us think. Tibe will slowly heal sub of your bisery.'

Everyone perked up - even Daphne - when Andy put the kettle on and passed round a packet of Frosted Fancies.

After the SPAM meeting I walked home, in the icy sleet, and, I might add, my so-called water-resistant, thermal lined, easy entry, zip fronted, weather-proof boots (mail order, £15), started leaking. Suddenly it hit me, like a lightning flash. Daphne and I are meant for each other. Just thinking about her makes my heart skip a beat.

Or could my heart skipping a beat be palpitations? Or possibly arterial fibrillation? To be on the safe side I asked Doc Ng to check my heart. I was hoping she'd send me for an electrocardiogram but no, she said heart flutters are caused by the 'fight or flight response' or by too much caffeine. She listened to my chest through her stethoscope, told me to stop smoking and to start taking cod-liver oil capsules. I know what's causing my heart to flutter alright. Ah Daphne! Cod-liver oil capsules aren't the answer.

Fact is Daphne is lonely. 'Come and be lonely with me, Daphne' I could say. Or rather 'Come and be lonely no more with me, Daphne.' By an uncanny co-incidence I have just this week been reading the Journals of Alice James, one of my bargain book buys, (Help the Aged, 50p). Alice was the sister of the long-winded, world-famous American writer, Henry James. She never married and spent much of her life confined to her bed with mysterious nervous disorders. On the topic of loneliness she wrote the following which I intend to copy out and show to Daphne.

> The ghastly days when I was by myself in the little house… how I longed to escape from the 'Alone, Alone!' that echoed through the house, rustled down the stairs, whispered from the walls, and confronted me, like a material presence, as I sat waiting, counting the moments as they turned themselves from today into tomorrow.

What Alice needed was an American SPAM equivalent. Anyway, I was thinking these things over, in the bath with a can of Scrumpy Jack when the phone rang. I jumped out of the bath. It was my Mum.

'Ronald! You there Ronald? Did you know that bowel cancer is the second biggest killer in the UK after lung cancer? There's a whole page about it in today's paper. Each year 40,000 people get it, and 16,000 die of it. Now listen to me, Son. You can now get a free stool-test kit. To get your stool-testing kit you phone this number, are you writing all this down Ronald?'

'Yes Mum, I always jump out of the bath stark naked holding a pen in case Mum phones wanting me to write something down—'

'Anyway the test kit contains spatulas, sample cards and a jiffy bag for three samples, which you send off by Freepost to a testing centre…'

What a woman. Talk about cheer me up. I don't think. She completely ruined my appetite for my late-night sausage sandwich.

'And so to bed', as Samuel Pepys used to say. 'Perchance to dream', as Shakespeare said. Dream? About Daphne perhaps? She brings out the Viking in me. No two ways. Good grief, I'm turning back into a teenager.

Regrets? I've had a few… the main one being that apart from a seven-day package holiday to Majorca in 1979, I've never visited any far-flung places. I've always been of the same opinion as the poet Philip Larkin (a great boozer and bosom buddy of Kingsley Amis) who said he'd love to go to China, or anywhere, as long as he could be home in time for tea. But it has of late become a fantasy of mine to embark on a world cruise stopping off at exotic ports of call. This is why, at this time of year when the icy blasts are whipping up my trouser legs, The Shack's letter-box is stuffed with glossy cruise brochures. Here's one that took my fancy – starting at Southampton it heads for the ports of Cadiz, Valletta, chugs along the Suez Canal, then on to Aqaba, Dubai, Muscat, Mumbai, Colombo, Singapore, Hong Kong, Yokohama, Honolulu, San Diego, Acapulco, Antigua, Barbados…. Just reeling off the list of exotic places gives me little shivers. Whew! Imagine. Four months of rolling across the ocean, stuffing my face, lolling on the sun-deck wearing a Hawaiian shirt, Panama hat, aviator sun-glasses, maybe a kaftan, glass of champers in one hand, plate of barbecued hog-roast in the other… All for £12,000. In your dreams, Tonks. Yet I always keep my passport renewed just in case. Ah me. Back to reality.

My toenails need trimming again. This is where a wife would come in handy. Not that the Nutcracker ever ventured within ten paces of my naked feet. Made an appointment to see Doc Ng. Who should be sitting in the waiting-room but Jinxie Wicks reading a magazine article – which I couldn't help noticing was headed 'BANISH YOUR BINGO WINGS' – and still giving me the cold shoulder. Doc Ng referred me to the chiropody clinic and gave me another Quit Kit. At the clinic they told me that they no longer cut toenails, apart from diabetics' toe nails, due to new Health and Safety regulations. What are they scared of? A sharp bit flying up and stabbing them in the eye? The only solution, they said, was to make a private appointment with a podiatrist. This costs £45. *Forty five* pounds to get your blinkin' toenails cut? Sheer madness. Good grief! I could fly to Spain and back for forty-five quid. Not that I want to fly to Spain. Thankfully my Mum came to the rescue. She spotted an ad for 'Long Reach Toenail Scissors' – '*the extra long shank not only saves you bending and stretching, it also provides excellent leverage for cutting the toughest nails*'. Eureka! I sent off for a pair. I still require some practice, but hopefully problem solved. It makes me wonder how our homo-sapiens ancestors kept their toenails trimmed before scissors had been invented. Sharp shards of flint perhaps?

So, toenails apart, I am sorry to report that there has been no progress on the Daphne front. I caught sight of her in the queue at the butchers and I experienced a little surprise twitch in the magic flute department. Too much information as Daphne might say. But at least there's life in the old dog yet. But how does an anxious, nervous, out-of-practice, wannabe romantic take the plunge?

To add to my heightened emotional state, there's been a drama at The Shack. A metal thief made off with my front garden gate. There's a nationwide epidemic of metal theft, with thieves cashing in on the high price of raw materials and pinching copper cables, railway lines, bronze plaques from graves and war memorials, drain covers, wrought-iron garden seats and even a famous bronze sculpture by Barbara Hepworth. It was one of those big, blobby numbers estimated to be worth £500,000 but only £1,500 in scrap metal. It wouldn't surprise me to hear that thieves have stripped the jumbo-jet sized arms (solid metal) from Anthony Gormley's famous Angel of the North. Network Rail estimates that metal theft has cost them £43 million over the past three years.

Anyway, the first I knew that my gate had gone was Bingo dashing out into the road and knocking someone off their bike. That someone was Daphne! Yes DAPHNE. Oh no! What a disaster. I was in my dressing-gown and slippers, peering through the window, and there was Daphne picking herself up off the tarmac, front mudguard buckled, a stack of cruise brochures spilling from her bike basket. As for Bingo he was on his back, legs in the air, stiff as a board. I shuffled outside to find Daphne just about able to stand upright, looking shaken, brushing herself down. A cup of hot, sweet tea was called for, I thought, recalling my Boy Scout's training from the 1950's.

'No, no I'm fine' insisted Daphne, retrieving her bobble-hat and cruise brochures from the middle of the road, 'It's your poor little dog, who needs seeing to'.

What was I supposed to do? Give Bingo the kiss-of-life? Holy-Moly! I was just preparing to do mouth-to-mouth when – thank the Lord – he came to and started frisking about. Daphne declined my invitation to come inside and have a cup of tea. This was a relief. A huge relief, I don't mind saying, my immediate worry being that Daphne might venture into The Shack's bathroom and notice that I've got one of those old-folks 'grab' rails on the wall, to help me get in and out of the bath. Not a cool look for the bathroom. Or she might spot my haemorrhoid ointment carelessly left on view. Or my foam arch-supports. So - thankfully, Daphne refused my offer and, pushing her bike, went on her way. I was in such a tizz I couldn't eat my sausage sandwich. Let's face it, the sight of Yours Truly first thing in the morning, in his dressing-gown and slippers, is hardly the sort of vision to get a woman's hormones in uproar. I spent the day worrying about it.

Walked to the High Street and spotted a bunch of tulips (reduced, 45p) in the Co-op. Paid a boy who lives along the road from me, twenty pence to deliver them to Daphne's house, with a note of apology about Bingo knocking her off her bike. I sent, with the flowers, the previously mentioned Alice James's item about loneliness copied out neatly in my best italic handwriting. Not for nothing did I attend Snodland Tech evening classes all those years ago. And would you believe it, RESULT! Three days later Daphne herself appeared on my doorstep with a package. No she couldn't come in. Couldn't stop. Very busy. Off to visit her grandchildren for a few days. She handed me the package explaining: 'I knitted this jacket for poor little Bingo to conceal his-ahem-bald patches' and flashed me a smile I could have poured on my porridge. Talk about a walk-my-way-and-a-thousand-violins-begin-to-play moment. Then she hurried off with a friendly wave. 'Poor little Bingo'? I could kill the little bugger. But he looks very natty (and warm) wearing his stripy knitted jacket. He seems full of beans, none the worse for his misadventure.

As for me, I am a lovelorn wreck. My re-awakened romantic imaginings have landed me in a worse anxiety state than usual. I am haunted by the undignified scenario that might unfold should Yours Truly actually find himself (and Daphne) in an under-the-blankets situation. I keep trying to imagine myself stripping off in a frenzy of rampant lust like the guys do in just about every play or film you watch on TV these days. Michael Douglas and Jeremy Irons are particularly dab-hands at it. But imagine me, Ronald Tonks, 71, well past the first flush of youth, fiddling around with his belt and braces. Whipping off his Y-fronts.

Imagine:

'Hang about, Daphne, while I unbuckle my titanium knee-brace.'

Or – mid-snog

'Hold your horses, Daphne… must nip down the corridor, dodgy waterworks.'

And what about my flatulence problem? It never happens to Michael Douglas or Jeremy Irons.

Let's get real. There are too many miles on my clock. Wenching, womanising and carnal indulgence is not for Yours Truly. Having come to that conclusion, my jangled emotions are beginning to calm down. I will henceforth worship Daphne from afar – 'She is as the heavens fair / No one as lovely in earth or air' as a poet (not Tozer) wrote. Too true. But, in my anxious state, a romantic dalliance would be too nerve wracking. Where Daphne is concerned I have decided to throw in the towel.

To take my mind off romantic fantasies I decided to sort out and re-arrange my books. This week I bought a massive doorstopper of a Dickens biography (RSPCA, £2) and a book about the writer and philosopher, Iris Murdoch (St Mildred's Hospice, 50p). What a woman! Now there was a female who wouldn't have permitted a chaps' ball-of-foot cushion or titanium knee-brace to put her off her stroke.

The book's author, A.N. Wilson (one of my literary heroes and a living legend if ever there was one) had become a friend of Iris Murdoch and her Oxford don husband, John Bayley, long before the celebrated Iris succumbed so tragically to

Alzheimer's. Wilson describes a visit he and his wife made, to dine with the famous couple at their London pied-a-terre. They were greeted by a scene of unimaginable squalor – reminiscent of the IRA Maze Prisoner's Dirty Protests – filthy bathroom, poop encrusted loo, gloops of black grease in the kitchen, unwashed crockery, unmade bed, heaps of discarded clothes on the floor, scatterings of books and papers… in fact it reads as if the Wilsons were taking their lives in their hands when they sat down for the meal. Admittedly they all knocked back plenty of high quality booze but, as the four of them engaged in witty, intellectual chit-chat, the meal Iris dished up consisted of one small pork pie cut into quarters, some salami that had seen better days and some fluff-covered olives. This was followed by one scrambled egg divided between four, cheese and biscuits and two packets of Mr Kipling's cakes. It is certainly not what you imagine of the Oxford intelligentsia. But as A.N.Wilson reminds us, Iris was a right live wire in her youth. He writes, *'Iris had clearly been one of those delightful young women – and continued to be such a person well into middle perhaps old age – who was prepared to go to bed with almost anyone'*. And you can bet that Iris in her prime, must have been the sort who would have had no hesitation in telling someone like Doc Ng what she could do with her ruddy Quit Kit. Mine has scared the living daylights out of me. Just a moment ago I was poised with a can of Scrumpy Jack all ready to light one of my roll-ups, but thought better of it. Or rather I though of Quit Kit's black envelop with its skull-and-crossbones on the front and the words:

WARNING: *contains disturbing information.*

Inside is a card with a picture of a cigarette topped with a long downward drooping bit of ash and the words 'SMOKING

MAY REDUCE THE BLOOD FLOW AND CAUSE IMPOTENCE'. A second card has a picture of a bed-ridden hospital patient and the warning that 'smokers are ten times more likely to develop vascular disease which can lead to AMPUTATION OF ONE OR BOTH LEGS.' Bloody hell. Life is one big worry after another.

Speaking of which, I was agitating about how I'd be able to afford a new gate. I mentioned the theft to Len when I bumped into him at Doc Ng's. He said he'd been walking along the beach on the lookout for firewood and had spotted a gate, buckled and rusty, in a skip opposite the Lifeboat station. I was round there in a flash and – lo and behold – there was a buckled and rusty gate very similar to my own. It *was* my own! What luck. No doubt the metal thief got cold feet. So now it's back at The Shack. And I'm all right Jack. Apart from the usual occasional twinge in my lower lumbar region. And here is the letter I dashed off to A.N.Wilson after reading his brilliant biography of Iris Murdoch.

To: A.N.Wilson

The Shack
Spratling Sea Road
Saltmarsh
Kent

Sir,

What a riveting book about Iris Murdoch! I couldn't put it down. You are very lucky to have been a friend of the acclaimed authoress. As a great bookworm myself I must admit that Iris Murdoch novels can be a bit over my head, all the colourful characters being rather posh and highly intellectual. I have never met anyone who talks or behaves like her characters – not even when I was studying at the Snodland Tech (evening classes) where any bloke who wore corduroy trousers or maroon socks got funny looks. And if any of the female students had carried on like Iris Murdoch did at Oxford, according to your book, they'd have been called 'sluts' and

'slags'. How times change! You might be interested to learn that I once saw Iris Murdoch on the London Underground (Northern Line) – stockings wrinkled, eating a pork pie, no airs and graces – you don't expect to bump into world famous authors on the 'tube'! I was kicking myself for not having one of her books to hand. I might have dared to ask her to sign it. I don't know HOW you do it – all those novels, non-fiction books, newspaper articles, TV documentaries. It takes me two days to write a shopping list! Hats off to you.
Yours truly
Ronald Tonks

The killer freeze has struck. Snow has swept across Kent as the Arctic chill tightens its grip.

Around the house I've been wearing my fingerless mitts ('Fagins'), fur-trapper's hat and dressing-gown over two layers of togs. I am now settling down in front of the coal-effect to enjoy a hot cup of cocoa. Phone goes. You've guessed.

'Ronald! Are you wearing your thermals? Your fur-trapper's hat? I just heard on the wireless that the Prime Minister has issued a level three Amber Cold Weather Alert for the attention of all pensioners! Can you hear me? Are you there? Did you know that freezing weather increases the risk of heart attacks, strokes and breathing problems?—'

'Calm down, Mum, over here in Saltmarsh there's a bit of frost but—'

'—How's your wheezy chest, by the way? Are you rubbing it with Tiger Balm? A hundred and fifty people have dropped dead from the cold in Eastern Europe. In the Serbian mountains eleven thousand people are trapped by snow—'

'No worries, Mum, we've only got a slight sprinkling here by the sea—'

'—starving wolves are roaming through the villages looking for food. And in the Ukraine thousands are being treated for frostbite and hypothermia – ooh, can't stop for more chit-chat – district nurse at the front door.'

Sometimes I wish I hadn't given her a 'Simple Sam' big button mobile phone for her ninetieth birthday.

Back to my cocoa. Bingo and I are now at daggers drawn. He snaffled my sausage while I was on the phone. But, big news! Jinxie Wicks and I have made it up! I'd been racking my brains trying to think up some damage limitation exercise. And, then, Eureka! I won first-prize in the *Saltmarsh Gazette*'s Valentine raffle. The prize? A 'luxury day-long pamper for two' at the Turbine View Hotel and Spa. Not my sort of thing, I'll admit, but right up Jinxie Wicks' street.

So, dropped her a card saying 'Time to let bygones be bygones'. Two days later we booked into the Turbine View Spa, surrounded by zombie looking people wandering about wearing white dressing-gowns. I thought we'd walked into a loony-bin. Piped pan-pipes. Dim lights. Just like *One Flew over the Cuckoo's Nest*. Before you could say 'Nurse Ratched' we were wearing white dressing-gowns and shuffling about in disposable flip-flops, and seating ourselves by the therapeutic Jacuzzis to select our 'treatments'. Jinxie Wicks went off for a *DEEP WRINKLE TREATMENT* (ever the optimist!) I tried out a fifteen minute relaxation session in the flotation tank. This involved floating on my back, bollock-naked in a shallow tank of warm salty water, in the dark. Every time the beginnings of a small sensation of relaxation began to steal over me a female voice from a speaker above my head would shout 'All right, Mr Tonks? Everything okay?' which jerked me back to thinking how ridiculous I must look. I was worrying that there might be hidden cameras, and that someone was having an almighty giggle at my expense.

Afterwards, along came this female massage therapist (Slovakian) who recommended a 'Lime and Ginger salt glow body scrub', proceeded by a 'Sole Delight Foot Treatment'. Foot treatment? Now we're talking. My toenails trimmed by an expert! The 'Sole Delight' lasted for thirty minutes. It tickled. My feet have never been so pampered. After half an hour in a ylang-ylang footbath they had acquired a new spring in their step.

By now I was getting a bit jumpy at the thought of what was to follow. What was I letting myself in for? Some Slovakian hanky-panky? You read about that sort of thing in the newspapers. Would I be allowed to keep my Y-fronts on? The thought of fingernails, especially female fingernails – Slovakian female fingernails – anywhere near my naked parts makes me very worried. Would it tickle? Would the magic flute start playing up? I once read about a chap who went for a first time massage at a posh health spa. His masseuse left him alone in the treatment room telling him to take off his togs and to put on a paper thong item, which was just big enough to cover the crucial bits. When she returned he was stretched out on the bed, face down, bottom up, with the thong pulled tightly over his head. Not having seen one before he thought it was some sort of facemask. Could happen to anyone. And what a relief. I was allowed to keep my Y-fronts on.

'Take off your robe, Mr Tonks and lie face down on the massage bed…' Panic stations! My knees were like jelly. All this was doing my blood pressure no favours. With the panpipes piping I had my torso kneaded, patted, pounded and buffed. Thank the Lord that the lights were dim. Thank the Lord that my flatulence problem didn't rear its ugly head. All in all it wasn't too traumatic apart form a couple of agonising spasms when the Slovakian fingers pummelled my lower lumbar region. Afterwards I smelt like a Thai takeaway. Relaxing? No way. I certainly wouldn't volunteer for a luxury Lime-and-Ginger-Salt-Glow-Body-Scrub again in a hurry.

But might as well be hung for a sheep as for a lamb, I always say. I entered the Eucalyptus Sauna (men only, phew! Yours Truly was the only one in there) where I had to remove my specs because they kept steaming up. I then went and sat on them by accident. Ouch. Bloomin' heck. Got a splinter of broken glass in my left buttock. Blood all over my white dressing-gown. Like a scene from Hitchcock. Nothing serious though. Nothing to worry about, apart from the repair bill for my specs. My 'final treatment' was a spray tan. I stood in a booth – bollock naked again – and was sprayed front and back. I ended up looking like Robert Mugabe minus the mad facial expressions. An important tip here for would-be spray-tanners. IT RUBS OFF. After one night my bed-sheets looked like the Shroud of Turin.

So, duty done. Once again I am in Jinxie Wick's good books. We had an enjoyable outing to the Dickens's Day, in Rochester, travelling by train. Rochester High Street was packed with Morris dancers, shantie singers, ye olde hot-chestnut sellers, and people roaming about in Dickensian clobber. I counted five Mr Pickwicks, two Miss Havishams, six Artful Dodgers, and four Bill Sykes on the grass outside the Cathedral, where a brass band was playing a medley from *Oliver!* A banner painted with *HAPPY BIRTHDAY CHAS DICKENS* was flapping between two lampposts. A chap wearing a top hat puffed past on a penny-farthing bike. Inside the heaving Betsy Trotswood Tavern I found myself crushed against yet another Miss Havisham. She was deathly pale, white lips, silver eyelids, a sort of tangled beehive of matted plaits down to her waist, a flimsy white frock, and torn white stockings.

'Ah ha! Miss Havisham, I presume?' I said in a larky tone.

'Yer wot? You speaking to me? I do the pub snacks.'

Turns out she wasn't in fancy-dress, just normal garb. Normal for her, that is. I felt a bit of a twerp. But I felt an even bigger twerp when I stepped into the Gents and was accosted by a Bill Sikes who sidled up to me and hissed out of the side of his mouth: 'Psst. Wanna do a deal, Grandpa?' Good grief. Was he trying to sell me drugs? He was. What a shock. Even during my 'turn on - tune in - drop out' days at the Snodland Tech evening classes I was never tempted.

'Come now, my good fellow, you've made a mistake...' I said.

Whereupon Bill Sikes winked, smirked, tapped his nose and said: 'No probs. Stay cool. Have a toke on me, Pops...' and thrust a small, foil wrapped package into my coat pocket. Excellent quality Harris Tweed, incidentally, reaches down to my boot tops, (The Red Cross, £8). I must admit that I felt a distinct tingle of wickedness ripple through my vitals or 'witals' as a Dickens' character would say. Life on the edge, eh? Could this be the start of the slippery slope?

When I revealed all to Jinxie Wicks on the return journey, she told me to never look a gift horse in the mouth.

'Bring it on, daddy-o,' she hissed, giving me a nudge. Has Rochester turned into a den of iniquity? Charles Dickens must be turning under Westminster Abbey's stone floor.

The upshot was that we retired to The Shack that evening, closed the curtains, dusted off my *Rolling Stones Greatest Hits* CD, and turned up the volume on my boom-box (Cancer Research, £3).

So, I stick the Rizlas together like the hippies do, and I roll a 'joint' (ooo-er! Criminal!) the first one I've ever rolled in my life. A spliff! A spliff! The little tingle of wickedness ripples through my vitals again. Woah! I light up, Take a puff.

Inhale. Jinxie Wicks takes a puff. Inhales. Nothing happens. Except my eyes go out of focus. But this could be because I'm wearing my out-of-date replacement specs while the ones I sat on are being repaired. Jinxie Wicks is hogging the 'joint' and getting lipstick all over the end.

I roll another. I take a long drag. Whoosh! I must have rolled it too thin. It bursts into flames and the contents are sucked down my throat. Five minutes later I'm skipping about with singed eyebrows and a big grin. Whomp! Whew! Wow! The pot has kicked in big time. Jinxie Wicks – in her padded mac and moon boots due to the freezing weather – is gyrating across the shag-pile rug (RSPCA, 50p) and thrashing her arms about.

'Let's rock n' roll, baby' she roars, and I'm up on my feet (have to keep my slippers on due to the icy draught blowing under the door) doing my snakey hip thrusts, pelvic jiggles, nifty little kicks on the off beats, a waggle of my elbows, jaw jutting, knuckles on hips. Whoo-hoo, sob your heart out Mick Jagger.

'Aahm-jumpin-jack-flash-itsa-gas-gas-gas…' Old Jinxie Wicks is hopping, bopping, stamping and shaking her bum about, when suddenly above the throbbing jangle of the Rolling Stones, there's an almighty loud banging on the front door.

'Oh my God!' squawks Jinxie Wicks, mid bop, 'it's a drug bust!'

'Oh no!' I yelp, at the same time, 'It's the Fuzz!'

More knocking and banging. Then a kick on the door. Panic.

'Quick, hide the stash' I hiss.

Jinxie Wicks grabs the foil wrapper and what's left of its illegal contents and hides it in the dog basket, under Bingo's blanket.

I unplug the boom-box. We can't stop laughing. We're rolling on the floor. Oh my aching sides! Into the silence comes another volley of knocks. Bingo barks.

A voice shouts, 'What's going on in there? Dad! Open up Dad!'

Total horror! Oh no! It's Terry. Fruit of my loins. Aaagh! I may not have mentioned my prodigal so far in these pages.

'What the bloomin heck's going on Dad? Open up!'

'Just coming Terry' I croak, head spinning, eyes still out of focus.

In comes Terry, knocking the snow off his boots.

'Dad? Jinxie Wicks? Good gracious, what's that smell? It smells like – DOPE. IT IS dope isn't it? POT! You're both stoned out of your skulls! Pull yourselves together the pair of you. What a disgrace. And stop that infantile giggling. At once.'

'Hey, you, Terry, get offa my cloud,' roars Jinxie Wicks and we both roll about on the floor again.

Well, the upshot is I get a right telling off from Terry. He threatens: 'I've a good mind to report you to Grandma, except the shock might finish her off.' And then Terry drops the bombshell. Says he wants to move in for a few weeks. A few WEEKS? I tell him that with his Christian ways and his happy-clappy church-going habit he'll drive me mad.

'Oh let him be, you hard-hearted old git, he's just trying to find himself' says Jinxie Wicks.

'Find himself? He's forty-five for God's sake'.

'Please don't take the Lord's name in vain, Dad. And while I'm here NO MORE DRUGS, no more substance abuse. Is that understood? Cannabis is a dangerous, mind-altering drug that can have disastrous effects on the brain.'

Creep! So can the Christian religion. Look at that smug, self-proclaimed, war-mongering Christian Tony Blair. At this point there is a strange, strangled gurgling sound and Bingo suddenly leaps out of his basket with a yelp, jumps on and off the sofa ten times, then keels over onto his side panting. His tongue is lolling out.

'Oh my God' screams Jinxie Wicks, 'he's swallowed your stash!'

Total panic. Visions of the R.S.P.C.A turning up and taking Bingo into care. Me appearing in court, in the dock, on charges of animal cruelty. Headlines – '*SHAME OF LOCAL PENSIONER IN DOG DRUG ABUSE SCANDAL*'. Daphne never speaking to me again. And me being forced to 'share' at SPAM. Oh the horror of it. Then, what a relief. Just as I am about to phone the emergency vet, Bingo coughs up the silver foil and its contents, starts wagging his tail, licks Jinxie Wicks' moon boots, gobbles half a tin of Chappie, slurps copiously from his water bowl, and returns to normal.

'I think we ought to thank our Lord for delivering Bingo from the jaws of death,' says Terry. To be honest I don't think Terry shares a single atom of my D.N.A.

The upshot is that Terry and his poncy laptop, iPod, smartphone, Cliff Richard CD's, King James Bible App and microwave (MICROWAVE? What do we do with it?) are now installed in The Shack's spare room. Yesterday we had words about me singing along to my Leonard Cohen CD.

'Bloomin' heck, Dad, Laughing Lennie is doing my head in. Talk about songs to slit your wrists by, do me a favour…'

At the time I was thinking of Daphne. Ah Daphne.

'We-met-when-we-were-almost-young-deep-in-the-green-lilac-park…' et cetera et cetera. Leonard Cohen has been there, has known heartache, has known love unrequited… A deep sigh escapes from Yours Truly.

SPAM was cancelled due to the snow. I saw Doc Ng who directed me to the district nurse to have a small remaining splinter of glass removed from my left buttock, Y-fronts off again, and gave me another Quit Kit. My specs repair cost an entire week's income.

Terry is sorting out his benefit payments. He has applied for a job as a professional mourner or mute, walking in front of the hearse and turning up to funerals of people who have no relatives or friends. This might keep him away from The Shack each day. Hallelujah! Oh yes. And here's the note I received from Jinxie Wicks:

Thanks, Ronald, for the fab day at The Turbine View Hotel and Spa. Here's a confession. I was the person who pinched your gate and dumped it in the skip. I'd had one too many. Come round for some of my faggots-in-onion-gravy any-time soon. — JW

MARCH 2012

It's driving me up the wall having Terry under my feet. To give him his due, he cooks an excellent sausage hotpot. During the big freeze Terry's hotpots have come into their own. But it's his nonstop nag-nag-nagging that gets on my nerves.

'Watch your language, please Dad.'

And: 'How's about me helping you to clear out some of your books? You've read them all, so why hang on to them?'

Philistine! He's inherited the Nutcracker's genes all right. Then there's his born-again Christian habit of muttering: 'For-what-we-are-about-to-receive' et cetera before tucking into his grub. Mumbo-jumbo. Some days I feel like running away from home, leaving a 'no one understands me' note propped up against the tomato ketchup bottle, legging it with my wheelie suitcase (St Mildred's Hospice, £1) in the small hours.

I've found a copy of Richard Dawkins' *The God Delusion* (Age Concern, 20p) to wave under Terry's nose. And I clatter round the kitchen singing Ira Gershwin's '*The things that you're liable / to read in the Bible / It ain't necessarily so...*'

Terry won't accept that Biblical stories are as much make-believe as Winnie-the-Pooh. Dawkins knows his stuff. For example, take the ancient biblical prophecy that Jesus the son of God, would be a direct descendent of King David. Dawkins points out that if, as the Gospels claim, Jesus was born of a virgin and if no human male (or female) had any part in his conceptions, then being a descendant of King David doesn't come into it. The prophecy is utter claptrap.

And if the Almighty knows everything, sees everything, and is 'omnipresent' i.e. always with you WHAT, for crying out loud, is the point of prayers? But you try mentioning that to Terry. He just gets the sulks and slopes off to his room to listen to his Cliff Richard CD.

Or else he comes on all heavy and says things like, 'Okay, Dad, you and your fellow atheists find it difficult to believe in God and the bible but I, personally, find it even more difficult to believe – as the Richard Dawkinses and other heathen boffins of this world believe – that the entire bloomin' universe was once contained in something the size of a pea, and expanded into something the size of an orange and then exploded into where we are now – the Big Bang Theory? Who can get their head round it?'

That's telling me isn't it? Matter of fact, Yours Truly also has problems with the Big Bang. No two ways.

But some good news! Bingo's hair is sprouting. Two weeks after he swallowed my stash his bald bits turned fuzzy. Could be onto something big? I delivered the following letter to the vet.

Sir,
I am writing to suggest that you consider putting cannabis on prescription for bald dogs. Why? Well, you will be interested to hear that the long-standing baldness disorder that has afflicted my dachshund Bingo, appears to have been cured overnight. How did it happen? Bingo accidentally swallowed a small quantity of cannabis (the circumstances of which mishap are not relevant here, and are, indeed somewhat hazy). Should you wish to pass on details of Bingo's cure to the powers-that-be at the top of your profession, or if you wish to publish it in The Vet magazine you have my full permission.
Yours sincerely,
Ronald Tonks

A week later I received a reply:

Dear Mr Tonks,

Bingo's sudden recovery is certainly good news. I was most interested to read your letter and have made a note of your suggestions, for which I thank you. Meanwhile make sure that Bingo receives all the vitamins, minerals etc. that are necessary to return his coat to full glory. Our own exclusive Saltmarsh brand kibble(with aloe vera), *Chomp 'n' Romp* – £36 a pack – is highly recommended for canine health.

Yours sincerely

Senior Vet

PS A complimentary trial sample of *Chomp 'n' Romp* enclosed.

A bit of a lukewarm, mealy-mouthed response, I thought. It worries me that the vet might be planning to steal my cannabis discovery, pass it off as his own, and rake in fame and fortune, within the veterinary world. I shall keep my ear to the ground.

Speaking of keeping my ear to the ground I hear that Daphne has been seen out on her bike again. Ah, Daphne. Hold my hand, I'm a stranger in paradise... Let's get real. Not a chance. *The rain falls down on last year's man...* as Leonard Cohen puts it so poignantly. But I can still admire Daphne from afar. Be a friend-in-need if I'm called upon. At least I haven't got myself into the same crazed state as William Hazlitt (1778–1830) – another famous son of Kent whose *Liber Amoris* I've just been reading (Barnado's, 30p). Bloomin' hell! Talk about unrequited love. Poor old Hazlitt suffered a mid-life crisis, divorced his wife and became obsessed with his landlord's teenage daughter. Disaster. He went completely doolally. 'My only ambition was to live with her and to die in her arms,' he told his friends, driving them to distraction with his rantings and ravings and repeated threats to top himself.

To one friend he wrote, '*I want a certain hand to guide me an eye to cheer me, a bosom to repose on; all which I shall never have, but shall stagger into my grave, old before my time, unloved and unlovely.*' This strikes a chord with Yours Truly. Especially the bit about a bosom to repose on.

The landlord's daughter thought he was barking mad, what with his declarations, dog-like devotion and his skulking about the house begging her to sit on his lap.

To another friend he confided, '*My heart has found a tongue in speaking to her and I have talked to her the divine language of love.*' The upshot was that the landlord's daughter ignored 'the divine language of love', gave Hazlitt the old heave-ho and took up with chap of her own age.

As for Daphne, there has been a right old rumpus at her end – the posh end – of town, on the leafy outskirts, following a *Saltmarsh Gazette* story headed SWINGERS CLUB SHOCK. Turns out that a newcomer to town, Mr Vladimir Piskov, owner of a six-bedroom detached house, has installed a dungeon fitted with spanking benches (whatever they may be), torture equipment and pad-lockable leather chastity belts. In the back garden he has set up two floodlit jacuzzis and a bouncy castle. Calling his house Shackles R Us he advertises theme nights – LESBIAN VARIATIONS, BONDAGE BARBECUE, RUBBER ROMPS, WICKED WANDA'S WHIPLASH and a hog roast event called DOGGIN 'N HOGGIN.

People hire the dungeon for private parties. Local residents, according to Daphne, are up in arms, fed up with the non-stop comings and goings, car doors slamming, screams, shrieks and giggles, the constant throbbing of the motorised pump that keeps the bouncy castle inflated, and the general hanky-panky and disturbance of the peace. Mr Piskov insists he is doing nothing illegal. He is now complaining about harassment and about nosey-parkers who invade his privacy and peer over his garden wall. Last week a coach-load of sightseers drove up (after Shackles R Us had been voted Swingers' Club of the Year). They parked, climbed out and started taking photos. Jinxie Wicks took a wander to have a quick nose over the wall hoping to see a Doggin 'n Hoggin session in full swing, but the place was 'dead as heaven on a Saturday night,' to quote Leonard Cohen again.

Back at SPAM there have been dramatic developments. I'm sitting there gearing myself up to take a turn at 'sharing', trying to decide whether to 'share' my ongoing 'worried-well' worries, or whether to share the fact that I'm always worrying about being worried, when Andy walks in wearing a T-shirt with HOW DARE YOU ASSUME I'M HETEROSEXUAL printed across the chest.

'How dare he assume anyone gives a flying fart,' sniggers Tozer, who is wearing odd socks and flip-flops.

Then Andy drops a bombshell. It turns out that, due to government spending cuts, SPAM is being axed and is being replaced by activity mornings for the elderly. These are going to be called Saltmarsh Pensioners Activity Mornings – so we're still called SPAM.

'I promise you, folks, that the new SPAM format will be much more participant pro-active,' says Andy, as Len, in all the excitement, drops the plate of Viennese whirls that he's passing round. 'We can look forward to Scrabble! Singing-for-fun! Bingo! Ping pong! African drumming! Exciting stuff, eh? You name it…'

'Yeah! Wet T-shirt contests! Wife-swapping! White water rafting! Bring it on!' shouts Tozer, spraying the air with Viennese whirl crumbs.

'Now, now, lighten up, Tex. Keep your hair on! Perhaps we'll have a poetry-reading or two, eh? Or keep-fit? Talks? Maybe Ronald Tonks can be persuaded to read extracts from his anxiety management journal? Hi there, Ronald. How about it? Keep up the good work, the Samuel Pepys of Saltmarsh, huh?'

Read extracts from my journal? Over my dead body. That would put the cat among the pigeons, no two ways. No, my journal is intended for posthumous publication I hope. From my writings, future historians will discover exactly what life was like for the undefeated old-timers of Saltmarsh at the beginning of the 21st Century.

Tex Tozer is still having a go at Andy, '… Naked mud wrestling! Strip poker! Doggin! Whoo-ee! Go for it!'

At that moment I notice that he has a stripy knitted scarf round his scrawny neck. An exact match for Bingo's doggy jacket, if I'm not mistaken. Oh no! Cupid's dart alert! Tozer and Daphne? My mental alarm bells start ringing. Then Andy rounds off the session with one of his jokes.

'A team of local police arrive at their police station to find that burglars have broken in and stolen all the toilets. What do the police say?'

Blank looks all round.

Then Tozer pipes up with his chainsaw chuckle, 'We've got nothing to go on'. Everyone (except me) roars. Daphne roars loudest of all. And then I notice a fleeting flash of eye-contact between her and big-head Tozer. Anguish. 'My heart is smitten, and withered like grass' to quote from psalm 102, which Terry has framed in his room. To cheer myself up I polish off the last Viennese whirl.

Back at The Shack, Terry, having announced he has given up sausages for Lent, dishes up a sardine hotpot. Pottering about in the kitchen afterwards doing the washing up I absentmindedly reach for my vitamin B tabs. By mistake I swallow four of Bingo's conditioning tablets. They look and smell identical to my vit B's and happen to be jumbled up with all my other vitamin bottles on the shelf. Panic attack! I'm in a dial 999 situation! I'm an emergency! Will it mean a stomach pump? Tubes down my gullet? My trembling fingers tap out Doc Ng's number.

'Help me, Doc!' I whimper, and explain what has happened. Long silence at her end. Followed by a sort of muffled, spluttering sound. 'Are you still there, Doc?' I ask, a cold sweat breaking out on my brow.

'No need to worry, Mr Tonks,' she replies. '...However, if you find yourself wanting to cock your leg against a lamppost or getting the urge to roll around in dead seagulls, you had better phone me back immediately. Oh yes, and by the way, what progress with your Quit Kit?'

I'll give her Quit Kit. And if Terry doesn't stop sniggering I'll ram his potato peeler up his nose.

In like a lion, out like a lamb, that's what they say about the month of March. Whoever invented the hot water bottle gets my vote for the Nobel Prize. Freezing estuary gusts are howling through the gaps round the windows. Walloping gale-force winds have hit town – dinghies cart-wheeling across the shingle, two beach huts blown down and smashed to splinters, a trampoline lifted out of a garden and left hanging from a telegraph pole. Jinxie Wicks had to spend the night at Daphne's (wish it was Yours Truly. If only!) due to worries that her static might blow over. When I ventured forth (after a bowl of Terry's runny porridge) with Bingo looking dapper in his knitted coat, what with the spray and the feeble sun bouncing off low clouds it was like walking into a painting by Turner.

I was en route to visit my housebound octogenarian neighbour, a visit I make regularly. Cyril, known locally as Brainy Cyril, lives ten minutes along Spratling Sea Road. In his front garden is an imitation tombstone with this verse written on it:

> *Beneath this stone*
> *Cold stiff and hard*
> *Is the last bloody cat*
> *That crapped in my yard.*

Cyril is looked after by his live-in, octogenarian, sister, Gladys. They are ex-colonial types – house full of elephant foot umbrella stands, African masks, rhino horns, zebra skins, elephant-hair fly whisks, voodoo dolls, Zulu spears, bongo drums, tiger-skin rugs, and what have you. First I do Cyril's shopping – large sliced loaf, jar of marmalade, margarine, 14 frozen cottage pies, 14 frozen chicken tikkas, a dozen eggs, two packets of digestive biscuits, 50 fags for Gladys, the usual… which I load into my trolley on wheels (Sue Ryder, £2). Once I've handed over the groceries to Gladys – 'you're quite the Good Samaritan, Mr Tonks' – I sit back to enjoy a few hours of high-brow chit chat. Talk about a man of intellect! What Cyril doesn't know about literature wouldn't cover a penny stamp. Ha. A penny stamp? What's that?

He is propped up on his day bed, surgical collar, oxygen cylinder and pill bottles to hand, tubes draped round his ears and up his nose.

'Ah, Tonks, my good fellow,' he wheezes, with Gladys hovering with his hot water bottle and extra blanket. 'Offer Tonks a finger, Gladys, and get him to pull up a chair.'

'Stop that ruddy dog cocking his leg against my bronze Zulu warrior, Mr Tonks,' snaps Gladys, tinkling about with sherry glasses and bottles.

There's a choking pong of Vic vapour rub mingled with paraffin heater fumes which to my way of thinking can't be helping with Cyril's bad chest.

I sip my sherry. Cyril dips a digestive biscuit into his. Due to his eyesight problems he has difficulty with the printed page so he likes me to read to him a poem or a chapter or two which we then discuss. In recent months Cyril has had an intellectual go at Coleridge's *Ancient Mariner*.

'It's bloody ludicrous, Tonks. An albatross, the world's largest flying bird, has a wing span of eleven foot. ELEVEN RUDDY FOOT! The Ancient Mariner – *Hold off! unhand me, grey beard loon*. Remember him, Tonks? Boring old fart that he is, would have been incapable of STANDING UPRIGHT, for God's sake, on a rolling ship with a damn great dead albatross hanging around his neck.'

Cyril has also, recently queried the mystery of Oliver Twist's posh accent.

'Answer me this, Tonks, how could a boy whose formative years were spent in the workhouse and in Fagin's den of thieves, speak in the educated tones of a Victorian gentleman?'

Culture with a capital 'C' eh? Old Cyril knows his stuff when it comes to literature.

His current passion is D.H. Lawrence. Myself, I'm in two minds about D.H.L. I'm more a Thomas Hardy man. In my view you can't beat *Tess of the d'Urbervilles*. This month Cyril is getting us started on *Lady Chatterley's Lover*. After asking Gladys to adjust his nasal tube and plump his pillows, Cyril takes a puff on his inhaler and starts pontificating.

'The important thing about D.H.L., Tonks, is that he was not afraid to call a spade a spade. Or come to that, a see-you-en-tee, a see-you-en-tee. Gladys, offer Tonks another finger, and top me up too…'

Gladys tops up and throws Bingo a digestive biscuit.

'Nothing wrong with good old Anglo-Saxonisms when used correctly, eh Tonks? Consider the vocabulary used by the working-class gamekeeper, Mellors, in the sex sequences. You may recall him saying to Lady C, *Tha's got the nicest arse… it's the nicest woman's arse as is!* – in chapter 15. You can take it from me, Tonks, there's not a woman alive who won't fall for a chap who tells her she's got a lovely arse. Or a lovely see-you-en-tee for that matter. I expect Gladys will back me up on that if called upon.'

Here Cyril's hacking cough gets the upper hand and Gladys is called upon to bang his back, rather than back him up by giving her views on the gamekeeper's salty wooing techniques. As for me, I'm having a ponder. Fact is if I had said – had ever dared say, *Tha's got the nicest arse* to the Nutcracker, she would have smacked me round the head. On the other hand is there a possibility that a Mellor-ism or two might work with Daphne? It's an interesting thought. Off with the Y-fronts and Yours Truly murmuring sotto voce into her ear in a fruity, Jeremy Irons' voice, *Tha's got the nicest arse*, Daphne. Hmm. In your dreams.

Anyway, a few days later, following up Jinxie Wicks' invitation I battled my way through the sleety gusts along the sea road. En route, by the bottle bank, I spotted something unusual. A hamster in a cage on the pavement. Someone had abandoned it, dumped it with a note attached saying, 'Please care for me. My name is Roger. My owner is out of work and can't feed me.' How much does it cost to feed a blinkin' hamster, for crying out loud? Dumping a pet hamster – which, I have to say, looked quite perky considering, scrabbling around its plastic wheel – has to be an act of desperation, as well as a sad sign of the times in these days of credit crunches and double-dip recessions. I decided there and then to write a letter to the Saltmarsh Gazette. Here's my letter as it appeared in print.

Hamster horror
Sir,
I was shocked and outraged to witness the sight of a pet hamster dumped, in its cage, by the bottle bank. A note explained that its unemployed owner could no longer afford to feed it. It is a national disgrace that in 2012 honest, out-of-work people cannot afford to feed their hamsters. It is also a sad sign of the times, and yet more proof that the country is going to the dogs. The MP for Saltmarsh should be told.
Yours sincerely,
Ronald Tonks

Editor's comment:
The Saltmarsh RSPCA reports that 35 hamsters have been dumped in recent weeks. The Hamster Rehoming Group urgently seeks loving homes for these abandoned pets.

Thanks to my intervention, Roger was rapidly rehomed by the Saltmarsh Infant School reception class. It is reported that he is very happy.

Arriving at Jinxie Wicks' static, still, despite the storms, in one piece I'm glad to say (the static, I mean, not Yours Truly) I handed her a can of Scrumpy Jack and stepped over the heap of cruise brochures scattered across the floor. Jinxie Wicks – like me – sends off for a load at this time of year. She too dreams of palm-fringed beaches, azure seas, coral islands where the balmy breezes waft, hibiscus flowers stuck behind each ear and so forth. Like me she keeps her passport up-to-date – futile or what – just in case her luck changes.

Even though the static was rocking and swaying in the wind, there was a welcoming waft of the famous faggots in onion gravy. Jinxie Wicks was wearing a jungle print, boiler-suit sort of affair. She looked like something off the BBC's *Wildlife on One*. We were soon tucking in, Jinxie Wicks entertaining me with stories about her recent online dating exploits. One chap turned up at the arranged rendezvous with his mum. Another described himself as 'tall, dark and handsome' and turned out to be five foot tall and bald. The only promising-looking one – invited her back to his bijou basement opposite the public conveniences.

Fidgeting with his dimmer switch he promised, 'Later babe, we can watch Championship Darts on my plasma screen TV,' which as chat-up lines go, is hardly likely to get a red-blooded woman on red alert. Out came his Tesco Lambrusco and the cocktail chipolatas. On went his Barry Manilow CD. Into the microwave went a frozen chicken tikka. Into the loo went Jinxie Wicks. Hanging on the wall was a floral-patterned porcelain plaque saying: 'If you sprinkle when you tinkle, be a sweetie, wipe the seatie'. Jinxie Wicks was out of the bijou basement and running home before the microwave had pinged.

Later that day, despite the freezing cold, I toddle along to the Friendly Winkle. Len is in the bar regaling regulars with a blow-by-blow account of a TV programme he'd watched called *Aircraft Confidential* about a Boeing 747 that rolled out of control in 1999 sparking a six-year investigation. Someone chips in to say that she'd read in the paper that long-haul flights cause hair loss.

'Is the world full of bald airline pilots or bald air hostesses?' scoffs Len, beer froth on his bushy moustache. 'No it is NOT. Don't believe what you read in papers.'

A bloke sitting nearby jokes that sex for seniors can be rather risky. The last time he and his lady got a bit frisky, she licked his ear and short-circuited his hearing aid. We all laugh our socks off. Even Len.

I then catch sight of Tozer, skulking at the corner table thumbing through the Friendly Winkle's stack of cruise brochures. Flashing his mossy teeth, he calls over, 'Care to join me for a tincture or two, Ronald?'

Against my better judgement, I join him, sipping my half pint while he whinges on about his absentee wife.

'She's mad as a box of frogs, but there you go, Ronald, grief is the price we pay for love.'

I notice that he is wearing THE hand-knitted stripy scarf. Grief? What does Tozer know about grief? Then Tozer suddenly pounds his fist on the table (splashing his drink everywhere) leans close, and hisses, 'I have measured out my life in toilet rolls, Ronald. Tempus fugit. I grow old, you grow old, we shall wear our trousers rolled. Once I wanted to change the world, now I can't change my socks without dislocating my back. What have I done with my life? What have you done with yours? God save us from ending up like those two doddery old farts two tables away. Look at them! Over there – two old topers – strawberry noses, droopy jowls, wobbling wattles, hang-dog expressions, dead eyes, brown stumps for teeth, boozing themselves to oblivion, sad old bastards…'

Over there? I look. I look again. Hang about!

'That's not two tables away, Tex. It's a mirror.'

Good grief. The man's barking. I escape from his gloom and doom into the ozone rich fresh air of the Saltmarsh seafront.

Next day, to the dentist. Further shocks await. Booking in for a check-up I'm told by the receptionist that the cost has trebled. TREBLED. Overnight the NHS dentist has gone private. I am informed of the fact by a stern-looking woman, a dead ringer for Wicked Wanda's Whiplash at Shackles R Us.

'Now look here, young woman,' I thunder, 'as a lifelong contributor to the welfare state, I expect to get what's left of my teeth and gums sorted out at a minimum subsidised cost.'

Is she concerned? Is she sympathetic? Not on your life. In a no-nonsense manner she says, 'Mr Tonks, as I explained, the situation has changed. We are now a private dental practice. I will make your views known to the dentist.' This put me on my guard. Never antagonise a dentist. There is no knowing what diabolical vengeance he might wreak with his drill, or whether your name might get into the dental world's black books. Out I go, tail between my legs.

Interestingly, in a biography of Thomas Hardy by Claire Tomalin (RSPCA jumble sale, 40p) I came across a Hardy quote:

Hurt my tooth at breakfast. I look in the glass. Am conscious of the humiliating sorriness of my earthly tabernacle.

Talk about Hardy hitting the nail on the head. *Humiliating sorriness.* What a great phrase for us old-timers trapped, as we are, in our earthly tabernacles. *Humiliating sorriness* might almost be a Leonard Cohen line.

Two days later I wake up to find I've been cast into dental darkness. Struck off. Here's the letter I received:

Dear Mr Tonks
I understand you wish to register with a new dentist.
In the circumstances I think this is the best course to take.
If any further problems arise I suggest you see your new

dentist as we are no longer able to accommodate you at this practice.

Yours sincerely… et cetera

Miserable git. Capitalist hyena! So now I'm obliged to traipse across Kent trying to track down a NHS dentist. Take it from me, NHS dentists are thinner on the ground these days than lamp-lighters and crossing-sweepers.

Talking teeth, no writer has written more harrowingly about his dental tribulations than the trailblazing young novelist Martin Amis. In his gripping autobiography *Experience* (Oxfam, 30p) he writes unflinchingly about his tooth torment. Martin Amis? Now there's a man who, you might assume, has everything – fame, literary stardom, an Oxford education, a stunning fire-cracker of a wife, the late Philip Larkin as his godfather, and probably a share of his late dad's royalties – everything that is, except his own teeth. Amis, afflicted by terrible dental problems in midlife, endured months of drillings, probings, wrenchings, tearings, jaw-bone graftings, gum stitchings, a choke-inducing bridge running from ear to ear, excruciating dental implants, X-rays galore, and a final bill big enough to buy – had he wanted to – a detached bungalow with parking space and solar heating panels on the leafier outskirts of Saltmarsh. And you can bet he didn't get all that fancy dental work on the NHS Incidentally it is from Amis' biography that I learnt that Lawrence suffered with his teeth. An acquaintance of D.H.L. recalled that his teeth *'were like black pumpkin seeds'*.

Must remember to tell that to Brainy Cyril. Meanwhile I'm stuck with throbbing gums and worries about where to find a NHS dentist. To calm myself down I dashed off this fan letter to Martin Amis.

To: Martin Amis
Sir,
How skilfully you write about your teeth! I could almost feel
the dentist's drill! And I was close to flinching at the painful
probings and pokings around that you so vividly describe.
As the old Ukranian proverb goes: 'Man is closer to his teeth
than to his family and relations'. Your harrowing descriptions
of dental procedures have scared the living daylights out of
Yours Truly prior to some forthcoming dental work. No
man is a hero to his dentist! Be we celebrated or humble
– educated at Oxford or the Snodland Tech – we are all
at the mercy of our gnashers – the great levellers! Bet you
had to do a fair bit of donkey-work with the old felt-tip to
stump (no pun intended!) up for all that dentistry! Keep on
scribbling! It's time you had a Booker Prize win. I am a great
fan of your late father's brilliant books. He is my favourite
author.
Yours truly
Ronald Tonks

Having posted the letter, I settle down with a can of Scrumpy
Jack, Bingo on my lap, and a book, and start pondering the
fact that I am more concerned about my teeth, even about
Martin Amis' teeth, than I am about – say – the war in
Afghanistan. I spend more time agonising about my teeth
than I do about the horrors of, for example, twenty-six women
and children being murdered by militia loyal to President
Bashar Assad in Syria as happened this week. Should I be
ashamed of my lack of concern about world events? Or is
it all part of *la condition humaine*? Nowadays the profound
quandaries of human existence seem to boil down, for me, to
the cost of dental treatment and the deteriorating sorriness of
my earthly tabernacle.

On the radio a chirpy voice is blaring 'Happy bicentennial
Charles Dickens – and here to celebrate it is Lionel Bart's

orchestral overture for *Oliver*...' My mental plasma screen lights up with a picture of Dickens lolling about in the great hereafter surrounded by the heavenly host flapping their wings, their radios turned up full blast. At this point my imaginings are interrupted by the phone ringing. I pick it up and get an earful of a shouty female voice.

'Mr Tonks? Mr Reginald Tonks? This is a call from the Community Police. We are with your mother, Mrs Doris Tonks. She has been stopped in the street for speeding on her mobility scooter, and we have reason to believe she has been drinking.'

At this juncture my mum comes on the line.

'Is that you, Son? I haven't touched a drop. All I've had is a dose or two of my special cough linctus. I swear on my mother's grave. Tell 'em, Son, and tell 'em I'm suffering from early onset dementia to get me off the hook...'

'I don't think you can get early onset dementia at 94, Mum.'

'— and tell her, Son, that I didn't mean to cause the Police any incontinence...'

Luckily the shouty female was of a benevolent disposition. My mum, drunk in charge of a mobility scooter? That's all I need, yet another thing to worry about. Luckily the situation was sorted out amicably, no charges. No repercussions. And so I fill my trusty hot water bottle, make myself a cup of cocoa, put Bingo in his basket and go to bed.

What a turn up. It's now hotter here than Morocco! Seventy degrees and rising in Kent. The warmest March since 1957. Off with the 'Fagins' fingerless mitts, on with a knotted handkerchief to protect my thinning dome from melanoma-causing sunrays. I was up with the lark to take Bingo for a run – well 'run' is putting it a bit strong, more a stop and start waddle (Bingo I mean, not Yours Truly) – with Jinxie Wicks. We stopped off at a riverside creek to sit on a seat which had a plaque with 'Ethel and Albert Cook enjoyed this view and hope you will too. RIP' fixed to the seat's back.

So there we are, quietly enjoying a slurp from our cans of cider, minding our own business, grumbling cheerfully about our aching knees and wondering how trade is doing at Shackles R Us, when a big, burly plod suddenly looms into view disturbing the peace with his crackling walkie-talkie.

''Ello, 'ello, 'ello,' says Jinxie Wicks out of the side of her mouth, in a jokey, *Dixon of Dock Green* voice. The plod marches over with menacing deliberation.

'Excuse me, sir, madam, may I draw your attention to the notice opposite.'

'What notice?' we ask, simultaneously, our cider tins poised.

'The notice informing you that you have entered an alcohol-free zone, and as such, the consumption of alcoholic drinks is forbidden. You are therefore perpetrating an infringement of the law.'

Pumped up pillock! Two harmless old-timers enjoying a little snorter in the spring sunshine and the next thing we know is we're about to be handcuffed and carted off to jail. It's getting worse than Russia.

'Oh push off, go and play with your whistle,' snaps Jinxie Wicks, glugging the last few drops. 'Why aren't you out catching rapists, murderers and terrorists, instead of harassing blameless senior citizens on a countryside ramble.'

To prevent the situation escalating into a full-blown crime scene I stare into the Plod's beady eyes, incline my head towards Jinxie Wicks, and make a circular movement against my temple with my finger. Plod glares back, catches on, winks twice, and says, 'Got it. Understood, sir. You'll know better next time. And you, madam, watch your language…' and pushes off.

Phew! Fact is we hadn't noticed the notice. Even if we HAD noticed it, we wouldn't have been able to read it without our specs.

As Plod walks away (in a westerly direction) a low-life sort who has been crouching, unobserved, behind an upturned rowing boat, pokes his head up and hisses, 'Is it all clear, mate?' He then lurches over, waving a bottle of the hard stuff and making a whooping, yodelling sound. Bingo starts growling. The chap sways towards us shouting, 'Bleedin' fuzz always making life a misery for us harmless pissheads, eh mate? Bastards! Just because we enjoy whetting our whistles now and again they think they can harass us from dawn to dusk. Tossers! Cheers!' He proffers us the bottle saying, 'One for the road, mates?'

Good grief! He thinks we're a couple of inebriates! Fellow dipsos! We depart with dignity continuing on our way along the tow path with Bingo frisking through the dandelions. The reeds rustle in the spring breeze, the cries of wild fowl echo across the glittering estuary and the sun 'pours down like honey' to quote Leonard Cohen. God's in his heaven as Terry would say. All's right with the world.

Days later and the sun is still shining. I rescue my trusty deckchair from its winter hibernation in the lean-to (or 'extension' as I like to call it) and set it up on the storm-blasted patch of shingle aka my back garden. A sailing dinghy bobs on the horizon. A windsurfer wobbles on a wave. A line of poetry by John Keats floats into my head.

Oh ye! Who have your eyeballs vexed and tired
Feast them upon the wideness of the sea…

Feast them indeed. And I do. I laze back in my deckchair, knotted hankie on my head, happily feasting my vexed and tired eyeballs. I am suddenly reminded of a recent newspaper item which had me laughing so hard I burst my braces. A Brazilian bather on Copacabana beach had been swimming in the sea, returned to his sun-lounger, flopped down, fell asleep and got a terrible shock when he woke up and tried to stand up. His testicles had become TRAPPED. The chilly sea had temporarily shrunk his testicles, but as they warmed up and returned to normal size they had become wedged between the wooden slats. He had to use his mobile phone to call the emergency lifeguard who managed to free him by placing ice cubes on the trapped testicles. Never use a slatted sun-lounger that's my advice to all male sun-worshippers. Oh my aching sides! Just thinking about it starts me laughing again, feeling glad that I'm safe on my canvas fold-up. Then disaster strikes. The seat splits and as my nether regions hit the shingle the chair folds up trapping my knees up under my chin. I am in shock, teeth (what's left of them) rattling like castanets. With my arms and feet dangling over the wooden cross bar and flailing about I spend the next half hour feebly shouting, 'HELP! HELP!' Fortunately Bingo's frantic barks alert a member of the public who happens to be cycling past The Shack.

It pains me to report that my rescuer is none other than – you've guessed it – Daphne! There am I, doubled up like a trussed chicken, looking far from my best. Blobs of sun cream on my nose, hankie on my head, knobbly knees exposed by my boy-scout shorts (Sue Ryder, 50p) and – worst of all – I'm wearing socks with my flip-flops. Not a dapper look for a man of romantic inclinations. The only consolation is that at least my horny yellow toenails are not exposed.

Daphne throws up her hands. She sets to, doing the fireman's lift, extracting me from the collapsed chair.

'Don't struggle, Ronald, just go limp,' says Daphne. NOT exactly the words I've fantasised about in my dreams. And it's certainly not the moment to attempt a D.H. Lawrence *Tha's got the nicest arse* line of chat-up. Just as I'm getting into the recovery position on the shingle and Daphne is soothing my sunburnt brow with a damp cloth, Terry turns up, having come straight from one of his funerals.

'Afternoon, folks. Hope I'm not interrupting anything!' chortles Terry, who is wearing his professional mourner gear, including a top hat.

'Oh my goodness,' exclaims Daphne, open-mouthed at the sight of Terry's togs. 'You gave me quite a shock. I don't think you're needed in the line of duty just yet!'

The upshot is that Terry puts the kettle on. I'm soon feeling right as rain and Daphne pedals off into the sunset.

And life goes on. Terry has been trying to sort out the TV set. Here in Saltmarsh we have lost our TV reception. The *Saltmarsh Gazette* reports that this is due to solar flares. These are apparently bombarding the earth's magnetic field this month at six hundred miles per second, sending a barrage of charged atoms to wreak havoc with broadcasting satellites, power grids and computers. None of us seniors have a clue what this is all about. All we know is that none of our TV sets are working. Andy has promised to invite an expert to explain all at the next SPAM meeting.

Later, looking at the calendar, I note that we are approaching Mother's Day. I have a very soft spot for my old mum. Took her a bunch of daffs last Mother's Day. She turned her nose up and said, 'They won't last five minutes.

Between you and me and the gatepost, Ronald, I'd rather have a nice bottle of gin.'

Fact is we Tonkses have never been touchy-feely types. If, when I was a lad, my mother had started cuddling and kissing me I'd have assumed she was on the booze.

Not everyone has a fluffy relationship with their mum. Some mums can be a nightmare. If ever anyone had a mother from hell it was the poet, Edith Sitwell. I must remember to tell Brainy Cyril about Edith's relationship with her mum on my next visit. She published her autobiography. *Taken Care Of* (Scouts' car boot sale, 10p) in the 1930s. Observations like, '*It was my mother... who made my childhood a living hell*' and '*my mother hated me throughout my childhood and youth*' make it clear that her mother was never likely to receive a box of chocs and bunch of daffs on Mother's Day. Her mother – the Hon. Ida Denison, who married Sir George Sitwell, who from all accounts, was fairly bonkers himself, used to work herself up into *tornadoes of fury* until she blacked out. Poor old Edith. She describes a childhood incident which shows how little affection she had for the tyrannical old boot. She was five years old and two kids of a similar age came to tea. They were dressed in black and Edith wanted to know why, and also why their mother wasn't with them.

'Our mother is dead,' replied the kids and started to sob. They went home soon afterwards. Edith asked her nanny why they had cried. 'Because their mother is dead.'

Puzzled, Sitwell replied, 'Yes, I know THAT. But why did they cry?'

Fascinating, eh? Brainy Cyril will be very interested. In spite of her mum, Edith Sitwell grew up to have a great sense of humour. She became a terrific character, no two ways. When she was 75 someone asked her how she was. She replied, 'Dying, but apart from that I'm alright.'

Anyway, off I go for my Mother's Day visit. Mum's council flat is in Margate, not far from Dreamland. What a wonderful place Dreamland was in its heyday with its Caterpillar, Haunted House, Flying Scooter, Ghost Train, Hall of Mirrors, Whip, Cup and Saucer and – admittedly rather small by today's standards – Big Wheel. Dreamland was once the nation's best-loved amusement park. Fun-fair fans flocked to Margate in their thousands to ride on Dreamland's famous scenic railway with its mile-long wooden frame. It had a thrilling, white-knuckle hill drop. You could hear the screams in the high street as the public roared down the drop.

Saltmarsh itself is not far from Dreamland, fifteen miles as the crow flies, one hour by bus from Canterbury. From Mum's kitchen window you can see the gaunt skeleton of the scenic railway, destroyed by fire in 2008. Dreamland today is a mass of rust and rot, twisted wreckage and puddles of greasy water. There's a joke does the rounds. The first raffle prize is a week in Margate. The second prize is a fortnight in Margate.

In I go and there's Mum, frizzy blue hair, yellow flyaway specs, frilly pink blouse, baggy leggings and green trainers. She likes her bright colours does Mum. She is perched on a booster cushion, in her riser-recliner by the window. On a side table is a magazine open at a page headed UNLEASH YOUR INNER SEXPOT WITH A WIG.

'Hello, Son. Come in. Wipe your feet. Put the kettle on. Got my bottle of gin?'

On the wall are framed photographs of dogs long gone, dogs that go back in to the mists of memory – Bobby, Sunny, Patch, Bonzo, Congo, Flossie, Darkie, Snuffles, Lassie, Batty… There's a photo of Yours Truly, aged about 12, holding Snuffles, wearing school uniform and round wire-rimmed NHS specs. Mum's flat is somewhat cluttered. Every surface – mantelpiece, window ledge, sideboard, coffee table and shelf unit – is scattered with ornamental china dogs. All sizes. All shapes. On top of the TV are two floral-painted, plastic urns containing the ashes of Charles and Diana, two poodles rescued by Mum from the Battersea Dogs Home, her last hurrah as a dog-owner.

Today's visit is typical. No hugs. No kisses. I pour nips of gin and squirt tonic into two glasses hand-painted with West Highland terriers.

'You're looking a bit peaky, Son,' says Mum, getting out her knitting needles. 'You haven't been eating Dutch sundried tomatoes, have you?'

'Matter of fact, Mum, I've NEVER ever eaten sundried –'

'Because they can be fatal. You hear me? FATAL. A sundried tomato alert has been sent out to all the big supermarkets. There's a deadly outbreak of Hepatitis A which is linked to Dutch sundried tomatoes, it was on the telly—'

'Mum. Watch my lips. I've never, ever, eaten sundried—'

'—the symptoms to watch out for are loss of appetite, muscle aches, headaches, stomach pains, itchy skin, yellow eyeballs. Here, come over to the light, let's have a look at your eyeballs.'

And so it goes on. A flowing of mutual affection, in an understated, taken for granted manner. The wall clock – a large Labrador silhouette – goes tick tock and makes a barking noises on the hour. Mum has moved on to a new topic. Walnuts.

'Miracle food, Son, packed full of anti-oxygen.'

I tell her how I recently cracked a tooth eating a walnut. Time flies. Four barks and it's time to put my coat on and slip a fiver under the life-sized china pug dog on the window ledge.

'Cheerio, Mum. Keep your pecker up.'

'Ta-ta, Ronald. Don't forget your cod-liver oil and your Tiger Balm chest rub.'

Like all mothers who once long ago powdered their babies' backsides, she can never accept that her baby has grown up.

APRIL 2012

Oh no! Good grief! I'm living in a horror movie! Phone rings as I'm stirring the porridge. It's Jinxie Wicks. 'Ronald! Urgent news! Nutcracker alert! The Nutcracker's back in town!'

Bloomin' hell! Knees wobble. Palpitations start up. Vitals turn to water. Then I twig. Ha-ha!

'Blimey, Jinx! Hee-hee-hee. You nearly had me there! Nice try. April fool to you, too.' Phew!

'RONALD,' yells Jinxie Wicks 'this is NOT an April fool. I saw the Nutcracker, large as life and twice as terrifying. She was in the Friendly Winkle knocking back a full English. She's let herself go, a bit, but there's no mistaking the Nutcracker. It was her, all-right. Defo. She's back in town and looks like she's on the war-path…'

Panic stations. Sweaty palms! Where can I hide? Five minutes later the phone rings again. Bingo starts barking. Some sixth sense tells me it's the Nutcracker. Ignore it, Tonks. God strike me stone dead if ever I speak to that woman again. Phone keeps ringing. Terry, who is still trying to sort out the TV digital switchover problem, calls out, 'Are you going to answer the phone, Dad, or shall I?' I answer it. Aaaagh! That voice! That donkey-like Nutcracker laugh! Talk about make me want to walk into the sea with lead weights tied to my flip-flops.

The upshot is that after a monosyllabic series of responses on my part 'Yup? No. No way. Don't care. What? No. No. No. No. Okay…' I agree to meet her in the Friendly Winkle. I put the phone down and suffer a violent Imodium moment.

Rush along the passage. Trip over Bingo. Fall flat on my face. Blasted dog. Not a word do I say to Terry. We never mention his mother.

So, on with my best bib and tucker. Don't want to let the side down. Besides, I want her to take one look at me and start thinking what a fool she was to dump such a fine figure of a bloke. I want her to be overcome with regrets and yearnings for *temps perdus*. '*Our days were a joy and our paths were through flowers*' as Thomas Hardy wrote. That might be putting it a bit strong if applied to me and the Nutcracker, but in the first flush of youthful passion we did have our moments. Although, I must admit, we got off to a bad start. I had just grown a moustache and after a snog on our first date I said, 'This is the first time I've kissed a girl with a moustache.' And she slapped me round the face.

Come 11 A.M., I stagger through a sleety April shower, the weather having turned wintery again, and attempt a brisk trot to the Friendly Winkle. The place is empty apart from an old boy with a white crew cut fiddling with his smartphone. Not wanting to be the first to arrive I walk on by, then retrace my steps. Twice. Perishing cold it is, too. I peer inside again. The place is still empty apart from the old boy. I need the Gents. I need a drink. Talk about collywobbles. In I go, settle myself down with half a pint. I take a slurp. Suddenly the old boy yells: 'Bloody hell! Ronald? Is it YOU! This is ME. Hello! Didn't recognise you!!'

Whaat? Oh no! The 'old boy' with the white crew cut is the Nutcracker. It's been fifteen years. Say no more. She's wearing khaki chinos with lots of pockets. Her head looks as if it's been recently shaved. She's got a badge on her chest that says 'A WOMAN WITHOUT A MAN IS LIKE A FISH WITHOUT A BICYCLE'. She clomps over to me in big, khaki commando boots laced up to her knees and slaps me on the shoulder: 'Look at YOU. Little pot-belly coming! You're getting a roof over your tool-shed, as the Aussie's say…'

Talk about pots and kettles. Her roof starts at her neck and ends at her knees. She's got a bum like a bouncy castle. Sit her on a bike and the wheels would buckle. No two ways.

'Fact is, Ron, I need closure.'

SHE needs closure? I need an ice-cold compress on my head. And a hi-alc snorter. Shock! She buys me one. With her own money. Talk about a world first.

'Fact is, Ron, I'm now batting for the other side…'

What's she going on about? Has she taken up cricket?

'Chrissakes, Ron, I'm trying to tell you…', she says offering me some pork scratchings and doing a double wink, 'I'm a Friend of Dorothy'.

Who the hell is Dorothy?

'I'm surfing on the other side of the shore. Bent as a butcher's hook. Queer as a clockwork orange.'

Is she speaking in code? Has she gone bonkers.

The barman's ears are flapping like dinghy sails. Then the penny drops. Stone the crows! Gobsmacked isn't the word. All that Imodium and booze must have slowed down the old brainbox.

'Wake up and smell the coffee, Ron. Hee-haw. Hee-haw. I'm out! I'm a ginger beer! I'm gay! I'm in touch with my true sexuality at last. You see sitting before you a radical, burn-her-bra woman's liberationist and – yeah – a lesbian!'

Blimey. I bet when she burnt her bra it took the fire department three days to put it out. But you have to hand it to the woman for getting her act together. Say it loud, say it proud and so forth. She tells me she's in a relationship with a woman with a big heart and an even bigger bank balance.

They are working together for the Stop Female Genital Mutilation Campaign and are shortly off to Sudan for the cause. Let's hope the Nutcracker decides to stay there.

I'm numb. I'm almost doubled up with the gripes. Off I scurry to the Gents – living proof of an observation made by the little-known writer John Lancaster Spalding, who said, 'There is nothing so humiliating as to know what a controlling influence the intestines have on the thoughts and ways of men'. Too true. I return to the bar where the barman is struggling to keep a straight face.

The Nutcracker is still rabbiting on. 'Let's face it, Ron, we had our ups and downs, but we had our good times, too. Remember Bubbles? Darling old Bubbles? That dog was the love of my life – dog-wise I mean.'

Bubbles? Good grief? Images of toilet rolls, cotton-wool balls and puddles of dog-vomit flash upon my inward eye.

'So, Ron, I'm here to say cheerio, draw a line and all that. I admit that when you got me you got the rough end of the pineapple. I blame it on my oestrogen plunges.'

Oestrogen plunges? That's a new one on me. The barman is convulsed, pulling faces and tapping his index finger on his temple behind the Nutcracker's back.

'Don't know what gets into me sometimes, Ron. On the other had I *do* know what doesn't get into me any more, if you get my drift? Hee-haw, hee-haw, haw, haw.'

Oh that nightmare bray. Followed up with one of the Nutcracker's painful nudges in the ribs. How did I survive all those years?

'So no ill-feelings, Ronnikins? Friends?' Hee-haw. Nudge. Nudge. We clink glasses.

She says, 'Bums up!' takes a swig and with a victory-V sign and a jaunty wiggle of the fingers, she clomps out. Talk about breathe a sigh of relief.

'Ronnikins!! RONNIKINS,' honks the barman, doubled up. 'Fancy a ginger beer, Ronnikins?'

Then she stomps back in: 'By the way, tell Terry he's often in my thoughts. Blood's thicker than water...'

Phew! A load has been lifted. As the commando boots march off into the sunset, I feel like Dorothy felt in *The Wizard of Oz* when she watched the wicked Witch of the West with the green face dissolve into a sizzling puddle of foaming bile. I almost break into a few bars of *Somewhere over the Rainbow*.

Despite the boggy terrain along the sea road, there's a new spring in my step. I hurry home with a song in my heart and – not to put too fine a point on it – alarming turbulence further down. I'm feeling so euphoric that I post off a cheque for £25 to the Stop Female Genital Mutilation Campaign, not my first choice of charity and not a pressing problem here in Saltmarsh, but you learn something new every day. And Jinxie Wicks assures me that the FGM campaign to put a stop to a heathen abomination is a very worthy cause.

Terry, busy at one of his funerals, has left a pilchard hotpot on the cooker, and a note to say he's fixed the TV Hurrah.

As I heat up the hotpot (six minutes in Terry's microwave, talk about twenty-first century!) I find myself pondering upon one of the great mysteries of *la condition humaine*, namely the dwindling of romantic passion. You meet a person, your heart stands still, you're walking on air, you can't eat, you can't sleep, you feel more alive and kicking than you've ever felt before. That person lights your blue touch-paper, invades your dreams and plays havoc with your hormones. Then, one day, the magic has gone. What happens to it? Suddenly the person dwindles into just another human being, someone who has to cut their toe nails, floss their teeth, hog the bathroom… I expect D.H. Lawrence had something to say on the subject. I must check it out with Brainy Cyril.

I'm ruminating on these matters and scraping the remainder of Terry's pilchard hotpot into Bingo's bowl when, glancing through the window, I see a large, briefcase carrying woman with hairy legs pounding up the front path. Knock-knock. Rat-a-tat-tat. I freeze with a spoonful of pilchard hotpot poised in mid-air. Is she a plain-clothes plod? Has Terry shopped me for my little spliff debacle? Has the vet reported me? My mental plasma screen lights up. I'm seeing flashing blue lights. Shouty drug-squads in hi-vis jackets are smashing the door down. Yours Truly is being dragged outside. Yours Truly is sewing mail bags.

Knock-knock. Rat-a-tat-tat. I open the door flashing my ever-aching choppers.

'Evening, Mr Tonks. I'm Edna Higgins, volunteer from Community Care. I'm delivering a complimentary Save-a-Flush loo pack to all Saltmarsh pensioners.' She explains that the Save-a-Flush is simple to use. Once installed it will save me one litre of water each time I flush. That equals 2,000 gallons of water a year. Or 35,000 cups of tea. All I have to do is flatten the Save-a-Flush and drop it into the lavatory cistern between the ball cock and the front panel. The instructions are all on the pack. Edna has more hair on her legs than Bingo.

And off she hurries. Save-a-Flush? Whatever next? Panic over. Back to the pilchard hotpot. Phone goes.

'Hello, Mum'

'Hello, Ronald. Everything all right? I'm phoning to warn you to watch out if the Community Care people give you a free gadget called Save-a-Flush. They tell you to drop it into your lav and it will save you using 2,000 gallons a year—'

'Not INTO your lav, Mum, you drop it into the—'

'Don't interrupt, Son… I'm warning you. I dropped mine and now the lav's blocked up. I think it was an April fool stunt.'

Good grief! What a day. And it gets worse. That evening, after I've dropped the Save-a-Flush into the cistern as per instructions, it expands to the size of a house brick and gets stuck under the ball cock. The flush won't work. Even as I'm writing this Terry is in the toilet, cistern lid off, banging about with a spanner and trying to get things working again. So much for Community Care.

Guess what? Yours Truly has become a music maker! Whoever would have twigged that beneath my thermal vest (St Mildred's Hospice, 50p) throbs the heart of a rockin'-rollin'-finger-pickin' dude with a boogie-woogie-tootie-fruity dream? Yo! I have joined the ukulele group set up by SPAM leader, Andy.

Good old Andy. I can say, hand on heart, that to be in a group all singing and strumming along to *Down By The Riverside*, say, or *Honolulu Baby* is, for Yours Truly, almost as good as it gets. Okay, certain killjoys like Terry, may scoff and make snide complaints about George Formby and his saucy innuendo. They may very well sneer at Formby's *Little Stick of Blackpool Rock* and *With My Little Ukulele in My Hand*, but THEY themselves ought to bloomin' well have a go at playing the humble four-string instrument. If they did, they'd soon realise that Formby was a giant among ukulele players, a genius, with fantastic musical skill. And what's more you can buy a ukulele brand new for only £12 (Sue Ryder). Take it from me, learning to play the uke when you're past the first flush of youth takes gumption.

The SPAM uke group meets in the Friendly Winkle's back room. Our uke instructor, Diesel, looks like something that's been dug up from a peat bog after 6,000 years – wrinkly, skinny, greasy grey ponytail that starts in the centre of his bald upper scalp, wispy beard, brown teeth. A Celtic cross dangles below his Adam's apple. He wears a scuffed, leather jacket with an eagle on the back outlined in metal studs. His flared jeans end three inches above his Cuban-heeled, winkle-picker boots. His tambourine-toting partner is Big Babs, a fine figure of a woman, Afro American, twenty stone, hair like a shag-pile carpet, teeth that outshine her face and an unpredictable, volatile personality. You wouldn't want to bump into her up a dark alley. But Big Babs bashing and jangling in time to old Diesel's skiffle-scarred vocals and nifty finger-work is a sight to behold and a sound for sore ears. At the uke group, Diesel demonstrates a new chord and – twang – off we go – plunk, plunkety, plunk, fumbling fingers, aching wrists as we work up some speed. 'Daddy, daddy cool...' we warble, jowels wobbling, Big Babs banging and caterwauling, while various sniggering non-uke players keep poking their heads round the door:

Jinxie Wicks: 'Oh no, not another plucking George Formby!'

Len: 'Right on, you mad old pluckers!'

Tex Tozer: 'If music be the food of love then ukulele music is the syrup-of-figs.'

We pluck on regardless. The word put about (frequently) by Diesel is that for more years than he can remember he travelled the world employed as a roadie to all the big names.

'All the living rock legends and some dead ones. All the greats. You name 'em...' rasps Diesel, tuning up his uke, fag hanging from lower lip, 'The Stones, Grateful Dead, Black Sabbath, Led Zeppelin, you name 'em...'

Oh yeah? Pull the other one.

'C'mon, let's get serious guys. Get pluckin', ' snorts Diesel, Big Babs handing him a pint of brown ale and shaking her maracas. So we get pluckin'. Bring it on daddy-o! Thanks to Diesel I managed to master four chords after two sessions. And here's the amazing thing. You can play hundreds of songs with just four chords. Literally hundreds. You should hear me doing *Blowing in the Wind* (only three chords – C, F, G7), after only two weeks. TWO WEEKS! If Bob Dylan could hear me he'd be punching the air. And my version of Leonard Cohen's *Bird on a Wire* had Terry, who was in the kitchen cooking one of his hotpots, standing with his mouth hanging open.

'Blimey, Dad, you'll be headlining at Glastonbury next,' he said, beating time with his potato peeler.

So, Monday nights I can be found at the Friendly Winkle strumming and warbling with twenty of so fellow strummers and warblers. True, it's early days and will be some time before I can achieve Diesel's fancy twanging techniques, calypso strums, four finger rolls and funky contrapuntal rhythms.

'Keep it basic, Deez,' we beginners entreat as he and Big Babs get carried away on wings of song and waves of rhythm.

Gamely we strum and pluck, chords off key, upstrokes too harsh, downstrokes too timid. Big Babs rolls bloodshot eyes.

So does Diesel, 'C'mon guys, take it from the top, start slow, in the key of C…' and away we go – '*What shall we do with the drunken sailor*' – getting up speed with each verse. Talk about scorching fingertips. Brilliant. If only the Nutcracker could see me now. Regrets she'd have a few, I don't mind saying. Walking home with my ukulele in its special case over my shoulder, I feel like some devil-may-care rock god. The Nutcracker (if she wasn't a ginger beer) would be throwing herself at my water-resistant, thermal-lined boots.

However, life's not all beer and skittles. I made my regular visit to Brainy Cyril. He was on good form, propped up on the day bed, his copy of *Lady Chatterley's Lover* open where we left off at chapter six.

'Strange chappie, D.H.L.,' Cyril begins, as Gladys tinkles about with the sherry glasses.

'Ruddy strange if you want my opinion,' snaps Gladys, turfing Bingo off Cyril's day bed. 'You're always wittering on, Cyril, about D.H.L.'s filthy Anglo-Saxonisms and admiring his way of calling an arse an arse and so forth, but let me remind you that he rarely calls a penis a penis. He calls it a "John Thomas". JOHN THOMAS, for God's sake? How infantile is THAT?'

Cyril coughs and splutters: 'As a matter of fact, Gladys, I did NOT ask for your opinion. And before you so rudely interrupted me I was about to inform Tonks that the man was in love with his—'

'John Thomas?' chips in Gladys, her eyes glinting friskily behind her bifocals.

'—in love with his mother, completely tied to his mother's apron strings. So, if you would be kind enough, Gladys, to hand me the D.H.L. biography, third shelf, second left…'

Gladys hands it to him, he blows the dust off and he riffles through, sneezing and wheezing.

'Ah ha! Here we are. Now, Tonks, this is what D.H.L. wrote in a letter to a lady friend: "Nobody can have the soul of me. My mother has it, and nobody can have it again." Interesting stuff, eh? Food for thought. A classic Oedipal complex in my humble opinion. Tied to her apron strings, no doubt about it, and, loving son that he was, did you know that he confessed to helping speed his mother on her way during her final illness by adding morphine to her milk?'

'Don't put ideas into my head,' says Gladys.

'So where were we, Tonks, with Lady C, chapter six? Let's get cracking.'

All this high-brow banter is making my head spin. John Thomas? We had a teacher at the Snodland Tech called John Thomas and no one batted an eyelid. Mind you, no one had heard of D.H.L. at the Snodland Tech. So I clear my throat and start reading:

He was naked to the hips, his velveteen breeches slipping down over his slender loins…

Gladys makes a snorting sound and says that she never wants to hear another word about the randy gamekeeper who is always wandering about the woods with his velveteen breeches' buttons undone, and that she'd rather spend the afternoon going through her cruise brochures. She flounces out leaving us lads to our literature and to our philosophical contemplations. An hour passes in peaceful reading and literary rumination. Before I say my farewells we have a good chuckle when Cyril informs me that when D.H.L. visited Majorca he described the local wine as tasting like '*the sulphurous urination of some aged horse*'. Must remember that phrase next time Terry offers me a glass of his homemade beer.

Leaving Brainy Cyril's I walk at a brisk pace (as recommended by Doc Ng) to the High Street, desperate for a gasper. Into the Saltmarsh Supermarket I go, where a message is flashing up on the cigarette counter's till screens – CUSTOMERS PLEASE NOTE THAT FROM MID APRIL ONWARDS WE SHALL BE HIDING OUR CIGARETTE AND TOBACCO PRODUCTS.

Stone the crows! Where will they be hidden? On the cheese counter? Among the baked beans? Behind the toilet rolls? Then I bump into Daphne. Heart pounds, knees knock. As I stand in the pain-relief aisle my mental soundtrack vibrates with the sound of soaring violins… 'Once I had a secret love,' et cetera. My manhood awakes, as Virginia Woolf might say. Daphne tells me that the hunt-the-baccy lark is due to new health and safety regulations. Fags and baccy will still be on sale in the same place but hidden on shelves behind newly installed doors. What will they start hiding next? Mars Bars (too dangerous for diabetics)? Pork pies (too tempting for fat people)? Haemorrhoid ointment (too upsetting for the easily embarrassed)? Speaking of which I need a tube but am certainly not going to reach out for one to put in my trolley with Daphne looking over my shoulder.

She tells me that she's started attending the SPAM poetry appreciation group. Hmm. Say no more. We loiter there in the pain relief aisle, flanked by shelves of haemorrhoid remedies, corn plasters and such like, Tex Tozer is the elephant-in-the-room as Daphne enthuses about a recent session on modern verse. In my view, I tell her, one of the great modern versifiers is Pam Ayres whose poem *I Wish I'd Looked After Me Teeth* speaks to ninety per cent of British pensioners. Warming to the topic I break into one of Pam's witty verses:

How I laughed at my mother's false teeth
As they foamed in the waters beneath
But now comes the reckonin'
It's me they are beckonin'
Oh, I wish I'd looked after me teeth.

Daphne greets my recitation with a tinkly laugh and says 'Oh, Ronald, you are a card, you've made my day…' she then looks around, lowers her voice and whispers, 'Have you heard about Jinxie Wicks?'

Oh my Gawd! Turns out that Jinxie Wicks has been up to no good trying to earn some extra spondulicks. I prefer to gloss over the ins-and-outs, suffice to say that she's been working for a phone-sex set-up called 'Filthy Grannies'. She sits in her static answering calls from kinky punters between 9 a.m. and 11 a.m. The going rate, so Daphne tells me, is 50p a punter per minute, plus a bonus if the call is over five minutes. How does Daphne KNOW? Well, she cycled over to the site and as she was undoing her cycle-clips outside the static door she could hear Jinxie Wicks panting and moaning and saying things like 'lick it Big Boy... suck it, rub it... Wow! Big Boy...' at which point Daphne wondered whether Jinxie Wicks had at last hit the jackpot with her online dating efforts, but then she noticed that the curtains weren't closed. She peered in and there's Jinxie Wicks sitting on the settee, tray on her lap, phone in one hand, forkful of spaghetti Bolognese in the other. Catching sight of Daphne she silently mouths 'Come in!' then carries on with her panting and moaning and '...more Big Boy, more' sort of stuff and while Big Boy at the other end of the line continues to get his money's worth, Jinxie Wicks silently mouths at Daphne, 'Put the kettle on' and does a few final pants, moans and a couple of 'Yes! Yes! Ye-es!' for good measure before switching off the phone.

'Of course, she disguises her voice,' says Daphne, her bag-for-life, I observe, still going strong, though my own started falling apart after two weeks. 'And talking of voices, Jinxie Wicks is certain that she recognised Len's voice when a punter dialled Filthy Grannies and started going on about – ahem, pardon my French, Ronald – 'Rumpy-pumpy' on a jumbo jet.'

Talk about Sodom and Gomorrah. But you have to hand it to Jinxie Wicks for her enterprising outlook. She's always been a girl to grasp the nettle. I leave Daphne rooting along the free-range chicken shelf and scuttle back to pain relief for my haemorrhoid ointment. Interesting fact: Diesel informed the ukulele group that Johnny Cash's song *Ring of*

Fire (only three chords, C, D, G) attracted the attention of an international haemorrhoid preparation company that wanted to use it in their TV ad – '*And it burns, burns, burns / The ring of fire…*' et cetera but lawyers for the Johnny Cash estate refused permission on the grounds that it would trivialise an iconic work of art. So, I pay for my ointment and baccy and as I'm walking out of the store a piercing alarm goes off and a beefy bloke clamps his hand on my shoulder and says, 'Come this way, please sir.'

Good grief. It's like living in North Korea. Daphne rushes up, in a flap, dropping her tomatoes and insists on accompanying me, with my mouth agape and an ominous spasm in my nether regions, into the 'office'. The beefy bloke opens my tattered bag-for-life. Oh no! Don't look, Daphne. PLEASE. She looks. Beefy holds up the tube of haemorrhoid ointment and a packet of tobacco. Hardly the stuff of a serious shoplifter. To cut a long story short I have my till receipt in my pocket. Daphne accuses Beefy of being a bully, Beefy grovels a bit, gets me a cup of tea and concludes that my titanium knee brace must have set off the alarm. 'I was only doing my job,' whines Beefy. So, I tell him, was Heinrich Himmler.

Things have been fairly mellow at The Shack. Bingo had a flea treatment (£45, daylight robbery). Terry had a haircut. I had my ears syringed. Made twenty pounds on a bundle of old *Dandy* comics, via my vintage bookseller friend. We have to keep our eyes peeled in the vintage and rare books business. We book spotters spend a lot of time in charity shops, riffling through the shelves, always on the lookout for valuable first editions in mint condition with dust-jackets, books by

Graham Greene, Ernest Hemingway, Virginia Woolf, all the literary giants or from the sublime to the cor blimey, early *Beano* and *Dandy* comics and annuals. Speaking of the cor blimey, mint editions of Enid Blyton's *Magic Faraway Tree* books are worth a bomb. In today's modern reprints of the Blyton books though, Jo is now Joe and Dick and Fannie have been changed to Rick and Frannie. Talk about censorship and political correctness gone barmy.

Also bought a bargain pack of pets' mince from a market stall, not sure what's in it, the stallholder said to keep it in the fridge. The big news is that I've signed on with a NHS dentist, Mr Wienczyslaw, a man with a good, strong set of gnashers himself – NEVER trust a dentist with dodgy teeth is my advice. Am seeing him next month. Made the mistake of mentioning the fact that I'm having some teeth out to my mum.

'Wha-a-at?' she squawks, at the other end of the phone, Englebert Humperdinck crooning in the background. 'You must be MAD! At YOUR age there's a terrible risk of getting DRY SOCKETS. Your Uncle Wilf DIED of dry sockets –'

'Dental procedures have improved since Uncle Wilf's day, Mum, what with antibiotics and—'

'Another danger is osteonecrosis – are you making a note of this, Ronald, that's O-S-T-E-O-N-E-C-R-O-S-I-S. I saw a whole page about it in the *Daily Mail*. Your gums and jawbone start to decay. It can start when the over-sixties have a tooth pulled out or get fitted with dental implants. Uncle Wilf would be alive today if he hadn't gone and got dry sockets—'

'That would make him a hundred and twenty, Mum, so let's not—'

'Okay, Son, must go. Your Aunt Maude, God rest her soul, had all her own teeth until the day she died at 103. Ta, ta.'

I remember Aunt Maude. She was the one who bequeathed me The Shack. When I was a little kid she used to say to me, 'Nip along to the corner shop, Ronnie, for 20 Craven A and a packet of Hacks for me chest.'

My tooth problems apart, Saltmarsh has become a hotbed of springtime, radical unrest. OAPs have been queuing right round the block at the Post Office, panic buying postage stamps before the price goes up later this month. The 'SPAM SAY NO' action brigade – brainchild of Len – were out in full force declaring that the postage stamp price hike is yet one more pensioners' stealth tax seeing as how it's only OAPs who still post letters and cards in these times of texts, emails and new-fangled electronic communications. Shoppers have been stripping the booze section of the supermarket before the post-budget price increase kicks in. Outside the Conservative Association the 'SENIORS AGAINST PENSION CUTS' have been urging passers-by to sign their petition. Then there's the 'SAVE THE BADGERS' group, the 'SAVE OUR LIBRARY' campaign, the ANTI-SHACKLES R Us movement with their 'SALTMARSH SAYS SHACKLES R NOT US' placards, as well as the 'BAN DOGS ON THE BEACH' group. Try to do your local shopping and you run the gauntlet of placards, banners, slogan-shouters and pens at the ready for petition signatures. The BAN DOGS ON THE BEACH group's banner reads 'THE POO FAIRY DOESN'T EXIST – SO PICK POO UP'. 'Poo fairy'? Who thought up that one?

As I was walking past, on my way to get Brainy Cyril's groceries, I noticed that one of the POO FAIRY bunch looked familiar. She caught my eye. I caught her eye. Our eyes locked. Ping! She stared long and hard. Then, waving her walking stick, she tottered towards me yelling, 'Yoo-hoo! Yoo-hoo!'

Stone the crows. I did a double take.

'Ronald? Yoo-hoo!'

'Rosemary?'

'It can't be!'

'Blimey, it is!'

And then we couldn't think of anything else to say to each other.

Fact is, I was lost for words. Gobsmacked. The doddery old dear flashing her horsey gnashers was a blast from my past, a reminder of some youthful 'O-be-joyfuls' and other rural shenanigans. Blimey again. She was certainly looking her age. For fifty years I've carried around in my head a picture of golden-girl, Rosemary, racing downhill on her bike, long legs pumping, skirt flapping, hair flying and Yours Truly zig-zagging along behind on my racer – cool as a cucumber – drop-handle bars and squealing brakes. No cycle-clips, me being a bit of a rebel. 'Where are the snows of yester year?' as the poet said. 'Where are they now, the old familiar faces?' as another poet said. Good question, especially after catching sight of those horsey gnashers. The gammy-legged Rosemary who was asking me to sign her POO FAIRY petition looked old enough to be my granny.

Okay. Okay. Pots and kettles. As Jinxie Wicks reminded me later, after I'd told her about my blast from the past, Rosemary would have been shocked too. She must have been thinking 'Blimey, old Ronald is certainly showing his age. He looks old enough to be my Grandpa.' This thought didn't cheer me up one bit. And mentioning grandparents reminds me that I saw a banner pinned to the railings by the Saltmarsh roundabout with these words daubed across it in red paint: CONGRATULATIONS GRANDMA ANGIE ON YOUR THIRTY-FIRST BIRTHDAY. Doesn't take two ticks to work it out.

The brief encounter with Rosemary unsettled me. It had me worrying about Time's winged chariot and so forth. To cheer myself up I made my way to the Friendly Winkle where the conversation turned to the Eurovision Song Contest. It takes place next month in Baku, Azerbaijan, a location not one of us could pinpoint on a map if asked. Britain will be represented by the veteran heart throb, 76 year old Englebert Humperdinck who has been in the crooning biz for forty-five years.

'Let's hear it for Englebert. Old codgers rule, okay,' bawled Jinxie Wicks who has dyed her hair – somewhat ineptly – a startling shade of orange.

'Englebert Humperdinck?' spluttered Len, spraying the air with peanut crumbs. 'What sort of message does that send out to the world?'

'It tells the world that – sadly – we Brits have no up-and-coming young performers good enough to represent Britain,' replied Daphne, looking as lovely as ever. Ah Daphne! Oh my aching heart. As Leonard Cohen remarked in a recent interview, 'I don't think anyone masters the heart. It continues to cook like a shish kebab, bubbling and sizzling in everyone's breast.' Too true. And incidentally, you wouldn't catch Leonard Cohen on stage at the Eurovision Song Contest.

'Yeah! There's no young performers good enough, Daf. Too right,' agrees Jinxie Wicks. 'It tells the world that they don't make 'em like they used to. Where are the Pat Boone's and the Perry Como's of today?'

It was generally agreed that no one under sixty watches the Eurovision Song Contest and that getting Englebert Humperdinck to represent Britain is a cynical ploy on the UK organisers part to attract the votes of all the old biddies across Europe. As for Humperdinck, he is not the *oldest* contestant. The Russians have thrown their hat in the ring with a quartet of singing grannies whose combined ages total 350 years.

Meanwhile it's lovely weather for ducks, as my old mum says. Call me a tedious old fart always droning on about the weather but when you've reached the age when each day is much the same as the next, the weather offers welcome variety. The headlines are telling us that it's the 'wettest April since records began' – rivers bursting their banks, flash floods, juggernauts aquaplaning across motorways, drain-covers forced off by jets of sewage, motorists trapped in their cars in rising water, the Badminton Horse Trials cancelled. At the Plucked Duck, according to the Saltmarsh Gazette, a chap rushed into the public bar yelling 'the toilets are exploding' as water and worse gushed out of the loos and whooshed through the ground floor.

At The Shack, due to the ongoing problems with the Save-a-Flush and dodgy drains, I found myself wading through six inches of water. Bingo was floating across the kitchen floor in his plastic dog bed. We've also had seventy miles an hour winds whipping up waves, uprooting trees, blocking roads and bringing down power lines. There's been beach huts blown over, yacht masts snapped, a porpoise washed up onto the shingle, deckchairs flying through the air and Jinxie Wicks' static listing an angle of forty-five degrees in a foot of sludge. But mustn't grumble. At least we don't have surface-to-air missiles parked on our roofs like the inhabitants of a tower block overlooking the Olympic site in East London.

The Starstreak high-velocity missile is part of the Government's so-called 'ring-of-steel' set up to deter terrorists during the Olympics. The ring-of-steel includes the warship H.M.S. Ocean, with eight Lynx helicopters, patrolling the Thames. London's streets are being pounded by sinister-looking, balaclava-wearing fuzz toting machine guns, pistols and stun grenades. Gone are London's British bobbies on the beat. How much is all this military might costing the taxpayer, I'd like to know?

As Terry pointed out as we discussed the missile madness, over one of his sardine hotpots with the rain lashing against the kitchen windows, these Starstreak high-velocity missiles on the roof won't alter the plans of any nutcase suicide bomber aboard a plane flying over London. And if the plane is shot at from the ground it will blow up and crash over a huge, densely populated area causing mayhem. Terry heard on the news that fifty-two armed police have been drafted in to guard the Olympic Torch. Who are they guarding it from? Metal thieves planning to melt it down for scrap? Talk about 'brave new world'.

MAY 2012

A postcard arrives from my vintage bookseller friend:

'Hi Ronald –
Hooray, hooray, the first of May
Outdoor shagging starts today.
(Chance would be a fine thing, eh, you old devil?)

Those were the days! But, away with vulgar sentiment, there has been a drama at The Shack! Arrived home from the ukulele group (Big Babs hot-footing it across the floorboards wearing a Union Jack pattern boiler suit and toot-tooting through a kazoo) to find an ambulance outside and Terry, with a drip in his arm, his eyes rolling, being wheeled out on a trolley. Panic stations!

'Food poisoning, Dad,' mutters Terry in a barely audible whisper, looking very green around the gills.

What to do? Should I climb into the ambulance with him? Does he need Yours Truly to hold his hand?

'No need, Dad, no need,' groans Terry. Ambulance doors close. Sirens blare and away he goes. I'm in shock, no two ways.

Opening the front door I am hit by an overpowering pong of disinfectant. Poor Terry. Make myself a cup of tea. Bingo keeps whining. It's way past his feeding time. I open the fridge. That's funny. What's happened to the bargain pets' mince I bought in the market? It's gone. Oh no! The penny drops. Terry must have used it to cook one of his hotpots! Holy moly. Sure enough there's a pan on the table containing hotpot leftovers. Chile con pets mince. The red kidney beans are all congealed on top. It smells terrible. Even Bingo turns his nose up.

Action is called for! I phone A&E to inform them of the likely source of Terry's mishap. The hospital people instruct me to bring in what's left of the 'source' to their lab for analysis. And to make it pronto! So, on with my titanium knee-brace. Jump on my bike, pedalling like the clappers, with the toxic leftovers in a plastic bag. As I screech to a halt at the hospital entrance my front tyre gets caught in a drain cover. Oops! I skid and topple over. No damage done but the plastic bag splits. Terry's hotpot is smeared and splashed all over my trousers. A chap in a white coat runs over, a passer-by parks my bike, and a woman wheeling a hospital trolley shouts, 'Looks like the poor old geezer's colostomy bag has burst – there, there, sir, don't worry – we'll soon get you cleaned up. You're in the right place…'

Luckily I am none the worse for wear, just a twinge in my lower lumbar area. Hospital staff wheel me inside with me explaining about Terry's hotpot while trying to scrape it off my trousers and back into the plastic bag. A bit of a whiffy undertaking. Gas masks on guys I joke. Luckily my rescuers appreciate the urgency of the situation. Rapid response is called for. What's left of Terry's hotpot is soon sent speeding on its way to the lab technicians. Clad in a hospital dressing gown I am wheeled into a cubicle next to Terry's and told to rest in a chair with a cup of tea until my trousers have been laundered.

'Dad!' whimpers Terry, a bit of colour coming back into his cheeks, 'What are you doing here?'

'Long story, son.'

Oh the joys of fatherhood! Then Terry's close friend, the Reverend Beverley – Bev the Rev – turns up to sing a hymn and say a prayer or two. I'm glad to report that Terry was back home after 48 hours. He has now become an obsessive vegetarian.

As for me, I don't mind admitting that the Nutcracker's jibe about having a 'little roof over your tool shed' rankled. Yes it RANKLED to such an extent that I had a try at toning myself up. Tried doing a press-up at the crack of dawn before frying my sausages and pulled a muscle in my groin. Agony. Rolled on the floor groaning. Terry came rushing out of the bathroom waving his toothbrush. Bingo started howling. My bad chest started playing up… The upshot was that Doc Ng recommended that I attend the seniors' weekly Keep Fit sessions. What a palaver. Jinxie Wicks helped kit me out with jogging pants, T-shirt with SEX AND DRUGS AND SAUSAGE ROLL across the front, and a pair of funky trainers (Barnado's: total cost £3.50 with a red headband and sports bra – ha! ha! - thrown in). I hope I don't bump into Daphne while I'm wearing my Keep Fit clobber.

The physical jerks session was one protracted hour of sheer torture. Thirty-two old-timers – two with portable oxygen cylinders plus attached nasal tubes, one wearing a neck brace – standing in a circle and limbering up with knee bends, leg stretches, jogging on the spot and flexing the buttocks, with *The Best of The Rolling Stones* CD thumping in the background. '*I – can't – get – no – sat – is –faction…*' and so forth, waggle, stretch, flex, jog, puff, pant and wish you were home in bed. Or dead.

The female instructor, who must have been all of eighteen and looks like she needs a decent square meal, yells, 'Now lie on your backs, guys 'n' girls, and draw your knees up to your chest.' A senior-citizen manoeuvre which is just asking for trouble in my opinion. As we creak, puff and draw our dodgy knees up to our chests the Rolling Stones are all but drowned out by a volley of farts. With Mick Jagger belting out '*You – shudda – seen – me – just – around – midnight...*' we attempt to stretch our legs ceiling-ward and do 'bicycle' in time to the throbbing rhythm. Mind you, I'm reminding myself as I windmill my spindle shanks in the air, Mick Jagger didn't get where he is today by lolling about with his nose always stuck in a book. Good old Mick hasn't let the roof grow over HIS tool shed. Oh no. And not many people know that a famous interior decorator, the late David Herbert, who settled in Morocco, had his guest room decorated with a blown-up portrait by Cecil Beaton of Mick Jagger's bottom in green and blue. You wouldn't get anyone wanting a blown-up portrait of my bottom in green and blue decorating their walls.

Then the music changes. We all stand and waggle our arms to '*Wild thing! You make my heart sing...*' A lumpy old girl steps on my toe. Bloody agony... '*If you think I'm sexy and you want my body...*' knees up, legs bend, buttocks twitch. One of the oxygen tank wearers is singing along and clicking his fingers as if he's at a rave. After the final knee bends and buttock flexings the bloke who has been singing turns blue round the mouth and has to be revived with an ice pack. Yours Truly has cramp in his right foot and a dull ache in his lower lumbar area. Never again. Roof or no roof.

To make matters worse, who should I bump into but Daphne (Wild thing! You make my heart sing...) who goes 'Way to go, Daddy Cool!' when she sees my T-shirt, and says that the red headband makes me look like John McEnroe in his Wimbledon heyday. When it comes to Keep Fit I go along with the great actor, Peter O'Toole, who said, 'The only exercise I take is walking behind the coffins of friends who took exercise.' And another thing he said was: 'When did I realize I was God? Well, I was praying and I suddenly realized I was talking to myself.' Speaking of O'Toole, several summers ago he was here, near Saltmarsh, all hush-hush, making a film along the beach near The Shack. First thing I knew about it was during a walk along the shoreline with Bingo. I was contemplating the way that 'dawn skims the sea with flying feet of gold', Bingo was frisking across the gravel patches and emitting playful little yaps, when a rough, sweary voice disturbed our peace. 'Sxxx, Fxxx, Fxxx… CUT! Get that bloody sausage dog out of shot, it's just ruined my take!' Whereupon a huddle of blokes with funny haircuts, fidgeting with clapper boards, microphones and walkie-talkie gadgets all started chasing Bingo. He gave them a good run around. There were wires trailing everywhere, and spotlights. The sweary bloke kept shouting at me, 'Put your soddin' dog on its lead and get off the bloody beach'. Little rat-bag. Telling me what to do! Insulting my dog! I shook my fist at him. Throughout the commotion, unconcerned and resting nonchalantly against the breakwater trying to look incognito, was Peter O'Toole himself – still looking like Laurence of Arabia all these years later but wearing aviator-style sun-specs. A small knot of locals were huddled by the beach huts craning their necks for a glimpse of the famous actor. He was having his sparse grey hair sprayed and brushed by a woman, while another woman was dabbing his face with make-up. The blokes with funny haircuts were still chasing Bingo, tripping over the electric cables that were snaking across the shingle from a noisy generator.

'Silence on set. Take two. Rolling,' shouted the sweary bloke. When the film is released I'll look out for Bingo in the background, paws up, tongue out, tail wagging, peering over a breakwater.

Days later I had a couple of strokes of luck. I found an early Rupert album in fair condition at a Bring-and-Buy which I flogged to my vintage book seller friend for £45.

More cash in the kitty towards the gas bill. Also found a copy of John Fisher's biography of ukulele genius, George Formby (RSPCA, 20p). Poor old George. His wife, Beryl, an ex-clogdancer, makes the Nutcracker look like a paragon of gentle womanhood.

So picture me. I'm reading the Formby book, sitting with Jinxie Wicks on The Shack's patch of shingle. A balmy May breeze rustles the marsh reeds. Every now and then I repeat some Formby fact to Jinxie Wicks who, I should mention, has given up doing Filthy Grannies because all the sound effects required had given her laryngitis.

'Did you know that Formby and Beryl's house was called Beryldene?' I say or:

'In 1939 Formby, with his comic songs, uke and banjo was Britain's highest paid entertainer earning £100,000 a year? That's five million in today's money, and bossy old Beryl, who took charge of all the cash only allowed him five shillings pocket money a day. AND she wouldn't have sex with him.'

Jinxie Wicks, who is studying her cruise brochures, keeps muttering, 'Well I never' or 'You don't say' and then 'Look Ronald, it's ruddy irritating when you keep reading bits out loud.' Fair enough. But I am riveted by the George Formby story. Old battleaxe Beryl was the driving force behind Formby's success, getting him into films, demanding bigger and bigger fees, and insisting that he had top billing at his shows. In 1932 he achieved his first huge hit with his song 'Chinese Laundry Blues' about Mr Wu who worked in a laundry. Off I go again—

'Here Jinx, you'll like this bit, here's a sample verse from Chinese Laundry Blues, it goes 'Now Mr Wu, he's got a naughty eye that flickers / You ought to see it wobble when he's ironing ladies blouses."

'Wa-ha-ha, hilarious!' chortles Jinxie Wicks.

'In 1936 his song 'When I'm Cleaning Windows' sold 150,000 copies in a month.'

'Well I'm blowed,' says Jinxie Wicks.

'In fact it was banned by the BBC. Snooty old Lord Reith declared, and I quote 'If the public wants to listen to Formby singing his disgusting little ditty they'll have to be content to hear it in the cinemas not over the nation's airwaves."

'No sense of humour in those days at the BBC, bunch of repressed ex-public school boys,' comments Jinxie Wicks.

'Beryl was so furious that she stormed into Reith's office at the BBC ranting and raving and demanding that he make an apology which he did, on the radio, but he didn't lift the ban.'

'Good old Beryl, good on her,' says Jinxie Wicks, helping herself to one of my roll-ups and to a slurp of Scrumpy Jack.

'And I bet you didn't know that King George VI and his wife – later to become the Queen Mother – arranged a private, uncensored performance of 'When I'm Cleaning Windows' at the Palace and enjoyed it so much that they presented Formby with a pair of gold cufflinks and Beryl with a gold powder compact.'

'Wow! Not bad for an ex-clogdancer. Some royal command performance!'

'Too right. And not bad for a Lancashire lad whose paternal granny had been a notorious prostitute. She was convicted 140 times for drunkenness, theft, vagrancy and brawling.'

'Good grief. I bet the Queen Mother wasn't told about *that*.'

'His dad was working in a cotton mill at the age of 12.'

'Poor little bleeder.'

'But sadly, by the 1950's Formby and Beryl had become very heavy drinkers. Formby had been smoking 40 cigarettes a day from the age of 12. When Beryl died in 1960, Formby got engaged to a much younger woman, but died, aged 57, two days before the wedding.'

'With his little ukulele in his hand, I wouldn't wonder,' quips Jinxie Wicks, at which point we are interrupted by a bloke in a bobble hat walking along the beach with a slobbering great boxer dog straining at the leash.

'Hi there,' says the bloke, stepping on to my patch of shingle. Believe me, Bingo's hackles would be well and truly standing up if he had a bit more hair on his back. The bloke in the bobble hat is the sweary bloke from the film crew. Bingo growls.

'Nice place you have here. Thinking of selling?' asks the bloke.

Blinkin' cheek. I am dumbstruck. The boxer dog is bearing its fangs, so is the bloke in the bobble hat, contriving to produce an ingratiating grin.

'I'm down from London, working on the Peter O'Toole movie – heel, Tolstoy, heel, down boy! – I'm on the look out to buy a weekend retreat with a sea view. By my reckoning your place would set me back two hundred and fifty grand.'

Two hundred and fifty grand? For The Shack? I nearly fall off my sun lounger (a replacement for the deckchair that collapsed – Help-the-Aged, £2.50). Jinxie Wicks' mouth is hanging open. The bloke in the bobble hat must be mental. The place is falling down. The WC hasn't worked properly since the Save-a-Flush debacle. The roof leaks. There's rising damp.

The upshot is that Yours Truly, Bingo and Jinxie Wicks send the bloke in the bobble hat and Tolstoy packing with a flea in his ear. It's not about money, matey. It's about ROOTS. My Kentish roots. The Shack doesn't need some cocky media type moving in and doing it up with poncy Farrow & Ball paint, and white curtains. Home is where your heart is and my heart is in The Shack and the environs around Saltmarsh. And never mind the dry rot.

In this vale of tears I can usually face the music. As long as it's not Englebert Humperdinck. God help me, I am still recovering from Andy's SPAM special Eurovision party. This took place in the usual Portakabin where a flat-screen TV had been set up so that we could watch – and hear (in stereo, I should add) the Contest as it was beamed live from Baku, Azerbaijan.

It blasted off with a migraine-inducing explosion of fireworks, flashing lights, crashing cymbals, pounding drums, sparkling tinsel, spinning glitter balls and teams of dancers hoofing across the stage like maniacs. Borderline hysterical, a female compere screamed, 'GREETINGS TO THE WHOLE WORLD FROM AZERBAIJAN! LET US LIGHT YOUR FIRE!!' in five languages, as showers of paper snowflakes tumbled through the air, acrobats dangled from the rafters and the music exceeded the pain threshold. Andy hurried over to turn down the volume. The female compere continued, 'WE HAVE 120 MILLION VIEWERS ACROSS EUROPE! WE HAVE 20,000 FANS ASSEMBLED HERE IN AZERBAIJAN'S FABULOUS NEW CRYSTAL HALL!' Again in five languages and whipping up the 20,000 assembled fans into eardrum-rupturing screams.

Cameras zoomed in for close-ups of champagne bottles and inebriated audience members waving their arms in the air. When Englebert Humperdinck – 'The Hump' – came on Andy turned the volume up again. We all gawped at the famous square-jawed crooner, much loved by female OAPs including my mum, with his mutton-chop sideburns and frilly shirt. None of us could remember the name of any of his big hits.

'Save the Last Schmalz for Me?' quipped Tex Tozer.

Daphne went into hysterics. When she'd calmed down she said, 'No, come on Tex, don't be mean-spirited, the poor man is 76 years old and is carrying the weight of the nation's hopes upon his shoulders.'

Jinxie Wicks, who was entering into the spirit of things, skipping about and handing round sausages-on-sticks, added, 'Not many people know that The Hump's real name is Arnold Dorsay. He still does 200 concerts A YEAR. He has sold an incredible 150 million albums. How's that for success?'

'Well, he has never sold one to ME,' snorted Tozer.

'Shhh. Sshhh. Sshhh,' hissed The Hump's loyal fan base.

Poor old Hump. He was the oldest solo contestant and they made him go first. He sang 'Love Will Set You Free', a dreary ballad that even Hump fans like Daphne had to admit was not his best. We all agreed that his Eurovision rendering of Love Will Set You Free was not his finest moment. And so the show thumped, flashed and glitter-balled on. An Albanian contestant stood spot-lit in a crimson cloud of swirling dry ice and reached a screeching high-note with what looked like a giant burst octopus on her head. Then came a sudden flash of laser beams and a Lithuanian contestant sang a raunchy ballad wearing a black blindfold, did a cartwheel and sank to his knees in a volley of cymbal crashes. Old Hump didn't stand a chance against the Lithuanian contestant.

Star performers were the Russian Grannies – the Boranovskiye Babushki. They came on wearing traditional folkloric costumes, singing a folksy sort of Russian song. The chorus went 'Boom! Boom! Boom!' every so often. When they got to the final 'Boom! Boom! Boom!' the Boranovskiye

Babushki punched the air and stamped their boots. 'THE GRANNIES ARE UNSTOPPABLE!' screamed the compere when they had stopped, whereupon the Grannies did another 'Boom! Boom! Boom!' for luck. The only contestant that got a lower score than The Grannies was The Hump. What with the flashing strobes and the TV cameras whirling around and 'in' for close-ups and 'out' for long-shots – up, down, up, down – we TV viewers were all feeling vertiginous and seasick. I, for one, was glad when it was all over and not a moment too soon. It was a relief to get back to The Shack. I can't for the life of me remember who won.

Next morning the first thing to meet my eyes was a copy of the *Saltmarsh Gazette*. Terry Tonks has hit the headlines! There he was – full-page article and photo – in their weekly series 'Good Egg'. Terry was the Good Egg of the week! See below:

The Saltmarsh Good Egg of the Week

Mr Terry Tonks (age 45), a regular church-goer, morris dancer and active STOP GASSING BADGERS campaigner is one of the few people in the UK who works as a full-time professional mourner. Employed by Saltmarsh's highly respected Mr Harry Podger of IT'S YOUR FUNERAL Funerals. Mr Tonks' almost unique job involves attending the burials and cremations of people who would otherwise make their final journey alone. Mr Tonks, who attends on average nine funerals a week, told the Gazette, 'People who now live into their nineties and beyond have often outlived their friends and relations. That is where I step in. My job is to keep the deceased company and give them a bit of a send-off as they set out for the Great Beyond.'

Mr Tonks, who currently resides in Saltmarsh with his father, Ronald Tonks, an amateur ukulele player, explained that with regard to funerals, dignity and respect, 'Down to Earth' is the Podger motto.'

For his official functions, Mr Tonks is attired in a black suit and a Dickensian top hat trimmed with black crepe ribbons. Recalling a recent 'scattering' in the Estuary he said, 'I had to wear a plastic mac over my suit and my top hat landed in the sea due to rough weather which rather spoilt the solemnity of the occasion.' He added, 'An unattended funeral is very bleak. Some people, my father is one, think that the job is a bit of a joke and say that I am being paid to put the "fun" back into funerals. This is definitely not so. I take my work very seriously.'

No sense of humour, Terry. Didn't even laugh when I pointed out to him the NO HOT ASHES sign on the litter bin outside the gates of the crematorium.

At last. Sunshine. Warm enough to sit in the back garden, recently tidied up by Terry, with a table and chairs he retrieved from a skip. The only thing missing is the tinkle-and-splash of the water feature which we are not allowed to use due to the hosepipe ban. It's been like a monsoon here for weeks, yet there's a hosepipe ban. Madness! On a sunny Monday I gave Bingo some tinned pilchards for a treat and settled down with a massive 1170 page biography of Dickens by Peter Ackroyd (The Red Cross, £1). And what did I discover? That Dickens himself had experienced his own Rosemary moment. Yes, Dickens, like Yours Truly, also had *his* romantic illusions shattered. At eighteen he had fallen in love with a teenage girl, Maria Beadnell. He described her as 'the angel of my soul' and hoped to marry her. But her dad had other plans and the heartbroken Dickens was sent packing. Twenty-four years later, having always carried a vision of Maria Beadnall in his head, he met 'the angel of his soul' again.

Gone was the small, pretty, golden-ringletted girl. Waddling into the picture was a fat, gushing, boozy old trout. Dickens, appalled, made his excuses and legged it. With his dreams shattered he turned matronly Maria into the grotesque giggling Flora Finching in *Little Dorrit*. A bit nasty of him I think because Maria couldn't tell her side of the story. I looked up the passage in *Little Dorrit* where Dickens describes Flora's one-time adorer meeting her face-to-face twenty-four years on, 'His eyes no sooner fell upon the subject of his old passion, than it shivered and broke to pieces.' Shivered and broke to pieces? Cor! I wish I could write like that. I expect poor old Maria Beadnall's own 'old passion' shivered and broke to pieces too. She probably took one look at Dickens, haggard, straggling grey beard, having lost his sparkle, disillusioned with his marriage and thought, 'Good grief. The old boy's looking his age. He could be my Grandpapa.' It was me and Rosemary all over. Not that Maria Beadnall would have ridden a bike of course, in those days of crinolines, her legs pumping, her hair flying in the wind...

Talking of legs pumping... I've started 'power-walking'. I power-walked along to a SPAM get-together where Len was in full spate going on about a new threat facing airline passengers namely 'laser louts'. These maniacs put lives at risk by shining blinding laser beams into the eyes of airline pilots as they are trying to land. 'A hooligan from Bristol was in court for temporarily blinding a police helicopter pilot...' ranted Len, eyelids twitching, specs steaming up, dewlaps vibrating, 'and another hooligan, from Liverpool, was fined for shining a laser pen at an Easyjet pilot landing at John Lennon Airport.'

Talk about doom and gloom. Escaping from Len's clutches I walked inadvertently into one of Andy's guest speaker talks. It was a talk titled 'Tips to Quit and How to Celebrate', which as talk topics go is really scraping the barrel in my opinion. Andy introduced the speaker, Maureen ('Let's have a big hand for Maureen from NiQuit'), who asked us to raise our hands if we smoke or have ever smoked. Most hands were raised. Tex Tozer, lurking by the tea table called out, 'I only came in here hoping for tea and biscuits'. Maureen wagged her finger and Andy unwrapped a packet of Fondant Fancies, which he then passed around.

Maureen informed us that people who want to quit smoking must create an 'optimal quitting environment'. You do this by throwing away your fags, baccy, ash trays and matches. You then have to get yourself a 'Quitting Buddy'. Tozer, stuffing his face with Fondant Fancies, started to walk out, shouting, 'Eat, drink, smoke and be merry, for tomorrow you may be stuck with looking after your Alzheimer-afflicted parents...' Daphne, who enjoys an occasional smoke as much as any of us, caught Tozer's eye and pulled her 'oh-you-are-awful' face. My hackles rose. Someone shouted, 'Right on'. Andy, whose vertical hair now has blobs of blonde on the tips, looked crestfallen. Several people were yawning. One woman had dozed off. Maureen soldiered on explaining that you need a Quitting Buddy because no one will understand the 'cold turkey' you are going through as much as will another Quitter. And, she advised, when the going gets tough, the Quitter must calm down by deep breathing or 'running for fun'. Maureen ended her talk on a metaphorical note telling all Quitters that 'If you have your eye on the summit, the climb can seem daunting, but if you focus on getting to the next base camp, suddenly it looks a lot less scary.'

Onwards to the next base camp, eh? 'Load of bollocks,' someone hissed, as Maureen dished out items called NiQuit patches. She promised us that these patches contained 'Built in, smart craving-control technology' that delivers nicotine into the bloodstream for twenty-four hours. Tozer, who was hanging around the exit door having a smoke, reckoned you could stick one on your arm, smoke a fag at the same time and get a double dose of enjoyment. No prizes for guessing whose tinkling, fragrant laughter was ringing in my ears as I power-walked back to The Shack.

But the big news is my session with my new dentist, Mr Wienczyslaw. I have remarked before, in this journal, that I worry about the revenge an unscrupulous dentist might wreak if you got into his bad books. Well, blow me down, I just read a newspaper item about an Eastern European dentist – Ms Mackowlack – who committed the ultimate dentist's revenge. She PULLED OUT ALL HER BOYFRIEND'S TEETH after he dumped her for a younger woman. Talk about the stuff of nightmares! A few days after dumping Ms Mackowlack, the ex-boyfriend (mad fool) turned up at her surgery complaining of agonising toothache. She knocked him out with a heavy dose of anaesthetic and yanked out ALL HIS TEETH! Nightmare! She then tied up his jaw with a bandage, advised him not to open his mouth until he arrived home because the cold air might irritate his gums. The poor sap arrived home, removed the chin-strap, looked in the mirror and the realisation hit him. Imagine the shock. Imagine the horror of peering into the gory, gummy abyss – a bit like looking at a Francis Bacon painting. In Poland a trial is pending, the ex-boyfriend is planning to sue. His new girlfriend has now dumped him because she doesn't fancy a man with no teeth.

I thought of repeating this story about his compatriot to Mr Wienczyslaw on my initial visit, but decided against. Don't want to go giving him ideas. Mr Wienczyslaw's waiting room has a wall covered with 'before' and 'after' photographs of film stars. 'Before' they are all snaggle-toothed and Bugs Bunny-ish. 'After', thanks to dental ingenuity, caps, implants, veneers, whiteners and so forth, each of the film stars flash huge, shiny, toilet bowl-white smiles. Tom Cruise 'before' had wonky, primrose yellow teeth. 'After', they look like they'd glow in the dark.

I'm in Mr Wienczylaw's surgery. The receptionist hands me a questionnaire about my drinking habits. 'What have my drinking habits got to do with Mr Wienczylaw?' I ask. Turns out it's a new innovation. Apparently dentists can spot the early warning signs of excessive alcohol consumption, such as tooth decay, cancer of the mouth, larynx and oesophagus. Good grief! Yet more things to worry about. And I can't be the only person in the world who never tells the truth about their drinking habits. All dentists and doctors must know that when someone says they have one glass of wine a day, the odd glass of cider, and a small scotch at the weekends, they really mean that they have a bottle and a half of wine a day, washed down with a couple of glasses of spirits, the odd bottle or two of beer and often struggle to remember what day it is. So I write 'fourteen units a week on average' on the questionnaire. Lying through my teeth, of course, which I probably won't have much longer to lie through.

After a check-up and a bit of poking around Mr Wienczyslaw recommends that I have a troublesome back molar removed there and then. My knees knock. Fact is, me and my teeth go back a long way, we've been together now for sixty plus years. I get a jab in the gum. Then a ten-minute wait for it to kick in. No probs. So far, so good. Back I go, laying back on the chair – oops! Gaze up Mr Wienczyslaw's nostrils (it's like a walk in the Black Forest up there) and think of Martin Amis. Using some clunky gadget Mr Wienczyslaw pushes my tooth to the left (loud tearing sound), pushes

it to the right (another loud tearing sound). To give Mr
Wienczyslaw his due, I don't feel a thing. Ah the miracles of
modern medicine.

'Ah ha, here he comes,' says Mr Wienszyslaw, like he's a
midwife delivering a baby. A loud cracking sound reverberates
round my skull. I'm worried that he might be pulling out a
chunk of my jawbone and that food will start falling out of my
nose when I'm eating, as happened to Louis XIV. Nightmare.

''At's 'at?' (What's that?) I croak in panic, through the
metal clamp keeping my jaws apart.

'Nothing to worry about, sir,' chuckles Mr Wienczysalw,
standing aside to allow the dental nurse to stick a gag-making
suction gadget like a mini-hoover on the back of my tongue.
'The tooth cracked, leaving behind two small splinters of
root…'

Oh my God!

''En-ow-aro-nd-ull-em-ou-ile-um-um-ods-say,' (Then poke
around and pull them out while my gum is numb for God's
sake) I beg through the metal clamp and the gag-making
suction gadget, and an absorbent wodge of cotton wool that
I've been told to bite down on.

'No. No. Must never do that, sir. When a tooth breaks it is
good practice to leave the splinters in situ in the gum.'

'Ull-i-ou-lease!' (Pull it out please).

'Not a good idea, sir. If I start prodding, the splinters
might move upwards, behind your zygomatic arch. If the
sinus is pierced – and this is worst case scenario – it could
lead to a fistula, then you'd be in big trouble.'

Zygomatic arch? Sounds like an item Terry might get
from the garden centre to install near the water feature.
Fistula? Isn't that something excruciating to do with the
nether regions? Didn't it finally finish off the aforementioned
Louis XIV?

This little dental ordeal set me back £75. At least it didn't HURT. Not until the jab wore off. Then I *still* had toothache. I also had a niggling pain in my jaw bone when I tried to chew. It was a sort of phantom pain, like the phantom pain amputees experience when their limbs have been amputated. Each time I got a twinge I started worrying about what was going on up there behind my zygomatic arch.

A week later I'm back in Mr Wienczyslaw's chair to have several of my top teeth extracted and a dental bridge fitted. No problems. No pain. No details necessary apart from the fact it set me back £300. One advantage of losing your teeth is that you stop worrying about losing your teeth. And by the time my permanent bridge has been fitted (two weeks) my gleaming smile will be flashing with all the allure of the Tom Cruises of this world. Ha!

On my power-walk back to The Shack I bumped into Jinxie Wicks who cheered me up with a story she'd found in the paper headed DENTIST'S SEX ACT AT 70MPH. The mind boggles. In the distant days when I could afford to run a car I couldn't so much as squirt the windscreen wipers or wind up the window, let alone commit a sex act while I was at the wheel. Not even if I was going as slow as 20 mph. The dentist pleaded guilty and has lost his driving licence.

JUNE 2012

Bunting ahoy! What a fiasco. The day of the Queen's Great Jubilee Pageant was a wash-out here in Saltmarsh. Raining cats and corgis. It bucketed down – soggy Union Jacks unable to flap, saturated bunting dangling from lampposts, street parties cancelled, sopping Morris Dancers throwing in the towel, the fire brigade pumping out water from the flooded Plucked Duck…

Jinxie Wicks went ahead with her efforts to take part in the 'all-across-the-nation Big Jubilee Lunch' as proposed by the Prime Minister in the hopes of encouraging neighbourhood get-togethers. Good old Jinxie Wicks, she never gives in, however daunting the circumstances. But thanks to the downpours her Big Jubilee Lunch could not take place al fresco, as planned, on the boggy grass surrounding her static. No. It had to take place indoors, a bit of a squash, no two ways. I squelched across the caravan site in my wellies, getting smacked round the head by festoons of saturated bunting. Talk about a quagmire! Jinxie Wicks greets me at her front door wearing flared, flapping Union Jack print trousers and a T-shirt printed across the chest with a grinning corgi wearing a tiara studded with diamante.

So picture us, four people – Jinxie Wicks, Terry, Daphne (gulp! Yes, I'm still carrying a torch) and Yours Truly all crammed into the static's dinette seating area where the windows are steaming up, *The Very Best of Buddy Holly* is blasting at full volume, the rain is rattling on the static's metal roof, and ominous gurgling noises are coming from the shower room somewhere beyond the kitchenette. No doubt due to the overflowing drains. What with the condensation inside and the biblical deluge outside, it's probably what being in Noah's Ark would have felt like, apart from *The Very Best of Buddy Holly*. 'It's like being in Noah's Ark,' says Terry, stating the ruddy obvious. To get us into festive mood Jinxie Wicks hands out cardboard Union Jack design hats which fix under our chins with elastic. Not a look I'm keen to adopt with Daphne in the room.

Corks pop. Fizz bubbles. Condensation drips off the bunting. Terry passes round a plate of Cheesy-Wotsits. Jinxie Wicks had suggested a potluck lunch (not *that* sort of 'pot', I should add, worse luck, not with Terry around) with guests bringing a dish and bottle. So we have vegetarian-pork-and-beans-without the-pork (Terry), chipolatas on sticks (Yours Truly), steak and kidney pie and a treacle tart – both homemade – (Daphne) and Jinxie Wicks' famous faggots-in-onion-gravy. Matter of fact I should have said five people are at the Big Jubilee Lunch. The gurgling noises from the chemical toilet turn out to be Tex Tozer.

So that's my day ruined. His contribution to the feast is a family-size Tesco ready-to-microwave Spaghetti Bolognese with a half price sticker on it. Stingy sod. He is wearing a T-shirt emblazoned with a portrait of a grinning, sticky-out-eared Prince Charles and the words 'You may laugh, but one day I'll be in charge' across the chest. He refuses point blank to wear his Union Jack design hat. 'Honest to goodness, I'd look a ruddy prat wearing that, like you do Ronald ...'

So there we all are tucking into the eats, wearing Union Jack design hats, eating off Union Jack design cardboard plates and drinking from Union Jack cardboard beakers. On goes the TV for the BBC's Great Jubilee Pageant coverage.

'Let's hope Her Majesty is wearing her thermals,' says Daphne as the Queen, buffeted by a squally gust, totters aboard the Royal Barge. A BBC commentator announces that the Royal Barge is, in fact, the redesigned barge, *Spirit of Chartwell.*

'Fartwell,' snipes Tozer, helping himself to a second slice of Daphne's pie.

'The Duke of Edinburgh is wearing the uniform of the Admiral of the Fleet,' continues the commentator.

'What fleet?' snorts Tozer, and Jinxie Wicks hits him over the head with a rolled up Jubilee Souvenir supplement.

There follows half an hour of close ups of flag waving loonies in plastic macs, interviews with nutcases who have slept all night on the pavement in pouring rain to secure a good view and grinning loyal subjects huddled under see-through umbrellas and shouting 'It makes you proud to be British!'

What with close ups of 'celebrities' that we've never heard of, footage of street parties in the rain, and the hot news that two babies born this morning have been named 'Jubilee', we all decide that the BBC coverage is a bit of a let-down. Where is the pomp and circumstance that the BBC normally lays on for the nation's historic occasions? Why are we getting this non-stop onslaught of chirpy drivel? And why are we getting shouting commentators who use the word 'iconic' every few seconds?

Unfortunately we can't tune in to a different channel due to the digital switchover not having yet successfully switched over here in Saltmarsh.

We all raise our Union Jack beakers (except for Tozer) and shout 'The Queen' as the camera zooms in on the Royal party.

'Look at the Queen! Eighty-six years old and not once has she sat down. She looks as if she's having a wonderful time…' burbles the commentator, as the redesigned *Spirit of Chartwell* Royal Barge sails past, the Queen grim-faced, rain drops dripping on her hat from the upper rails.

The rain is still rattling on the static's metal roof. The caravan site's boggy grass is a foot deep in water. I remark that you'd think that the Queen, being Defender of the Faith, might have plenty of influence with God. She ought to have been able to persuade him – the old party pooper – not to let it rain on her parade.

'Now, now Dad, don't take the name of the Lord in vain,' says Terry, nibbling a Cheesy Wotsit, still sticking rigidly to his vegetarian diet.

'Horseface! Strumpet! Marriage breaker!' roars Tozer, making us all jump as the camera zooms in for a close up of Camilla, Duchess of Cornwall.

The camera then zooms onto Kate, the Duchess of Cambridge, wearing a red, racy, short-skirted get-up and a red saucer affair with feathers on her head.

'Oooh!' shrieks Jinxie Wicks, 'believe it or not, but I used to have a twenty inch waist and a flat stomach like hers and long, shapely pins.'

'Red hat, no drawers, as my old Dad used to say,' roars Tozer. Daphne laughs so hard that she starts choking on her faggots-in-onion-gravy. I bang her on the back. Tozer dashes into the kitchenette for a glass of water.

Terry grumbles that no one is showing any interest in his vegetarian pork-and-beans-without-the-pork.

'Who's the old bloke with the red face next to the Queen? – Oops! It's the Prince of Wales,' shouts Tozer.

The thing we are all waiting for is the Big Moment – the much-heralded flotilla of a thousand vessels surging down – or is it up – the Thames. We are waiting to see the spectacle – the 'iconic spectacle' – which the TV commentators keep referring to as 'The Canaletto Moment'. For weeks, the media have been promising 'The Canaletto Moment', a sight never seen before and never to be seen again.

And, at last! Just as we're getting stuck into Daphne's treacle tart we get an aerial view of The Canaletto Moment – barges, kayaks, gigs, gondolas, rowing boats, launches, fifty Dunkirk 'little ships', the Royal rowing boat called *Gloriana*, a Kiwi war canoe with painted-faced paddlers chanting and sticking out wiggling tongues, pennants streaming, flags flapping, Handel's *Water Music* quavering above the howling wind and the hissing slap of choppy water. Amazing. Brilliant. 'How iconic!' gasps Daphne. But then, when we're on the edge of our seats, spoonfuls of treacle tart poised in mid-air, waiting for Tower Bridge to open up, the cameras cut away to a commentator in a funny hat wittering: 'There's lots of horns and stuff going off... There are rowing boats, iconic boats, historical boats...'

'Oh shaddup and let's ruddy well see them,' we all shout.

'What's happened to The Canaletto Moment?' shrieks Jinxie Wicks.

By now Terry is in a sulk because his vegetarian-pork-and-beans-without-the-pork has not been touched. Tozer has started slurring his words. Above a half-hearted rendering of the National Anthem being warbled by a group draped in plastic macs on Tower Bridge, he remarks 'Fans of the late Queen Mother may be unaware that she had a penchant for music hall songs. According to the memoirs of the composer, Sir Richard Rodney Bennett – a great friend of the Queen Mother – her particular favourite was "Auntie Mary had a canary up the leg of her drawers..."'

At this point Jinxie Wicks produces a sherry trifle. This is the sort of sherry trifle that would have even the privileged

Royal party, now sailing down the river towards their slap-up banquet, licking their chops and drooling.

In fact the Royals have turned blue around the gills. Hypothermia could very well be setting in. Talk about the Dunkirk spirit. Observing these remote and enigmatic beings, as we are, from the cosy interior of Jinxie Wicks' static, we marvel how the Queen and Duke – OAPs both – seem untroubled by dodgy bladders. Not one toilet break in four hours! No nipping to the cabin below for a call of nature. Or for a little nip of Glennhoddle come to that, to warm the old cockles. Ramrod straight, the Queen and Duke stand there in worsening wind and rain. A floating bell tower ding-dongs past. A barge full of state trumpeters chugs by. Then a pipe and drum band.

Suddenly there's some fleeting TV footage of an anti-royal demo. A sopping flag is unfolded saying *ANTI-JUBILEE COALITION* 'Right on, boyo, right on!' bellows Tozer. The cameras zoom in. A small huddle of anarchist banner-wavers are shouting, 'Lizzie, Lizzie, Lizzie! Out! Out! Out!' drowned out by a large huddle of Union Jack wavers shouting, 'Lizzie, Lizzie, Lizzie! In! In! In!' Then there's more footage of a 'celebrity' in a funny hat and plastic mac doing the conga, and another 'celebrity' at a dog's fancy dress party.

Looks like we've had our 'iconic' Canaletto Moment. And all too brief a moment it was too. There's a newsflash announcing that the rail network is in chaos because thousands of revellers have swamped platforms after being turfed off overcrowded trains as they struggled to get to the Jubilee celebrations.

We polish off the sherry trifle. The Queen and Duke look as if they are both thinking: 'For how much longer is this hell going to carry on? I'm frozen, I need the loo, my feet are killing me...'

Daphne says, 'Poor devil, the Duke standing about in the wet and freezing cold at his age. He's ninety-one for God's sake. What he needs is an ankle-length, ex-army padded greatcoat. Not wearing a heavy coat is just asking for trouble...'

'What he needs are some hot faggots,' says Jinxie Wicks.

'A bowl of my steaming vegetarian-pork-and-beans-without-the-pork would do both of them the world of good,' says Terry.

'Not many people know that in 2010 when the Duke visited Tana in the South Pacific, where he's worshipped as a god, the locals presented him with a gift of a traditional straw penis sheaf,' says Jinxie Wicks.

'Anyone fancy a banana?'says Tex Tozer.

In the opinion of Yours Truly, the Duke's expression caught on camera seems to say, 'At last! This bloody fiasco is coming to an end, thank God.' But no. The grand finale is still to come. The Royal College of Music chamber choir sail by, drenched and dripping, on the open top deck of a motor cruiser called Symphony. On the deck below them the London Philharmonic Orchestra is huddled (under a tarpaulin). The Royal College of Music chamber choir – and hats off to them for sticking it out – are soaked, hair plastered to their scalps, rain trickling off their noses and dripping into their microphones. Bravely defying the elements they sing *Land of Hope and Glory*. Marvellous! 'Makes you proud to be British,' as everyone keeps saying. Then the orchestra strikes up with the Sailors' Hornpipe which has the Royals gamely attempting a half-hearted last-night-of-the-proms sort of bobbing up and down. You can tell that the Duke is thinking, 'Ye Gods! We've still got the bloody flypast, gun salute, fireworks and the National Anthem... to get through.'

Suddenly there's a whoosh and a gurgling. A gush of brown liquid streams across the floor of the kitchenette.

Jinxie Wicks' drainage system has backed up and packed up. And so, the Big Jubilee Lunch comes to a dramatic end. We phone the emergency services. Tozer starts singing, 'Auntie Mary had a canary up the leg of her drawers' and offers to walk Daphne home, smarmy Welsh git. Terry helps Jinxie Wicks to clear up and await the plumber. I battle my way along the Spratling Sea Road, back to The Shack. Did the Jubilee Pageant make me proud to be British? Not really. Would I sleep on the pavement in the rain in the hopes of catching a glimpse of someone famous? Not bloomin' likely. Well, I might if that someone was Leonard Cohen. But not if my bad back was playing up. As for Terry's vegetarian-pork-and-beans-without-the-pork, not even Bingo would finish it off. Terry brought it home and put it outside for the seagulls. Serves them right.

Hot news. Saltmarsh is no longer the heaving Sodom of the North Kent coast. Mr Vladimir Piskov of Shackles R Us has done a runner. Turns out he was heavily in debt, his assets have been seized (and, presumably his spanking benches and padlocked leather chastity belts and all his kinky bondage clobber) and his house is on the market. No more coach loads peering over the wall. All decency restored. As Jinxie Wicks says, 'Shame! Boo!' Excitement over. Speaking of excitement, I was just about to tuck into a double-decker sausage sandwich when the phone goes. Surprise! It wasn't my mum for once. It was Daphne – Oh be still my beating heart – 'Hi there, Ronald. This is all a bit last minute, but I'm organising Tex Tozer's poetry reading at the SPAM Portakabin first Friday in July at 3 pm Would you like to come?'

My silent response was, 'Hell, no, I blinkin' well would NOT,' but I didn't want to upset Daphne.

'Oh dear, oh dear, what a shame, that date clashes with my long awaited optometrist appointment,' I replied, lying through my dental work. Am I a cad? Am I a mean-spirited guy with a grudge? Yes I am. The phone goes again. It's my mum.

'Oh my Gawd, Ronald, panic stations. Don't let Bingo out of the house.'

'Morning Mum, what's new?'

'A killer dog disease, that's what. It's in the paper. It's rampaging across Britain. Dogs are dropping down dead all over the country, it's called Alabama Rot—'

'Never heard of it, spell it out, Mum.'

'A-L-A-B-A-M-A R-O-T. It has swept across the U.S.A. wiping out half the canine population. In Scotland two cocker spaniels died of a mystery illness, the vet did tests and – guess what – confirmed that the dogs had died of Alabama Rot—'

'Scotland is a fair distance from—'

'So is the U.S.A.! The Kennel Club is telling all members to be on red alert and to see their vets the minute their dogs look peaky. Check up on Bingo. Now.'

'He looks fine, Mum, apart from his bald patches and—'

'Which reminds me, here's a designer dog joke. If you cross a cockerpoo with a labradoodle what do you get? Answer, a cockerpoodledoo!'

'Ha, ha, ha. Good one, Mum.' (You have to hand it to her, bright as a button at ninety-four.)

'And here's another one. What do you get if you cross a bulldog with a shihtzu? Answer, bullshit!'

'Ha, ha, again. Must go now, Mum, time for Bingo's walk. Duty calls.'

Returning to the kitchen I find that Bingo has climbed onto the table and gobbled my double-decker sausage sandwich. I try walloping him one with the fly swatter but he dodges under the table with a fun-loving gleam in his eyes. It's a funny thing how dogs – smelly creatures that cause no end of mess, inconvenience and expense – manage to worm their way into your heart. It must be to do with their non-judgemental devotion. Dogs don't mind if you've got no teeth, gravy down your jumper, broken specs, dirty socks, bad breath, a little roof over your toolshed… to a dog, you are God. From a dog you receive unqualified adoration. I often wonder what goes on in Bingo's brain. I feel almost tearful when I witness his desperation to communicate. The American writer John Updike put it like this:

> *Dogs perch on the edge of understanding, their bright eyes polished by the yearning to comprehend.*

Too true. Even as I'm scribbling this, Bingo has crawled out from under the table and he's gazing at me, tail wagging. I can almost read his mind. He's thinking, 'Look at the daft old bugger. He loves it when I tilt my head slightly to one side – here I go, tilt, stare him in the eyes, wag my tail. Yay! Soppy old Two-Legs is a pushover when I do a tilt, a gaze and a wag. Works every time, there he goes, over to the doggy treats tin…'

Over I go to the treats tin for a Meaty Morsel.

'Sit, Bingo, good boy!'

I am putty in that dog's paws. When he's curled up on my lap, ears and tail twitching, snuffling and snoring, and I run my hands over his wiry back (avoiding the bald patches – yes the baldness problem has struck again) I marvel at how dogs have so craftily adapted to living with us humans. But let's face it, they are always just dogs. I'm reminded of the Snoopy cartoon in which Snoopy says, '*Yesterday I was a dog. Today I am a dog. Tomorrow I'll probably still be a dog.*'

Matter of fact I've been reading Inside of a Dog by Alexandra Horowitz (RSPCA, £1) a professor of animal behaviour. She has spent years looking into the doggy mind and studying the ways dogs communicate. To make himself noticed by his Human a dog will gaze, whine, woof, push him with a wet nose, nuzzle, thump his tail or simply drop loudly onto the floor with a deep sigh. The intense gaze is the dog's best of all attention grabbers. When Bingo does the intense gaze it feels as if he is not just looking at me but into me. Very disconcerting it is too. The gaze can mean, 'Time for my walk' or 'Lift me up onto the settee' or 'How would you like to be evicted from your warm basket last thing at night, and booted out into the pouring rain...?' et cetera.

I often think to myself, 'If only Bingo could talk'. Take today for example. I go into the kitchen first thing and Bingo looks up from his basket as if he's saying, 'Hi Two-Legs! How's tricks this Sunday morning?'

As I fill the kettle, I can see that he's thinking to himself, 'Just look at him, bless his heart, padding round the kitchen... If I do a tilt and a gaze I'll get a juicy bit of his breakfast sausage.' Then, as I'm fiddling with the frying pan and Bingo keeps getting under my feet, he suddenly pricks up one ear and scoots back into his basket, clearly thinking, 'Oh no, here comes boring Terry.' Little does Terry suspect, incidentally, that yesterday I used the bowl that he's about to pour his muesli into for Bingo's mince. Bingo licked it clean and I put it back on the shelf without rinsing it first.

When Terry walks in wearing his shorty dressing-gown and new novelty slippers, I can see from Bingo's expression that he is thinking, 'Hi Terry, you tosser, how's about giving me a friendly pat on the head, just for once?'

Dogs have an uncanny knack of reading your mind, and of anticipating events and actions. No two ways. According to Dr Horowitz's book, a dog recognises his human by their pong. When we move about we leave behind clouds of 'molecules' – whole trails of dead skin cells to scent the air with our personal pong. In fact the dog's sense of smell is amazing. Human noses have six million receptor sites, a dog has 300 million. How do the boffins discover these facts, I wonder? It's all way above my head. What's more when we stroke our dogs, our stress hormones get less, so does our blood pressure. Then the 'feel good' hormones kick in (nature's heroin, called endorphins) and the effect is as good any prescription drugs. Not as good as a can of Scrumpy Jack, though.

Anyway call me a sentimental old fool, but, against my better judgement, I let Terry talk me into taking Bingo to Bev-the-Rev's 'Bless our Pets' service at Saltmarsh's Saint Mildred's Church. Pet owners, including Yours Truly, congregated in a field next to the church, where the Christian youth band – The Holy Hipsters – was setting up speakers, amplifiers and what have you. The Holy Hipsters comprised a keyboard, drums, violin, guitar, kazoo and football rattle. They had that crazed, happy expression common to evangelical Christians. Terry has it too. Always off putting first thing in the morning over porridge.

Lady vicar – Bev-the-Rev – was wearing baggy Bermuda shorts and a polo-neck T-shirt with 'FIGHT TRUTH DECAY, BRUSH UP YOUR BIBLE' across the chest. The only way you'd know she was a vicar was by the small stretch of clerical dog collar across her polo neck. To my way of thinking vicars should always wear their cassocks when they're on duty. You wouldn't catch the Pope cavorting about the Vatican in Bermuda shorts, would you? Or the Archbishop of Canterbury, sunbathing in the cathedral precincts wearing his budgie smugglers? Men of the cloth – and women – should behave with a bit of dignity and decorum.

'Greetings, Terry,' shouted Bev-the-Rev, spotting Terry at the raffle table. 'The Good Lord is smiling on us today! Must have heard our prayers, the rain seems to be holding off...'

In my opinion the good Lord ought to have better things to do than keep the rain off Bev-the-Rev's 'Bless our Pets' service... And just as Bev-the-Rev said, 'The rain seems to be holding off' there was an almighty clap of thunder which startled Bingo to the point where he did what a dog does and he did it bang beside Bev-the-Rev's orange orthopaedic sandals. Oops! Luckily I had a pooper-scooper to hand. And a handy bin was provided.

But, my goodness, what a turn-out! There were dogs, cats, tortoises, rabbits, two chickens, a goat, a goldfish, a sheep, a micro-pig, stick-insects and a pet rat.

Edna Higgins was there with her corgi. Mr Wienczyslaw with a huge slobbering bulldog. Roger, the abandoned hamster re-homed at the Saltmarsh Infant School, was there, escorted by two small girls wearing Brownie uniforms. The Holy Hipsters struck up with 'The animals went in two by two. Hurrah! Hurrah!' with a great deal of ear-splitting feedback from the microphone and amplifiers. The micro-pig had a panic attack and had to be restrained in a special crate. Then Bev-the-Rev stepped up to the microphone – more piercing feedback – and asked everybody to switch off their phones.

'Let us stand and praise God for His creation,' she began, raising her voice to be heard above a chorus of yaps, clucks, cock-a-doodledoos, bleats, barks, a silly ringtone from a phone that hadn't been switched off and the micro-pig's squeals and snorts. A small boy yelled that his guinea pig had escaped. Edna Higgins rushed to the rescue. Then the micro-pig broke free. Bingo tried to chase after it, I held on to his lead for dear life. Up with the umbrellas again. The Holy Hipsters' violinist played a little riff, the band struck up with *All Things Bright and Beautiful*;

Each little flower that opens
Each little bird that sings... et cetera,

during which Mr Wienczyslaw's slobbering bulldog tried to mount Bingo who wasn't having any of it and nipped the bulldog on the rump. A group of youths from the nearby council estate started rampaging across the field and jeering at The Holy Hipsters. 'Yah! Jesus creepers! Bible bashers get a life!' but they were quickly rounded up and escorted away by Edna Higgins. Salt of the earth that she is.

Then Bev-the-Rev interrupted The Holy Hipsters by announcing, 'Will the owner of a white corsair in the church car park please move it as it's blocking the entrance.' It turned out to be Mr Wienczyslaw's corsair and he asked Bev-the-Rev to hold his slobbering bulldog. Bev-the-Rev was dragged across the grass until Terry jumped over the raffle table and came to her rescue.

By now the yaps, meows, barks, clucks, bleats and snorts had reached a crescendo. The Holy Hipsters were firing on all cylinders, *Nellie the elephant packed her trunk...* et cetera. Then Bev-the-Rev stepped up to the microphone again and instructed us to place our hands on our pets and to insert our own pet's name into the Prayer that we were all to say in unison. This is how it went:

128

'Lord, thank you for BINGO, and for all our animal friends... Please Lord, bless BINGO and all the pets gathered together here in the name of the Father, the Son and the Holy Ghost.'

Bingo wagged his tail. I could tell that he was thinking, 'What is all this Jesus-bollocks about? Has boring Terry been brainwashing my Two-Legs?' Then the sun came out. Umbrellas were shaken and closed. Edna Higgins' corgi suddenly dashed across the grass and pounced on a guinea pig.

The Brownie pack sang, '*If I was an elephant, I'd thank you Lord by raising my trunk / If I was a wiggly worm, I'd thank you Lord by giving a squirm...*'

The *Saltmarsh Gazette*'s photographer took snaps. The Holy Hipsters played a final number and downed instruments. Bev-the-Rev announced, 'A big hand for the band!' A smattering of applause rippled through the assembled throng. 'I hope that all you good people have enjoyed this service and that you will stay for a beaker of orange squash and make new friends.'

Not to put too fine a point on it I was out of there and straight into the Friendly Winkle. Then I was straight out again when I spotted Tex Tozer holding forth at the bar. Instead I walked along the beach and sat on a breakwater while Bingo snuffled round the pebbles. I wonder if he feels any different now that he has been blessed. I wonder whether being blessed by the Lord will make his baldness better? I expect it would take a trip to Lourdes to make that happen.

Len wandered past jabbering on about an Air France Flight 447 that plummeted into the Atlantic Ocean in 2009. It took two years for air crash experts to recover the black box flight recorder.

Back at The Shack I phoned my mum:

'Hello Mum. Have you had a nice day? I took Bingo to…'

'Listen to me, Son, whatever you do keep Bingo away from slugs. You hear me? SLUGS.'

'It's fairly dry down by the beach and—'

'—don't interrupt, Ronald, all the recent rain has caused a slug invasion, and dogs can get deadly lungworm from eating infected slugs. Look out for any symptoms – vomiting, wheezing, coughing, nosebleeds, lethargy – remember LUNGWORM can be fatal. Lungworm kills! See you soon, I hope, cheerio…'

One more thing to worry about. And from the room next door I can hear the *whump! B-poc! B-poc! B-poc! Love fifteen!* blaring from the TV… *New balls, please!* Terry is watching re-runs of the Andy Murray matches. What a Wimbledon – female tennis players with tattoos, shrieking and grunting and sounding like a porn film soundtrack. Not that I've ever seen a porn film. In 2009 a female Portuguese player was recorded emitting a squeal akin to a plane taking off. Monica Seles emitted a scream with the same noise level as an electric drill. It's just not British. Then there's John McEnroe with dyed hair, spectators whooping, chanting, hollering, wearing novelty headgear and doing Mexican waves as if they are at a rock concert. Andy Murray has so many straps, splints and bandages on his knees, wrists and ankles that he looks like Frankenstein's monster. The special sparrow hawk, called Rufus, that keeps the pigeons away from the Centre Court, has been birdnapped… As I put the kettle on I can hear, coming from the next room, the commentary: 'Murray to serve – oh, what's happened? One of his balls has dropped out…'

Whaat?

Holy moly! I dash into the TV room to witness the drama. Panic over. Turns out the pockets of Murray's shorts are too small to retain the spare tennis ball that he stuffs into them before he serves.

'Oops! A second ball has popped out, he'll have to watch his balls or he could slip on one and suffer serious injury...' continues the commentator.

Clearly Andy Murray needs to get himself some shorts with deeper pockets.

Yes, it's a funny game. What with points, sets and games, the complicated scoring system certainly keeps you on your toes. As for the 'tie-break' I still haven't discovered how it works. And the scoring method – 'fifteen, thirty, forty, game' what's that all about?

'Who invented the tennis scoring system, Terry?' I ask, bringing in the mugs of tea.

'You can google it, Dad, I'll get my laptop...'

So Terry gets his laptop. I tap in 'who invented the tennis scoring system?' Click. Lo and behold, the answer appears. The French invented it in 1450. They based it on the minute hand of a twelve-hour clock. So – fifteen, thirty, forty – except that if this were the case it would be *forty-five* if you think about it? The word love as in love, fifteen comes from the French for egg, 'l'oeuf'. Clear as mud.

Meanwhile, Terry has switched to a re-run of the Wimbledon Final. Two multi-millionaires – Andy Murray and Roger Federer – slogging it out. *Poc! Poc! Wallop!* Crowd roars. *Poc!*

'He's got new shorts today, his balls safely tucked away,' says the commentator.

Bingo is sitting near the TV screen his head going from side to side as he follows the ball. Murray trips, skids, falls flat, twists his ankle, camera zooms in for a slo-mo shot of him writhing in agony. He staggers up, limping. He complains about wet grass. Federer serves a 120-miles-per-hour ace.

'Federer's ball striking and timing is pitch perfect, sheer poetry in motion,' enthuses Terry, mug of tea in one hand, packet of pork scratchings in the other. 'Federer has got to be the Leonardo Da Vinci of tennis…'

Bingo makes a lunge for the pork scratchings and scampers round the room with the packet dangling from his jaws. Federer wins in four sets. He stages a euphoric collapse onto the turf. It's his seventh Wimbledon win, he's made tennis history. The TV cameras zoom in onto Murray. It's his fourth Grand Slam (what does Grand Slam mean?) defeat. He is numb with emotion. His chin is wobbling. His upper lip a-tremble. His eyes are welling up. He is blubbing. The Duchess of Cambridge in the Royal Box is blubbing. The Prime Minister is blubbing. All 60,000 spectators on the Centre Court (apart from Federer's family) are blubbing. It's a nationwide blub-fest. Terry is mopping his eyes and blowing his nose. Only in Britain could the blubbing loser of the Wimbledon's men's singles make the front pages of every next day's newspapers. Readers had to turn to the inside pages for pictures of Federer, the seven times winner – Federer, the tennis genius champ! I blame all this touchy-feely, blubbing business on the tabloid newspapers and ridiculous TV talent shows. And on the late lamented Princess Diana. And I blame born-again touchy-feely Christians like Terry. Oh well, 'whatever', as the young of today say.

We said that it would all end in tears. The day after the Canaletto Moment the Duke of Edinburgh was rushed to hospital with a bladder infection. That's what comes of standing about on the Royal Barge for four hours in the wind and rain at the age of ninety-one. But why does the nation need to be told that he has a 'bladder infection'? Poor old sod. Too much information as Daphne would say. If I was the Duke of Edinburgh I'd like my bladder behaviour kept private. But no doubt the Duke's bladder is in good hands. It's a safe bet that he won't be sent home with a bottle of antibiotics and a Quit Kit.

But now for the exciting news. There have been interesting developments on the Daphne front. She phoned to ask if she could call in at The Shack to discuss something that's on her mind. Call in at The Shack? Of her own volition? Was I in a tizz, or what? I was out of bed at 5am tidying the place up, putting the carpet sweeper over the floor (Help the Aged, £1.50), hiding my medicaments, dusting Bingo with flea powder, spraying my freshly-showered self with lavender and rosemary relax fragrance. Silly mistake. This turned out to be room-spray, when I found my specs and read the label. No matter. I had another shower to wash it off, went to check that the loo seat was down just in case Daphne... Oh no!! I opened the door, water was gurgling over the seat, the Save-a-Flush was playing up again. Banged on Terry's door. No joy. He'd left for a funeral. Phone goes. It's my mum:

'Can't chat, Mum, got a plumbing problem—'

'Oh my Gawd! That's you and the Duke of Edinburgh both—'

'No, Mum, it's the ball cock playing up—'

'Like I said, you and the Duke, balls, cocks, comes to the same thing whether you're mighty or humble, once you're an OAP.'

At this point Bingo starts barking. Through the window I can see Daphne – my heart skips a beat, or maybe it's a recurrence of the symptoms of atrial fibrillation, must get it checked again by Doc Ng.

Mum is still rabbiting on:

'Well, Son, you just look after yourself. Hope you haven't got Legionnaires' Disease. Have you been opening bags of compost? Not many people know that the Legionnaires' bug is found in compost. It was in my paper. Last week a man in Scotland cut his finger while using compost, another man inhaled some compost and – guess what? – they both got Legionnaires'.'

Jesus wept, as Terry would never say. In comes Daphne, her usual radiant self – 'When e'er she speaks, my ravished ear / no other voice than hers can hear' – and so forth... I flash my new (partial bridge) smile. Turns out she wants to confide in me.

'You may have guessed, Ronald, I am sort of 'seeing',' (she makes wiggle marks with her fingers around the word 'seeing') 'Tex Tozer and I would value your advice.'

Gutted isn't the word. 'Seeing' Tozer? All the Leonard Cohen songs I've ever listened to jangle upon my inner ear. Let's face it. The writing has been on the wall for weeks. Wake up and smell the coffee, Tonks.

'He is a dear, complicated man, of great intellect and sensitivity, but when we are alone together...'

Alone together – the phrase is like a knife twisting in my vitals.

ALONE? With that boozed-up fat fake? Oh Daphne. Farewell my tranquil mind, farewell content...

'... he never commits... he treats me like a *sister*, he goes on and on about his writer's block and his feelings being numb. He quotes his poems, he tells me that he yearns for a sympathetic woman to save him from his demons...'

Don't we all, Daphne, don't we all, I'm thinking. I make her a cup of tea, and assure her that not one word alluding to her emotional outburst will ever pass my lips. The upshot is that she is planning to hold a dinner party in Tozer's honour. It's Daphne's make or break gesture. Her plan is that Tozer will fall for her feminine allure as well as her home cooking. I'm invited, so is Jinxie Wicks and Andy and his 'plus-one'. She wants me to arrive early to help with setting up the table and arranging the chairs. To my way of thinking, Daphne's dinner is going to be like a scene from a Harold Pinter play.

Daphne, then tells me a good joke, which I must try to remember to tell to Jinxie Wicks.

'A woman recovering from major surgery came round and informed the surgeon that during the operation she had left her body, had an 'out of body experience' and spoken to God. God told her not to worry, she would make a full recovery and live for another fifty years. So as soon as she was out of hospital she went on a diet, lost two stone, had liposuction, a face lift, a boob job, tummy tuck, buttock lift, Botox and dyed her hair. On the way home she was knocked down and killed by a bus. On meeting God, she told him how cheesed off she was and grumbled 'I thought you said I had another fifty years.' God replied, 'Sorry about that, I just didn't recognise you"

At this point Daphne gives me a sisterly hug (teenage-type tremors tingle up my trousers) and says, 'Ronald you are my tower-of-strength,' pats Bingo who is giving her 'the gaze' and drooling. I know how he feels. Then departs on her bike. It's like all the lights have suddenly gone out.

But, mustn't dwell... went into the back garden (wearing overcoat and scarf due to unseasonal cold weather) to sit in a sun lounger that Terry has rescued from the skip, and to ponder things in my heart like Mary pondered things in her heart after her visitation from the Angel Gabriel. No doubt about it, Terry's Christian ways are beginning to get to me.

Next day the sun is shining. Jinxie Wicks knocks on The Shack's front door. I open it flashing my gleaming 'bridge' and she says, 'Wow! Hi there, White Fang!'

We decide to go on a jaunt into Canterbury.

This is no easy undertaking, involving as it does a mile long walk to the bus stop, then a three quarter of an hour bus ride. By the time we arrive we both urgently need the loo. No public conveniences in sight. We go in to a café called ASK and ask to use the loos.

''Fraid not, pal,' says the man behind the till, 'the floors just been washed and it's wet.'

'We don't mind, we're not intending to take our shoes off,' says Jinxie Wicks.

''Fraid not, lady, it's health and safety regs. With the floor wet, there might be an accident.'

'Too right,' snaps Jinxie Wicks, 'there bloomin' well might be an accident – two accidents – all over the ruddy floor, if you don't help two seniors in distress. And then where will you be, huh, with your health and safety regs?'

The man behind the till shows no mercy. Even my ingratiating White Fang flash cuts no ice. He turfs us out. We cross our legs and stagger into nearby British Home Stores. Up the escalator to the loos on the first floor. The situation becoming desperate. Utter dismay. The WCs are locked. Jinxie Wicks shouts for a manager. He turns up, looks about sixteen and incapable of understanding the urgency of the OAP bladder situation. He explains that in order to increase 'customer satisfaction' a new system is being 'trialled'. The WCs can now only be used *after* a customer has made a purchase. The customer's till receipt will be printed with a special daily pass-code which the customer taps into the loo's entry security lock. Bloomin' heck. How much longer can my sphincter last out? He then goes on, 'The company wants customers to enjoy a happy experience when they use the British Home Stores' loos.'

Jinxie Wicks, at the end of her tether shouts, 'A happy experience? Now I've heard everything! Customers would have a much 'happier experience' if they could just walk in and use the ruddy loo – without all the hassle of queuing up first to buy something, and without having to read the smudgy small print on their till receipt.'

Has the world gone made? What are things coming to when a pensioner can't answer a call of nature in peace?

The upshot is that with my waterworks in spasm I queue up to buy a shirt. But then having obtained my till receipt, neither me or Jinxie Wicks can read the pass-code numbers having both forgotten to bring our reading specs. We then summon the manager again. He reads it for us, and taps it into the WC entry security lock. What happened to human dignity? At last – what a relief. So, do we have a 'happy experience of the British Home Store's loos'? No more than usual. Then I return the shirt to Customer Services for a refund. We cock a snoot at the manager and leg it. What a fiasco.

Then it's off on a Canterbury Charity Shop crawl. Life in the fast lane, huh? Jinxie Wicks stocks up on clothing while I bag some bargain books. (Two 'Biggles' books in good condition which I sell later to my vintage-book seller friend for £30). And a couple of china dogs for my mum. In the coat section we bump into Len who starts jabbering on about a near disaster aboard an Air Canada Boeing 767, reported in the papers.

'The pilot was half asleep – it's called 'pilot fatigue' – and mistook the planet Venus for an approaching aircraft mid-air,' says Len, rubbing his bulbous nose and twitching with agitation. 'Then in a panic, he rammed the control stick forward, plunged 4,000 feet and sent the plane into a terrifying nose-dive. Luckily the captain saved the day by grabbing the controls and setting the plane back on target. Sixteen passengers and crew were injured...'

We escape from Len, buy two cans of cider and a pasty each to enjoy in the public gardens, before catching the Saltmarsh bus home. Jinxie Wicks plans to write a letter of complaint about the BHS loos to the *Saltmarsh Gazette*. During the bus journey she regales me with details of her latest Soul Mates encounter.

Her blind date suggested they meet at an off-the-beaten-track hamlet at an olde-worlde inn that it took Jinxie Wicks an hour to reach by bus. She goes in, peering round for the bloke who had emailed that he'll be wearing a blue jumper, carrying a copy of Golf Monthly magazine and will have his dog with him. The inn is packed full of blokes with dogs, reading Golf Monthly. But there's only one bloke wearing a blue jumper.

'Hello,' says Jinxie Wicks, joining him at the bar.

'Hello,' says the bloke.

'Nice dog,' says Jinxie Wicks, patting the dog which is a large slobbery sort of dog with spools of drool dangling from its jaws. Before the bloke has even shaken hands or got onto first name terms he launches into a monologue detailing his dog's history: Abandoned on a motorway as a pup. Saved by a kindly pensioner. Pensioner dies, dog re-homed. New owner neglects dog. R.S.P.C.A. called in. Dog covered in sores. Re-homed... the bloke is unstoppable. He goes on and on. Jinxie Wicks orders herself a drink, the bloke orders himself one, saying to the barman 'Paw (ha, ha, pun) me another beer.' Guess who pays for both drinks? Not the bloke. He is spouting on about how the dog – called Dog – once swallowed a golf ball and the vet's bill was £300. Dog ate a chocolate rabbit and, chocolate being poisonous for dogs – Dog required emergency surgery, vet's bill £400. Dog ate two pounds of green grapes, also poisonous for dogs, emergency vet's bill £350. Vet made Dog vomit, two pounds of grapes came up looking as good as new, not even squashed. 'Fascinating,' says Jinxie Wicks, eyeing up the menu board on the wall – duck in orange sauce, steak au poivre, lamb shank in mint gravy – just the job she is thinking hoping that the bloke will suggest lunch. No such luck. He hasn't asked her a single question about herself. Not even whether she owns a dog. Bloke finishes off his beer, says 'must be off now, time to feed Dog. Nice to meet you.' And pushes off, leaving Jinxie Wicks to pay for the drinks. Into the Ladies she goes to powder her nose. As she comes out she sees, rushing in and out of breath, a tall, athletic-looking bloke with fair hair and piercing blue eyes. 'Phwoar! Testosterone-on-legs,' thinks Jinxie Wicks. He is wearing a blue jumper, carrying Golf Monthly and has a black, frisky, pointy-eared dog with him. 'Hi,' says the bloke to the barman. 'I'm very late, I should have been here an hour ago, has a woman been in who answers to the description, 'Bodywork good, some respraying, Kentish Lass, very young-looking?' Barman replies, 'Nah – young-looking? No one like that's been in today, mate.' Jinxie Wicks, feeling that the cards are stacked against, her, slinks out crestfallen. Never judge a book by its cover I tell her, as our bus bumps over the potholes, doing my lower lumbar area no good. Look at it this way, Jinx, I tell her, old 'Testosterone-on-legs' might have got her libido firing on all cylinders but did he look like a gentleman? Was he the type who'd pay for the drinks and stand a lone woman a pub lunch? Jinxie Wicks shakes her head and says, 'Fact is, Ronald, if any bloke could get my hormones pinging, well, even if he was wearing socks and flip-flops say, or had gravy stains down his jumper, I'd be willing to put up with cheese on toast and a glass of water.' Good grief. To be honest women are a great mystery to Yours Truly. Who knows *what* goes on in a woman's mind? As I remark to Jinxie Wicks as our bus chugs to a halt outside the Saltmarsh public conveniences, love conquers all except toothache and heavy snoring.

The following week, fired up by our British Home Stores debacle, Jinxie Wicks organised a demo! Our multi-functional SPAM SAYS NO! banner was once again waved aloft as a small group of protesters congregated outside British Home Stores to complain about them locking the loos. The dreaded Rosemary and some of her poo-fairy crowd also got in on the act, giving out leaflets that read 'NO LOOS IS BAD NEWS'. Slight problem though. The bus journey to get there had taken an hour and what with standing in the drizzle holding up the SPAM SAYS NO! banner, we were all desperate for the WC, the only ones in the vicinity being in British Home Stores – locked, but opened by a special code. Hoist by your own petard as the saying goes. Problem solved by Rosemary who offered to go in, buy something and to then give out details of the pass code. So the demo fizzled out. All I can say is that British Home Stores had better start looking to its laurels before angry mobs of pensioners start smashing locks on the WC doors.

JULY 2012

A big hand for Wiggo! I want to be like Wiggo! Yes. Bradley Wiggins – Wiggo – the first Brit to win the French Tour de France. The sight of thousands of spectators waving their Union Jacks and singing, 'God Save the Queen' in the Champs Elysees was certainly one in the eye for the Frogs. And the sight of Wiggo gasping for his bottle of water after slogging up to the peak of a 6,000ft mountain – the first of four that he would slog up that day – had me jumping off the settee and punching the air. Thirty-two years old and winner of the world's toughest race. What a hero. On the day before the finish one of the newspapers had the front page headline, ''Ere Wiggo! 'Ere Wiggo!' and a blank face-space mask of Wiggo's mod hairline and sideburns. The chap in the papershop had cut it out and stuck it on a poster of the Queen, so that Her Majesty's face was framed with Wiggo's hair and sideburns. Brilliant.

The day after Wiggo's momentous sporting triumph I was up at 6 a.m. and on my bike for a five-mile sprint (on the flat) along the Spratling Sea Road and back. And, I might add, I have blown an entire month's pension money on a pair of gel-padded Lycra cycling shorts, an orange hi-vis Lycra cycle jersey with fine mesh ventilation panels, and a red, lightweight, aerodynamic, head-retention system cycle helmet. Cool or what? Watch out Wiggo, here I come. All I need is a racing bike. To be honest I'm not sprightly enough – what with my lower lumbar problems and knee brace – to get on and off a racing bike. I'm happy to stick to my small-wheel Raleigh Shopper with its handy basket and saddlebag.

So off I pedalled, whizzing along to the papershop where I bumped into Len who took one look at me, and fell about laughing. Rather uncalled for I thought. Okay, so everyone – except Wiggo – looks a prat wearing a cycle helmet, especially if they also wear specs, but Len's guffaws where completely out of order.

'Wah-hah-hah,' he spluttered, holding his sides, tears spurting from the corners of his eyes, 'Oh my good Gawd! Wah-hah-hah – you wear the pointy bit at the back, you pillock…'

So I had my cycle helmet the wrong way round? We all make mistakes. No need for such hilarity. When Len had calmed down and lit a fag, he drew my attention to an item in the *Daily Mail* headed PILOT ERROR CAUSED JET PLUNGE, and started rambling on about loss of lift, malfunctioning airspeed sensors and the jet hitting the sea at high speed killing all on board.

In my view if anyone still needs Anxiety Management counselling it is Len. Definitely.

'Lighten up, Len,' I said, not for the first time, 'you can get killed crossing the road.' Then I told him about a motorcyclist in Stoke-on-Trent who was killed last week by a flying pheasant that flew out of a hedge and hit him in the helmet sending him and his 2500cc Kawasaki cartwheeling across the tarmac. You can bet that it had never crossed the poor bloke's mind that he would one day be killed by a flying pheasant. Stuff happens, as the young say.

'Point taken. Off you go. Talk about Blazing Saddle!' shouted Len as I pedalled away. 'With all that prize-money Wiggo's getting he'll soon be able to buy himself a car and not have to go everywhere by bike!'

On the topic of Anxiety Management I have just had my SPAM final assessment. No forms to fill in this time. No questions about my sexuality. Just a lot of matey chitchat about 'coping strategies'. The anxious looking assessor – Miss Box – wearing a droopy green cardigan and orthopaedic sandals kept tapping her computer keys throughout. She asked me how I'd been coping. How had my condition affected my day-to-day activities? Had I entertained any thoughts of self-harm?

'No,' I replied, 'I just feel my usual, anxious, every day self.'

Miss Box tapped her computer keys and said, 'So tell me, Mr Tonks, any progress with your NATS?'

Talk about embarrassing! I'm not happy going into details about my nats (funny word for them) with some stranger. Doc Ng at a push, but not Miss Box.

'To tell the truth, my – erm, ahem, ahem, NATS, as you call them don't appear to be getting any bigger. Doc Ng told me I could stop worrying—'

'Ah!' interrupted Miss Box, holding up her hand, palm facing me. 'We're at cross purposes here, Mr Tonks. NATS is short for Negative Automatic Thoughts, for which you have a propensity.'

She could say that again. Especially when my thoughts turn to Anxiety Management counsellors, my health, mobile phones, seagulls, dentists, happy-clappy Christians, Terry, Tex Tozer, you name it. Miss Box sneaked a peak at her wristwatch. She fixed me with an intent look. 'So tell me, what situation would be likely to trigger your NATS?'

'Apart from being here, with you, you mean?'

'Indeed.'

'Well, I'd definitely start to feel anxious if I was planning a trip to London for the 2012 Olympics for example. So I'm not planning any such trip because it would make me too anxious.'

'Why would such a trip make you anxious?'

'Well the train might be delayed, due to rail strikes. A suspicious unattended package might be found in one of the carriages. The train could be packed with hooligans rampaging through the carriages grabbing people's mobile phones and laptops. I might not be able to find my ticket when the inspector comes along. The Gents may be out of order…'

'Woah!' said Miss Box, holding up her hand, palm facing me again, 'Stop right there, Mr Tonks. NATS galore! Lots and lots of NATS! Why on earth, for instance would the lavatories be out of order?'

I had a good answer for that, no two ways. I told Miss Box about my experience last time I took the train to London – four years ago. As the train approached Chatham the guard announced over the intercom, 'Ladies and gentlemen, we regret that the toilets are not in use on this train. If you require toilet facilities please alight at Chatham where the train will wait for you.' What a palaver. Believe me nothing makes a person of my age suddenly want to use a WC more than being told that there isn't one, right? So off the train I got, as advised by the guard, and by the time I'd finished and emerged from the Chatham toilet facilities there was the London train vanishing at high speed into the distance. I was left stranded without a valid ticket.'

'Hmm,' said Miss Box, 'hmm. Be realistic, Mr Tonks, is the same scenario likely to be repeated?'

'Knowing my luck…'

'NATS, Mr Tonks, NATS Just listen to yourself. Any other thoughts on why you might be anxious about making a trip to London?'

'Well. The train might be overcrowded, standing room only. I might get pushed over in the stampede at the London ticket barrier. I might fall down, break a hip, be carted off to a London hospital 40 miles from home where none of the nurses speak English. They say that a broken hip is the beginning of the end if you're over sixty…'

Mis Box is tapping the words 'depressive', 'borderline paranoia' and 'cognitive somatic assumptions activated' onto her computer screen.

'…Otherwise, Miss Box, I'd say, I've been feeling relatively mellow of late. Quite chirpy in fact. The warm weather helps.'

She signed me off. An era has ended. As we shook hands I remarked, 'Hope my bike hasn't been pinched. I forgot to bring my lock.'

'NATS again, Mr Tonks, negative thinking!'

The upshot was that I left with a spring in my step and a feeling in my bones that Anxiety Management may not be as positive as it's cracked up to be.

So off I went, on my wheels, whizzing along a little detour towards Tex Tozer's neck of the woods, right past his cottage in Bogshole Street. He lives at number 2B – where he has stuck a wooden sign on the paint-peeling front door that reads '2B or not 2B, that is the question'. Swanky prat. Oh no! There, leaning against Tozer's mildew-covered, falling-down garden fence was Daphne's bike. DAPHNE'S BIKE! Oh haggard and woe-begone Tonks! Another twist of the knife. Don't get your NATS in a tangle, I told myself, and raced past at high speed so that if anyone – Daphne – happened to peer out of Tozer's window they would have seen no more than a blur.

So, full speed ahead to the Friendly Winkle for a bevvy. Andy was there wearing a T-shirt with FALL IN LOVE NOT IN LINE across the chest. Jinxie Wicks was there celebrating the fiftieth anniversary of the Rolling Stones. She was holding up a photograph of the four longest-serving

Stones – Mick, Keef, Ronnie and Charlie (combined ages 272 years), the first time that the famous wrinkly rockers have got together in public for four years. In the photo they were all wearing thread-bare jeans, trainers (Mick's were blue) and the sort of jacket you can get for a couple of quid in the Saltmarsh charity shops. Keef, with his wonky hat and aviator sunglasses, looked like one of those blokes you see sleeping in a cardboard box in the Canterbury underpass. All of them would have looked at home at the Saltmarsh Help the Homeless Centre. Everyone in the Friendly Winkle wondered why the Stones dress like we have to dress when they are worth an estimated £190 million (Mick), £175 million (Keef), £20 million (Ronnie), £85 million (Charlie). You'd think they would all fork out for some posh togs, wouldn't you?

'Whatever way they dress, just remember that Mick and Keef are Kent born and bred,' said Jinxie Wicks, who swears that she once enjoyed a knee trembler with Mick after a jive competition at the Dartford Co-op Hall. 'Yeah. Mick and Keef are two of Kent's finest sons. As for Keef, never mind his swollen finger joints and his not being able to remember the words of the songs anymore, he is still the world's most indestructible rocker, bless his heart, and he has promised his fans that he won't retire until he croaks, so there.'

Three cheers for the Stones. Everyone applauded, at which point, Tex Tozer walked in thinking the applause was for him. Big-head.

Tozer said that his favourite Rolling Stones revelation is how, on Mick and Bianca's wedding night, Bianca retired to her bed early, only to be woken up several hours later by Keith Moon of The Who abseiling past the bedroom window stark naked apart from novelty sunglasses and a pair of ladies knickers on his head. We all agreed that the Rolling Stones, OAPs all, are definitely not the sort of blokes who pat their pockets checking for their bus passes and reading specs every time they leave the house. Bet Mick doesn't go 'ooof!' when he sits down on a settee. Mind you, as Terry recently remarked, there is something weird about old geezers in their seventies capering about on stage singing 50 year old songs about pulling teenage 'chicks'. And who was it who said Mick had 'child-bearing lips'? Brilliant. Kingsley Amis, maybe?

Then it was an energetic pedal back to The Shack. I'm just giving Bingo his mince when the phone goes.

'Ronald? Listen, Son, stock up on tins of cocoa. And bars of plain chocolate. Do you hear me?'

'Hello, Mum, I was thinking about you this morning when—'

'There's this Doctor Glorambattista Desideri from an Italian university who has discovered that a daily dose of chocolate staves off Alzheimer's. None of us Tonkses have ever caught Alzheimer's, but there's always a first time.'

'Matter of fact, Mum, Alzheimer's isn't CATCHING. It's not like flu or –'

'Like I was saying, this doctor found that a daily dose of chocolate works after trying it out on a group of over-seventies. It's all to do with something called flavanols – I'll spell it – F-L-A-V-A-N-O-L-S, got it?'

'If I'm not mistaken, Mum, you get flavanols in red wine, and I drink plenty of that whenever I get the—'

'Must go, Son, *Cash in the Attic* is just starting.'

Following Mum's call I settle down with a can of Scrumpy Jack (does a can of cider count as one of my five-a-day? It's made of apples, after all...) and a vegetarian sausage sandwich (low fat following Terry's advice) and get stuck into *The Austerity Olympics* by Janie Hampton (St Mildred's

Hospice, 25p), a book about the time the Games came to London in 1948.

There was no ten billion pounds of tax payers' money to play around with that year! No armed guards or surface-to-air missiles on roof tops. No posh Olympic Village for the athletes. They even had to bring their own towels. They slept on straw filled mattresses in RAF camps, colleges and schools. Some were housed by volunteer families who made up beds on their settees. The cyclists had to make their own way to the velodrome on their bikes. Britain was, in fact, almost bankrupt, most of it a bombsite. As visitors approached Wembley Stadium they were greeted by a notice saying, 'Welcome to the Olympic Games. This road is a dangerous area.' Food was the big problem. It was still rationed in 1948, everyone being allowed only 2,600 calories a day. Even the Royal Family was still eating Spam and powdered egg off their gold plates. What with the shortage of tinned fruit, eggs, butter and sugar, British athletes were dependent on food parcels from Canada and Australia. Horlicks tablets, which they ate by the handful, were a real treat. When you consider how much the 2012 competitors knock back, it's no wonder that new records are set each Games. Take American Olympic medallist, Michael Phelps. Terry googled his diet on the laptop. We learned that he eats 12,000 calories a day. Which is probably as much as Yours Truly and Terry combined eat in one week. For breakfast he has three fried egg sandwiches with a lot of cheese, lettuce, tomato, fried onion and mayonnaise, two cups of coffee, a five-egg omelette, a bowl of grits (maize porridge), three slices of French toast with sugar and three choc-chip pancakes. And that's just for breakfast. It's all a far cry from the 1948 Olympics when the British weight lifting team was captained by a man who had been a prisoner of war in a Japanese death camp in Burma.

When repatriated in 1945 he weighed less than five stone but amazingly recovered, despite the austerity diet to take part in the Olympics. The opening ceremony consisted of the Boy Scouts, Girls Brigade and several choral societies offering up a rousing display of British values and traditions.

At this point in my reading, Terry interrupts with the news that a gannet has notched up the record for being the fastest bird in the British Isles. It travelled 722 miles in one day. Its average speed was only one mile, and an hour slower than the speed Wiggo achieved in the Tour de France time trial. Terry made one of his rare jokey remarks saying that it leaves you wondering how much faster the gannet could have gone if it had been on a bike.

The evening being balmy I decide to take the plunge and go for my first dip of the year. Down to the sea's edge I pick my way, wearing my green Bermudas (Barnado's, 50p). Into the foaming brine I wade, up to my neck, doing my side-stroke doggy paddle, keeping my head out of the water to avoid getting water in my ears. I notice that the water is forcing air up into my Bermudas around my rear quarters. They are inflating like a balloon. I doggy paddle through the waves, rear quarters billowing up out of the water. Swamp monster! Just as I'm getting into the swing of things, my billowing baggy Bermudas keeping me afloat, a sudden freak wave – no doubt caused by the wash from a passing oil tanker visible on the horizon – hits me, propelling me forward and making me crash into the breakwater. Oh no! Calamity! Disaster! My dental bridge is dislodged, knocked out and falls into the sea. I see it spiralling downward, down, down and out of sight. To cut a long story short I was walking about with my hand over my mouth for the next week. Luckily Mr Wienczyslaw came up trumps, and pretty pronto, but it's set me back another few hundred quid that I don't have.

The day of Tex Tozer's poetry reading arrived. Notices had been stuck up in several shop windows announcing:

PRIZEWINNING LOCAL POET TEX TOZER READS FROM HIS NEW COLLECTION, *THE GRATING ROAR OF PEBBLES*, ALL WELCOME.

Prize-winning? Hmm? Pull the other one. When someone tackled Tozer in the pub demanding to know WHAT prize, he laughed his shaggy head off and said, 'I won first prize in the Lifeboat Fund raffle.' Everyone roared, even Yours Truly. To be honest I'd been feeling guilty about boycotting Tozer's Big Moment. So my conscience pricking I decided to attend after all, arriving a little late. Hand over mouth to hide the absence of my bridge. As I approached the SPAM Portakabin Tozer's Welsh lilt was audible from half way down Spratling Sea Road:

> *'She sucked the boiling marrow from my bones*
> *And scorched the throbbing life-pump in my chest…'*

What's all *that* about? Pam Ayres he is NOT. My entrance coincided with a smattering of applause from the four people in the audience. That's not including Daphne who was perched behind the refreshment table. Tozer looked like something let out of Broadmoor for the occasion. Specs awry, he was standing behind a lectern which had a sheet of cardboard taped to it which read: PRIZEWINNING POET TEX TOZER READS FROM HIS LATEST COLLECTION (SOON TO BE PUBLISHED).

With dramatic hand gestures, and his flies undone (hope Daphne hadn't noticed), he told us that the title of his collection *The Grating Roar of Pebbles* was taken from Matthew Arnold's sublime cry of despair, the epic poem

Dover Beach. With a flourish of his notebook he announced that the next poem, called *Elemental,* was dedicated to his estranged wife. 'Here goes,' he said, and off he went, eyes turned heavenwards:

> '*Come wailing winds, tempests, battering storms*
> *Shatter my eardrums with your grating roar of pebbles*
> *Bruise blue my blood-blasted, bleeding—*'

He was interrupted suddenly by the fire alarm going off. Terrible racket. All six of us, including Tozer, stampeded for the exit. Turned out that hooligans had been tampering with the electrics, so no damage done. However, Tozer's poetic flow had been staunched. The reading was postponed until further notice. For Daphne's sake I muffled my laughter.

But biggest laugh of the week award goes to Mr Wienczyslaw's dental practice. Not that I'm complaining, Mr Wienczyslaw sorted out my replacement bridge with no delay. I get a phone call from someone called Joyce inviting me to 'pop in' for a complimentary one-to-one consultation following my dental extractions. Anything that's free and I'm game. It turns out to be a mini counselling session on the subject of 'coming to terms with tooth loss'. Joyce (who I note, has a 'White Fang' smile similar to my own) sits me down with a box of tissues and warns me that regret and sadness about lost teeth should never be bottled up. She say that distress is normal, thoughts of impending death common. We must learn to love our dentures, but it may take time.

'All denture wearers have a dread of catching sight of themselves in mirrors without their teeth in,' explains Joyce, who is sitting in front of a tank full of tropical fish. Fronds of water-weed are waving out of a giant set of false teeth. Fish dart in and out, nibbling. Water snails slide along the pink plastic gums. '… This is because what we see, namely the collapsed contours, creased lips and empty gum sockets, remind us that we are losing our physical attractiveness, our youth and our sexual allure.'

'Hang about – er – Joyce. I can't take mine out. I've got a partial bridge,' I interrupt, all too aware of the fragility of life et cetera after my original bridge got knocked out by the water. Turns out I've been offered the 'Coming to terms with tooth loss' talk by mistake. Do me a favour, Joyce! I escape with two free samples of anti-bacterial mouthwash.

On a more sombre note, Edna (of Save-a-Flush) turned up at The Shack to say that following Terry's bout of food poisoning, Doc Ng has recommended that we empty out and thoroughly disinfect our fridge and clean up the kitchen. That's telling us. But Doc Ng is right. It's bacteria heaven in our fridge. It's like a chemical warfare stash. There's a pack of festering sausages one year past their sell-by, a decaying tomato, some decomposing ham slices, a dead bluebottle, half a tin of baked beans sprouting grey fluff, chunks of mouldy cheese sprouting blue fluff, a bottle of curdled milk, a floppy cucumber, a slimy lettuce, something grey and stiff that looks like a dead mouse – it is a dead mouse. If Edna and Doc Ng were to see this they'd have me carted off to a care home before you could say Jeyes Fluid. So on with the rubber gloves…

And yes, a big clean up went into operation. Edna came up trumps by discovering a special 'emergency fund' for needy OAPs and by booking 'Hire-a-Hubby' for a day.

A bloke roared up in his Hire-a-Hubby van, with an industrial sized Hoover, drain unblocker, buckets, mops and disinfectant. While Terry was out at one of his mourning mornings Hire-a-Hubby gave Bingo a bath, sprayed his basket, dusted the books, zapped the fridge, de-greased the cooker and scrubbed the kitchen floor. Amazing. My kitchen floor was clean enough to eat your dinner off by the time Hire-a-Hubby had finished with it.

'Helluva lot of books you got here, mate,' he observed, flapping his duster about.

'Yes, my friend, they are insulating the walls of my home against the outside world,' I replied, sounding a bit like Tex Tozer.

'Oh, right, mate,' responded Hire-a-Hubby, 'any chance of a cuppa? Milk and two sugars?' I plugged in my sparkling, de-scaled kettle for a brew up. At which point Jinxie Wicks called in to borrow my cruise brochures. She didn't have time for a cup of tea, but she did have time to give Hire-a-Hubby a come-hither look and said, 'You can come and fix my ballcock any time,' before waving cheerio.

Hire-a-Hubby slurped his tea and remarked, 'You'd be amazed some of the things our clients, the divorcees in particular, want us to do, know what I mean, eh? Laugh – heh, heh, heh... twiddle their taps and fiddle with their fuse boxes... heh, heh, heh... but mostly, I must admit, it's sorting out flat-pack self-assembly kits.'

'You won't find any taps to twiddle or fuse boxes needing to be fiddled with here,' I retorted as Hire-a-Hubby got cracking in the bathroom. And I'm glad to say that he removed the Save-a-Flush and threw it in the recycling bin.

Later among the books that Hire-a-Hubby had remarked upon I discovered my very battered copy of *The Penguin Book of English Verse* (War on Want, 25p) and checked out Matthew Arnold's poem, *Dover Beach*, written in 1851. It begins, 'The sea is calm to-night / The tide is full, the moon lies fair' which is pretty much true of the view I can see from The Shack's window as I'm writing this. At the end of verse one I came across Tex Tozer's inspiration:

… Glimmering and vast, out in the Tranquil bay,
come to the window, sweet is the night air!
Only, from the long line of spray
Where the sea meets the moon-blanch'd land,
Listen! You hear the grating roar
of pebbles which the waves draw back, and fling…

Now that's what I call poetry! Tozer has a long, long way to go poetry-wise. No two ways.

Big news! Things have taken a political turn at SPAM. It's all thanks to Len who turned up wearing a T-shirt with THAT'S MY BRAIN YOU CAN HEAR WHIRRING across the chest. He has recently grown a droopy grey moustache that makes him look like an old walrus. As Andy handed round the HobNob biscuits Len was raring to go. He held up a double pager from the *Saltmarsh Gazette* announcing plans to build a multi-million pound hub airport in the Thames Estuary. An AIRPORT! Almost bang opposite The Shack! Over my dead body! Len whipped us all up into a fury as he explained that a new airport will destroy the Kent Marshes. All the thousands of wild fowl and wading birds that depend on the marshes for survival will vanish (not that a few million gulls would be much missed by Yours Truly, matter of fact), and the grazing sheep will disappear.

'Here in Saltmarsh we'll have ruddy Jumbo Jets roaring over our heads every few minutes,' shouted Len, his jowels wobbling with importance, holding up a plan of the proposed airport. 'The whole of North Kent will become a blinking great building site, bulldozers moving in to carve up acres and acres of the Kent countryside. It's Armageddon we're talking about here, guys, ARMAGEDDON nothing less.'

SPAM was in uproar. Tex Tozer (to give him his due) fired us all up even more with one of his diatribes.

'We must fight them on the local beaches – and fight some more – to prevent the iconic landscapes that inspired Charles Dickens from being turned into mile after obscene mile of concrete,' he roared, Daphne hanging on his every word with a 'my hero' look on her face, I noticed.

'...Dickens adored this part of Kent. He lived and died in Higham. He had his honeymoon in Chalk. He liked to walk to Cooling, where the lozenge gravestones inspired him to write the scene where Magwitch meets Pip in *Great Expectations*. Dickens loved the Kent marshes. We all love the Kent marshes and we must fight to stop them disappearing beneath a ruddy great hub airport.'

For once, I found myself in agreement with Tozer. Everyone applauded. Jinxie Wicks shouted that she would chain herself to the lych gate at Cooling Church in protest.

Andy said he was proud of the way SPAM was getting involved.

The lady members volunteered to make a banner. Andy asked for slogan suggestions.

'How's about SAVE OUR MARSHES FROM THE BASTARDS,' someone suggested.

'JUMBOS OUT,' suggested someone else.

'FLYING IS FOR THE BIRDS.'

'SCRUB THE HUB.'

It was finally agreed that we'd stick to our regular multi-purpose, *SPAM SAYS NO!* banner. A future group protest is on the cards.

Then a week later, after many hours on the library's Internet, Len came up with news that will definitely put the kybosh on any proposed airport. It turns out that 70 years ago an American cargo ship, the SS Richard Montgomery loaded with explosives was grounded on a sandbank off Sheerness. After a major salvage attempt half the munitions were removed, then the ship suddenly flooded and efforts to retrieve the remainder had to be abandoned. There are 1,400 explosives still on board!

'There's enough explosive to send a sixteen foot tidal wave onto the Kent coast and to blow out every window in Saltmarsh and Sheerness,' bellowed Len, his jowls vibrating with outrage.

Blimey!

'What's that got to do with building the airport?' asked Daphne. 'What is a HUB airport anyway?'

'I'm just coming to that,' said Len as we all sat there with our mouths hanging open at the excitement of it all, 'the sunken warship with its deadly cargo is still on the sandbank. That sandbank, to the East of the Isle of Grain, *is the exact spot where they want to build the airport.* The sand is constantly moving, the wreck is unstable, if the ship was disturbed – well use your loaf. A recent investigation concluded that the shifting of the cargo could cause an explosion that would *wipe out Southend.*'

Phew! Heavy! The people should be told!

Andy said that one M.P. has called the airport plan 'bonkers'.

Tozer said that he wouldn't want to travel from, or to, an airport, let alone work there, with a deadly unstable sunken ship from World War Two about to explode any minute on the doorstep. Scrub the hub!

Fired up with protest fervour various SPAM members retired to the Friendly Winkle to plot our campaign strategies. A fat, yacht-club type was hogging the bar, perched up on a bar stool, telling jokes. He was wearing a jaunty hat and a chunky navy blue sweater with 'OLD SAILORS NEVER

DIE, THEY JUST GET A LITTLE DINGY' across his chest.

'There was this chav, takes her four children to the doctor…'

'What's a 'chav', you posh git?' interrupts Jinxie Wicks.

'A 'chav' my dear lady, belongs to a certain sub-strata of society – wears high heels, short skirts, fake tan, says 'innit', claims benefits, watches Big Brother…'

'A member of the working class, in other words?' says Jinxie Wicks.

'Look, madam, do you want to hear my joke or not?'

'Not really,' says Jinxie Wicks poking out her tongue.

The yacht-club type, flashes a cocky grin and takes a swig of his scotch.

'Anyway, chaps, as I was saying… this chav takes her four children to the doctor. Doctor asks the eldest one's name. 'Wayne,' replies the chav. And the second one? 'Wayne'. And the third? 'Wayne,' Chav says. 'They're all called Wayne, so that when dinner's ready I can shout 'Wayne' and they all come running.' Doctor asks, 'So what happens when you want to speak to them individually?' Chav replies, 'No probs. I just call them by their surnames."

Everyone (except Jinxie Wicks) roars. The fat, yacht-club type roars loudest of all. Someone else who doesn't roar is single mum, Tracey, who's in charge of the pub snacks. She wears high heels, short skirts, fake tan, says 'innit', claims benefit, watches Big Brother and has a son called Wayne. Tracey tells the fat, yacht-club type what he can do with his chicken-in-a-basket-and-chips in no uncertain terms.

Arrived back at The Shack, where the phone was ringing. No prizes…

'Ronald? What have you been up to?'

'This and that, Mum, having a bit of a laugh about –'

'Whoa! Watch out, Son. Laughter can be dangerous. It's not always the best medicine! A team of Oxford University boffins have discovered that laughter can lead to serious health complications –'

'Aw c'mon, Mum, a good chuckle never did anyone –'

'WRONG! In the *Daily Mail* it said that people with racing heart syndrome have been known to collapse and die after a fit of the giggles. Laughing can trigger asthma, epileptic fits, hernias and a sudden tearing of the gullet…'

I'll have to keep a straight face in future, won't I? And maybe persuade Mum to start reading a different newspaper.

And then, just as I'm settling down to watch the sunset and peruse the *Saltmarsh Gazette* it falls open at its 'Good Egg of the Week' spot. Tex Tozer has been chosen as Good Egg of the Week! Talk about make my blood boil. Phoney toe-rag. This is what the *Gazette* printed – with a photograph of Tozer looking like an escapee from a high-security prison.

The Saltmarsh Gazette Good Egg of the Week

Prize-winning Welsh poet and Saltmarsh resident, Mr Texas Tozer (74) recently delighted the audience with his powerful recitations at the Saltmarsh pensioners' headquarters in Turbine View Terrace.

Reading from his acclaimed slim-volume, *The Grating Roar of the Pebbles*, a title taken from the Victorian Poet, Matthew Arnold's epic poem, Dover Beach, Mr Tozer was rewarded by enthusiastic applause.

Much respected as a colourful local character, Mr Tozer is often to be found in the Friendly Winkle holding forth on topics of national importance as well as sharing his philosophical views. He told the *Gazette*, 'I was a poet from the cradle – insightful, a loner, a wanderer, a philosopher – we poets have a great capacity for unhappiness.'

Mr Tozer recalled how he was orphaned at an early age, played barefoot in the Welsh valleys, spent his youth picking up coal that fell from coal lorries and eventually made his way to London. Here he lived in a cardboard box, feeding himself on food thrown away by West End hotels.

'At one point I went through a Hare Krishna phase – orange robe, dot on forehead, finger cymbals, lentils, smiling all the time. But London palled. In my opinion the man who is tired of London, is not tired of life, as Johnson said, but has suddenly grown up. I hitched a lift and arrived in Saltmarsh which has been my home for fifty years.'

Estranged from his wife, who is the inspiration for a slim volume privately published in a limited edition of 10, titled *Full Scream Ahead*, Mr Tozer remarked, 'My chief memory of my estranged wife is the running commentaries she used to provide during every TV programme, movie or play that I wanted to watch.'

In his lilting Welsh accent often likened to that of his compatriot poet, Dylan Thomas, he added, 'The hard times of my youth have caught up with me, my body is a temple and my temple now certainly needs a redecoration job. Ah me, boyo, I am but dust and to dust I will return.'

Also hitting the headlines this week was Jinxie Wicks. On the front page of the *Saltmarsh Gazette*, under the heading BIKES IN THE BUFF was a photo (in colour) of a team of naked cyclists pedalling through Canterbury. 'Good grief, that one towards the back looks a bit like Jinxie Wicks,' I spluttered, when Terry showed it to me. Stone the crows! It *was* Jinxie Wicks – bold as brass, wearing nothing but a kiss-me-quick hat and a pair of orthopaedic sandals. She had been snapped taking part in the World Naked Bike Ride, part of National Bike Week, for which – according to the *Saltmarsh Gazette* – 'the dress code is 'bare as you dare' with no mandate to cover intimate parts'. The annual event has been going on since

2003 to celebrate the benefits of a car-free lifestyle. The rules forbid any lewdness and insist that any male participant who finds his manhood awakening (Virginia Woolf again) must immediately cover himself and duck down behind his handle bars. Terry says that the country is backsliding, reverting to profane and heathen behaviour. He thinks it's time that the Government got a grip. And you certainly wouldn't catch Wiggo starkers on a bike without his Lycra get-up and hi-viz cycle helmet.

AUGUST 2012

Bring on the banner! Storm clouds are gathering as a small huddle of SPAM activists assemble on the sea wall to protest about plans to build an airport in the Thames Estuary. Fired up with revolutionary fervour we unfold the good, old, multi-purpose SPAM SAYS NO banner, and hold up our placards printed with SCRUB THE HUB and NO ESTUARY AIRPORT. A splinter group from Friends of the North Kent Marshes arrive and several members of the Dickens Fellowship. A surprise supporter is Diesel (no sign of Big Babs) who tunes up his ukulele, twangs a few chords and launches straight into a 40-fags-a-day, rusty rendering of 'We shall overcome, we shall overcome…' Not a bad turn out for a nippy Saturday morning. Even Tex Tozer – the Bard from Bogshole Lane – has arrived in his mud-spattered duffle coat and wellies. No sign of Jinxie Wicks who has been lying low of late, her Hire-a-Hubby activities being more pressing than the SPAM demo.

We are nicely warming up – 'We shall overcome some da-a-a-a-y' and getting into the swing of things with our chants of 'Hub, hub, hub! Out, out, out!' Then just as the *Saltmarsh Gazette* photographer is lining us up for a group photo, the blasted Poo Fairy Does Not Exist – Pick Poo Up brigade (led by Rosemary) turn up. They plonk themselves bang in front of the camera.

'Stop hogging the camera!' roars Len, brandishing a *SCRUB THE HUB* placard in a menacing manner, 'This is a SPAM demo, back off! It's nothing to do with dog's muck or poo fairies…'

'Hub, hub, hub! Out, out, out!' the rest of us shout. 'Scrub the hub! Scrub the hub!'

'We shall not, we shall not be moved,' croaks Diesel.

Luckily Rosemary's lot take the hint and shuffle off to protest further along the sea wall. The photographer hot-foots it back to his office and Edna Higgins arrives with mugs of hot Bovril. Very welcome they are too, especially when Len tops his and mine up with a splash from his hip flask. Then Len and Yours Truly each take one end of the SPAM banner which is flapping wildly in the wind.

'Hub, hub, hub! Out, out, out!' we shout, admittedly a bit half-heartedly due to the fact that passers-by are rather thin on the ground. In fact only three pass by during the entire demo. From his end of the banner, Len starts rabbiting on about an item he's seen in the paper.

This turns out to be a news report about a male passenger who was thrown off a Trip Airline flight in Brazil after he objected to the pilot being a woman. 'Poor devil, he was paralysed with terror,' explains Len, raising his voice to be heard above the roar and flap of the billowing banner, 'just before take-off he stands up and screams, 'Help! Someone should have told me the pilot is a woman. I'm not flying with a female at the controls, no way!" Len adds that the Brazilian police were called and the other passengers booed and hissed the man as he was led away shouting and gesticulating.

At this point a sudden gust catches the banner, tugging it from Len's grasp. It drags Yours Truly off the sea wall and into the foaming brine. 'Hub, hub, hub – aaargh…' Splash! Woah! What a shock. Not that the brine is foaming much, due to the fact that it's almost low tide.

'Summon the lifeboat! Dial 999! Summon the lifeboat!' bellows Len.

'Steady on Len, it's only six inches deep,' I squawk, up to me knees in seaweed.

'Summon the ambulance! Summon the ambulance!' roars Len.

'Don't be so blinkin' daft. I've got nothing worse than wet feet and saturated trouser bottoms, that's all.'

Edna Higgins comes to the rescue reaching down from the sea wall (which is only about ten inches high) to give me a leg up. My titanium knee brace comes into its own. No ill effects, bar a few extra twinges in my lower lumbar area. The SPAM banner has to be retrieved from the shallows where it is floating on tangles of seaweed, being washed gently to and fro by the lapping ripples. Further along the sea wall Rosemary and her Poo Fairy brigade are snorting and sniggering and holding their sides.

So even though the demo ends sooner than planned, we all agree that it has drawn public attention to a potential environmental catastrophe. So what if only a handful of Saltmarshians have witnessed our democratic protest? Great oaks from little acorns grow as my old mum says.

Here follows the Saltmarsh Gazette's report – getting the wrong end of the stick as usual – which appeared beneath a photo of Rosemary flanked by her mob, all waving their poo fairy placards. Behind them you can just see a blurred huddle of heads belonging to us SPAM activists and the top edge of the SPAM SAYS NO banner. Diesel is on the left of the photo, ukulele over his shoulder, smoking a fag.

PROTEST ENDS IN NEAR TRAGEDY

The Saltmarsh lifeboat sped to the rescue when a freak gust blew Mr Ronald Tonks (71) of The Shack, Spratling Sea Road, into the sea. Thanks to the quick thinking action of volunteer care worker, Ms Edna Higgins (59), who clung fiercely to Mr Tonks as he battled to keep afloat, he survived the ordeal. Mr Tonks is a keen campaigner for the anti-dog-fouling group 'The Poo Fairy Does Not Exist – Pick Poo Up'. Spokesperson for the group, Mrs Rosemary Betts (70) told the Gazette, 'The Tonks incident did not marr our highly successful demo which aimed to alert the public to the disgusting irresponsibility of certain dog owners who fail to clear up after their canine companions.' Mr Tonks is expected to make a complete recovery, he had no comment to make before the Gazette went to press.

So, that blasted opportunity-grabbing woman managed to hijack the Scrub the Hub demo. Talk about steam billowing from my ears! The reason that Yours Truly had no comment to make before the Gazette went to press is because no one asked me for one. At the time I was making my way back to The Shack, with the sniggers of the Poo Fairy mob ringing in my ears and with sopping wet trouser turn ups. In fact I walked past Jinxie Wicks' static where the Hire-a-Hubby van was parked. Second time this week. Say no more.

A few days later, fully recovered from the demo but still inwardly fuming about Rosemary's blatant act of sabotage, I was sitting outside on my shingle patch, reading the paper, listening to the sea swishing across the pebbles and to the sparrows twittering around my bird feeder (St Mildred's Hospice, £2), when suddenly the peace was shattered. A woman sprawling ten yards away on the break water, was shouting at the top of her lungs into her mobile phone. And I was forced to overhear her one-sided ranting. This is what I heard: 'Yeah, well, it was itching, stinging terrible... yukeroo... Yeah, green... You can say that again, yeah course I told him, you bet, the bastard... Yeah, yeah, you said it, they're all pond scum... oooh! Too much information, Shaz! Yeah, so the doc says... right, you got it in one. What d'ya mean you hope my nose don't drop off? Not funny, Shaz. No laughing matter.... Tests, more tests... metal instruments, anyways to cut a long story short... Antibiotics... Steroids? Huh? Did you? You as well? Blimey... Not surprised... Toerags, every one of them... Ha-ha-ha, don't make me laugh. Sometimes it's hard to be a woman, huh...'

And so on and so on.

It was putting me right off my cup of tea. Clearly the woman must have experienced a medical flare up of some sort, not that I wanted to hear the details. Her shouty diatribe continued for over half an hour. I was at the end of my tether. Bring back the pre-mobile phone era. Those were the days back in the 1950s when it was a novelty for a household to own a telephone. That was a time when the telephone stood on the hallstand by the front door. If someone was using it, they did so, discreetly, standing in the hall, to avoid being overheard. How times have changed... Anyway, driven mad by the woman's loud outpourings and with Bingo frolicking at my heels, I stepped nimbly over my low boundary wall (ignoring a twinge in my right knee) and politely approached the woman. The encounter went like this:

'Forgive the intrusion, Miss, but I thought you might –'

'Hold on a mo, Shaz, dirty old man accosting me – yeah? Whadya want Grandad?'

'I think that you should know that I can hear every word of your phone conversation—'

'So? So what? It's a free country. No law against using a phone on Saltmarsh beach.'

'Indeed not, but I thought you might be embarrassed – very much so – to know that a bystander can hear every detail—'

'Well, I'm NOT. OK? I don't give a flying f***. Feel free to earwig if it floats your boat. Now do me a favour. Piss off. And take your filthy, stinking dog with you. Dogs ought to be banned on beaches, crapping all over the place, spreading their disgusting germs... So, where was I, Shaz? Before the perv poked his nose in? ... oh yeah, this rash, oozing ...'

Is this aggression the result of Women's Lib, I ask myself? Is this the new feminism unleashed and out of control? Crestfallen I go back to The Shack. Catch sight of Edna Higgins' hairy legs scuttling away down the front path. No doubt she's just delivered one of her leaflets. Last month it was an instruction leaflet explaining how to hang the Union Jack the right way up. Today it's a STAY HEALTHY DURING THE 2012 GAMES leaflet.

The four glossy pages begin, 'We want everyone who comes to London 2012 Olympic and Paralympic Games to have a happy, safe and healthy experience...'

Happy experience? Strikes me that the youthful manager from British Home Stores, responsible for the locked WC crisis, may have had a hand in composing this daft leaflet. Same sort of lingo. Not that Yours Truly is likely to attend the London Olympics, what with tickets for the opening ceremony, for instance, costing up to £2,000. Then there's all the hassle of getting there – overcrowded trains, delays, traffic snarl ups, bag searches, pick pockets, armed police, surface-to-air missiles poised ready for action... nightmare.

The leaflet includes, 'Enjoy the sunshine safely. Eat well. Stay hydrated. Drink sensibly. Travel well. Carry your medication with you.

Talk about the nanny state gone mad. Turn to the back page and there's, 'Your check list for a healthy London 2012' with the following advice; 'Before you set off for your day out remember to take a bottle of water / medication / health snacks / sunscreen and a hat / travel information and maps / Games information and tickets / travel pass / comfortable walking shoes / water-proofs / health insurance / and please remember that containers of liquid taken into Games venues must hold no more than 100ml.'

It makes a visit to the games sound more daunting than a trek through the Brazilian rainforest.

And why 'healthy' snacks? It's a day out, for crying out loud. Why not a sausage-and-salad-cream sandwich? A paper-bag full of chocolate donuts? And a cream cake? Terry worked out that 100ml rules out your average Thermos of hot tea. 100ml is roughly the equivalent of a normal sized mouthful. Or a quarter of a mouthful, for those with a mouth the size of the mobile-phone woman on the beach.

In fact the 2012 Olympics (cost £9 billion) more or less passed me by. Andy organised SPAM get-togethers for the opening and closing ceremonies where we sat eating dip-dab-duck-bites and goggling, but the picture kept breaking up. As usual the Saltmarsh reception kept going on the blink. Len said that the specially commissioned Olympic sculpture looked like a helter-skelter wrapped in chicken wire, like something abandoned at Margate's Dreamland. None of us could recognise half of the celebs. The glum-seeming Queen looked like she'd rather be back at the Palace with her feet up watching it all on TV. The Duke of Edinburgh looked more disgruntled than he did at the Jubilee. The Archbishop of Canterbury, sitting behind the Queen, looked as if he didn't know what day of the week it was. No one at SPAM knew what a 'mosh-pit' was. Still don't in fact. Jinxie Wicks thought that all the old rockers wheeled on looked more hip-replacement than hip. She reckoned that old blokes singing young songs look weird. Paul McCartney for example. Tozer said that old blokes should always avoid wearing tight-fitting leather trousers, leather trousers being non-absorbent, if there's the slightest risk of leakage. 'Tell me about it,' grumbled Len.

Where are the Rolling Stones we wanted to know? Where was Mick Jagger? 'They've got too much bloomin' sense to appear in a mish-mash show like this,' said Jinxie Wicks. When a children's choir came on singing John Lennon's *Imagine*, Tozer got up on his high horse and started ranting, 'It's mawkish, a ruddy mawkish dirge. And anyway, what did John Lennon ever actually DO for world peace with all his millions? He rented a multimillion-dollar apartment in New York just to keep his own and his wife's fur coats stored at the right temperature. That would have built a few schools in Africa. Or hospitals. Or supplied mosquito nets and medicines, not to mention water purification plants.' By the end of the Olympics Britain had won 29 gold medals and 65 medals in total. And then the Olympic Park was closed until future plans are put into operation. But we all enjoyed the fireworks.

By the way, Terry is back in my good books again for giving me his old mobile phone. I know, I know... I may have been rather anti mobile phones in the past, but now that Terry has shown me the ropes and how to do text messages a new world of communication has opened up – so long as I can find my specs, otherwise I hit the wrong keys.

Just settling down to tackle my first text message, when the landline phone rings. No peace for the wicked:

'Evening, Mum, what new with you this bright—'

'Be warned, son, there's news in my paper that deadly mosquitos have been spotted flitting about the Kent marshes, and—'

'Well IF that's so, Mum, I'd better get a mosquito net and light my anti-mosquito candle—'

'Yes, you bloomin' well better had, my lad, these killer mosquitos have invaded Kent in the tyres of long distance lorries arriving in Dover from France and – I hope you are taking this in, son – they carry the deadly West Nile virus! Once bitten the victim—'

'Okay, okay, Mum, I'll be on the lookout for—'

'I'm warning you, Ronald, if you go and get West Nile Virus you'll know all about it – fevers, fits, swelling of the brain—'

'Blimey! Sounds nasty! But let's face it—'

'And worse news is to come, scientists have discovered another type of mosquito – the Asian Tiger mozzie from South East Asia. It's heading our way, straight for the Kent marshes, one bite and you can die of dengue fever –'

'Right Mum. Flit spray's at the ready! Over and out.'

Good grief. Killer mosquitos? In Saltmarsh? West Nile Virus and Dengue Fever? Has anyone told Doc Ng? I'd better get down to the surgery to check whether she will be able to cope in an emergency. And I'd better ask for some anti-malaria pills just to be on the safe side.

Anyway after the interruption I sent my first text. To Rosemary (whose mobile number is on the Poo Fairy leaflets):

'SABATEUR! COW! R.TONKS.'

Sent my second text to Jinxie Wicks:

'R U UP 4 A BEVVY L8TER?'

She replied:

'C U 8ISH, FRNDLY WINKL'

Yay! Welcome to the twenty first century, Ronald.

The big day dawned. Yes, the day of Daphne's do. I was in two minds. On the one hand I was chuffed to be invited to Daphne's house (at last!) and to be of help in her hour of need. On the other hand I was in torment – yes TORMENT to think that Daphne's dinner party would be in honour of the so-called poet, Tex Tozer. Scruffy Welsh windbag. What's Tozer got to offer that I haven't? The great poet, Philip Larkin – a bit of a weirdo himself but a REAL poet, in the opinion of Yours Truly – once said we all want poets to be better than the rest of us, but the only thing that they are better at is writing poetry. Which certainly doesn't apply to Tozer.

Anyway, morning had broken and I was in the kitchen humming along to Leonard Cohen's 'There ain't no cure, ain't no cure for love'. I was frying a sausage – 'I'm aching for you, baby... tra-la-la' – when Terry came in wearing his shorty dressing gown and saying he *wanted a word*. Heart sinks.

'Morning, Dad. The good, old Jeremiah of Tin Pan Alley getting your day off to a chirpy start, is he?'

'Now, now, Terry, sarcasm is the lowest form of wit.'

He has been hinting at some sort of confession for weeks. Is he going to tell me he's gay? He's a porn addict? He's in contact with the Nutcracker? He's lost his Christian faith? I am agog.

Turns out that Terry wants to tick me off for being a racist.

'Now look, Dad, you can't keep referring to Tex Tozer as a 'Welsh git'.'

'Why not? He's Welsh. He's a git.'

'He *might* be a git, or he might not, that's a matter of opinion, but to bring in the fact that he's Welsh is being racist.'

To be honest I don't get all this new-fangled politically correct business. To say Tozer is a Welsh genius would be okay. To say he's a Welsh git is not okay. British hero, okay. British bastard, not okay. I can't get my head around it. Last time I went to London (four years ago) I boarded a bus and saw that I was the only white passenger. A ticket inspector came round and when he reached me he said, 'Listen up, honky bruv, your ticket ain't valid during peak travel time, remember next trip.' Apart from the fact that I was worried that someone on the bus might pull out a gun, or a machete, I didn't feel the urge to report the inspector for calling me 'honky'. Definitely not. I felt as if the inspector was being cool, like it was matey and normal to be using nicknames in the ethnically diverse, multi-cultural society to which we both belong. 'Honky bruv' made me feel a bit of a dude to be honest. One of the guys. But you try explaining that to Terry.

'So tell me, Terry, what's the harm in calling Irish men 'Paddy', French men 'frogs', German men 'krauts', Liverpudlians 'scousers' et cetera?'

Terry chomped on his muesli before replying – spraying the air with raw nuts and oats --

'It's all about respect, Dad. And by the way, do you know what the French call the English? It used to be *les rosbifs* due to our partiality to that dish. Nowadays they call us *les fuckoffs* due to the almost universal use of that vulgar expression across the entire country. When the ticket inspector called you 'Honky' he was being racially abusive. He was using unacceptable language. Remember, Dad, all races are equal in the eyes of God.'

'Oh lighten up, Terry. All races are equal yes, except maybe the egg-and-spoon race.' Joke! What a way to start the day.

Next stop, call in on Gita Chudhury, widow and not very mobile, at her bungalow on Turbine View Avenue to trim her hedge. For the past few years I've helped Gita out with her garden. In exchange she cooks me the occasional curry to take back to The Shack as a treat. Last Christmas she said she wanted to give me a thank you gift. No need I told her, but if you insist a book is always welcome. Anything to do with Dickens. Forgot all about it until a package arrived on my doorstep. As a result there is now a big, never opened tome about chickens – All You Ever Wanted To Know About Chickens – wedged under the settee where the leg fell off.

Chickens? Dickens! Laugh! As my old mum says, it's the thought that counts.

Next I was off to the library, battling my way past Rosemary's Poo Fairy banner-waving bunch hogging the pavement. At the library I was in for a shock. No desk. Vanished. No friendly librarian chatting about the recent publications and recommending good books. There was only one of the familiar friendly librarians on duty, stationed beside an unfamiliar machine, demonstrating how to use it – scan your card, press a button, tap a screen, scan your book and so forth. I couldn't get the hang of it. Good job the librarian was on hand to help. But in my opinion having her standing there defeats the object. She might just as well be back at her post, behind the desk, like in the old days, i.e. last week. Progress gone mad.

From the library I went into the RSPCA shop and bagged myself a snazzy tie (50p) and a light-coloured safari suit, as good as new, with slightly flared trouser legs and a belt across the back (£2.50) to make a seasonal fashion statement. Stick a pith helmet on my head and I'd look like one of the Brit explorers in *The Curse of the Mummy*. Very dapper.

And so, 6.30 p.m. arrives. Splash on the Lynx for Men. Check the nostril hair. Flash the choppers. All present and correct. Shoulders back, stomach pulled in. We have lift off. On my bike, stop at the Co-op for a bunch of blooms (reduced 50p) and a bottle of pink fizz (£3.75). I know the etiquette rules! It is always appreciated if you present your hostess with a token gift on arrival. I pedal past The Shackles R Us house and observe the For Sale board still there since Mr Vladimir Piskov was run out of town. I take a left turn towards the outskirts of Herne Bay – or Hernia Bay as we locals call it. Along a potholed lane I spot a notice hanging at a strange angle and falling apart:

'YOU ARE ONLY 10 ½ MILES FROM DREAMLAND'
Ah Dreamland! What a great place it was in its glory days.
Another couple of miles on the flat and I'm in Daphne's
road. Then I'm outside Daphne's bungalow. Heart pumping.
Collywobbles. Haven't eaten since breakfast due to anxiety.
Park my bike. Unstrap my ukulele. Get the blooms and
bottle out of my saddlebag. Ding dong. Daphne opens the
door wearing an apron and flustered expression.

'Ronald! Come in! How kind... oops! Watch your jacket.'

Blasted lilies have sprayed pollen down the front of my
safari jacket. Try to brush it off. Make it worse. A big yellow
stain appears on my lapels. Into the lounge I go. Wonderful
waft of cooking. Chopin waltz tinkling from the stereo.
Candles. Lace curtains.

'Are you going to take your cycle clips off, Ronald?' says
Daphne ushering me into the kitchen. 'Tonight could be the
night, oooh, wish me luck...'

Over my dead body, I'm thinking. Daphne says she's been
preparing the dinner all day and that she's spent a fortnight's
food money on tonight's meal. Crab tartlets, smoked salmon,
celeriac roulade, fillet of beef in puff pastry, you name it. Talk
about gourmet cuisine. For afters – or 'desert' as Daphne calls
it, being a bit posh – she's made something called Eton Mess.
Sounds like the sort of afters the Prime Minister and his
school chum cabinet ministers used to wolf down for school
dinners. All in all Daphne's dinner is a meal that would make
any TV celebrity chef worth his salt kiss his fingertips and
whip off his chef hat to Daphne.

Next stage is to pull out the extra leaf on Daphne's dining
table. Then arrange the chairs round it. SIX. Tablecloth.
Place mats. Coasters. Whew! COASTERS. If Terry could
see me! Posh knives and forks, serving spoons, serviettes,
or 'napkins' as Daphne calls them. NOT paper ones, note.

Classy, no two ways. Next we work out who's going to sit where. Then Daphne pours herself a large vodka and soda, tells me to make myself at home with the vodka bottle and disappears to 'get ready'.

What a woman! As James Joyce put it so well in Dubliners (The Red Cross, 50p): *My body was like a harp and her words and gestures were like fingers running upon the wires.* What I wouldn't give to have Daphne's fingers running on my wires...

First to arrive is Andy and his 'plus one' – his film-star looking Ethiopian partner, Winston. I inwardly remind myself to watch that I don't make any non-P.C. remarks – no gay jokes, no racist comments, no mention of my 'honky' experience on the London bus. Andy has his vertical hair gelled into a sort of quiff that looks like a ginger meringue. Winston is wearing tight black jeans, black bomber jacket and razzle-dazzle reflector sunglasses. He proffers Daphne a bunch of blooms, like the ones I bought from the Co-op, as she makes her entrance in a floaty frock, high heels, glimpse of cleavage, a sight to behold – Shall I compare thee to a summer's day and so forth.

'Ooh lovely. Lilies, how kind. Pop the cork, Ronald,' says Daphne.

'Have you spilt egg down the front of your jacket, Ronald?' asks Andy.

'Nice one, Daphne. I hear that alcohol consumption is on the increase, especially among the people who drink. Boom. Boom. Cheers!' says Winston.

Jinxie Wicks arrives in her jungle print get up. Hands Daphne a bunch of blooms.

'Ooh. Lilies. How kind...'

'What's that down the front of your jacket, Ronald? Looks like a urine stain,' says Jinxie Wicks.

Pink fizz all round. Andy tells one of his jokes, 'Have you heard the one about the divorce judge who asked the wife, 'So you want a divorce on the grounds that your husband is careless about his appearance?' and the wife replied, 'Yes, Your Honour – he hasn't made one for three years."

'Ha ha ha,' we all go attempting to liven things up. Winston wants to know whether I've seen the newspaper story about the Hong Kong property tycoon who is offering a 40 million dollar reward to any man who can convert his lesbian daughter, Gigi Chao, into a heterosexual. He has promised to pay out when she gets married in a traditional wedding ceremony.

'Sing if you're glad to be gay, sing if you like it that way, hey!' warble Andy and Winston in unison.

'Ha ha ha,' we all go again.

Phone rings. Daphne rushes in from the kitchen looking distraught. But no, it's Terry wanting to speak to Your Truly.

'Hi Dad, Grandma wants to speak to you, shall I give her Daphne's number?' Phone goes again. It's Mum.

'I know you're out on the razz, Son, but I want to warn you – DO NOT DRINK ANY COCA COLA. You hear me? Don't touch it. It has a chemical in it that is being linked to cancer. I just heard about it on the news. It's called 4-methyllmidazole.'

'Mum, I've never in my life drunk—'

'So be very careful, Ronald. Just stop and think what all that fizzy brown stuff with all its chemicals could be doing to your insides—'

'Mum, it's the fizzy pink stuff I'm more interested in at this precise—'

'—and did you know, cancer risk notwithstanding, that 1.6 billion cans and bottles of Coke are gulped down EVERY DAY around the world? And that only two people alive –

yes, ONLY TWO – know the secret ingredients? They never travel on the same plane in case it might crash and the secret formula gets lost for all time – anyway, mustn't keep you any longer, don't want to interrupt your rave-up. Cheerio!'

No wonder I'm one of the worried well.

Daphne hands round some nibbles and looks at her watch. The elephant in the room – Tex Tozer – is now half an hour late. Someone's stomach rumbles (probably mine) and Winston says, 'Did you know that there's enough acid in a person's stomach to burn a hole in the carpet?'

'I think my mum will be interested to know that,' I respond.

'Well, well, would you believe it?' says Jinxie Wicks.

'And did you know that the name of the United States Assistant Chief of Protocol is Randy Bumgardner?' says Winston, trying to keep the conversation flowing.

Daphne looks at her watch again. Then, attempting to sound casual, she says, 'Now let's see, who's not here yet? One missing? Who are we waiting for – oh yes, Tex Tozer, wonder where he is?' I've said it before and I'll say it again – that woman could give Vanessa Redgrave a run for her money, no two ways. Round go the nibbles once more.

Into the kitchen goes Daphne to check on the beef in puff pastry.

'Better not put the vegetables on yet. Help yourselves to drinks,' she calls from the kitchen.

Twenty minutes later we are still on the nibbles... and drinks.

Winston tells a joke: 'Two nuns walking along the seafront are suddenly accosted by a flashing vicar. The first nun has a stroke, but the second nun couldn't reach.'

Jinxi Wicks laughs her head off.

Andy looks embarrassed and goes, 'Ahem, ahem, can't take Winston anywhere.'

'Oh yes you can, baby,' says Winston, 'anywhere, any way...'

I chuckle politely. Daphne keeps nipping in and out of the kitchen and looking at her watch. Andy says he read in the paper that we had the wettest June in Britain since records began.

Glasses are topped up again.

Daphne says she's going to put the vegetables on and if Tozer isn't here by the time they're cooked we'll have to start without him.

Ignorant Welsh git, I'm thinking. Then I change my thought to 'ignorant git' to be politically correct.

'Daphne's big do is going pear-shaped thanks to the ignorant Welsh git,' hisses Jinxie Wicks.

'Tell you what, I brought my ukulele with me,' I say in an effort to ease the tension. 'I'll get it and we can have a bit of sing song.' No one looks keen.

'Aloha! Let's hear it for the ukulele!' says Jinxie Wicks, always game for a bit of a sing song.

So I tune up – *twang, twonk, ping, boing* – and start strumming, 'I've got a luverly bunch of coconuts – da-da-da-da-da,' and singing away.

The others are half-heartedly tapping their feet.

'Come on guys, join in the chorus – roll-a-ball-a-bowl-roll-a-ball-a-bowl...' *Twang.* Strum. *Twonkety-twonk.*

No one joins in. That's life. You try to get things going with a swing and it all falls flat. '*I've got a luverly bunch of coconuts—*'

Ding dong. Ding dong.

Daphne dashes from the kitchen, whipping off her apron, patting her hair. Into the hall she hurries. We hear her open the front door. We hear Tozer's lilting Welsh tones, 'DAPHNE! I knew you wouldn't mind me bringing my young friend. Holly, this is Daphne. Daphne, this is Holly...'

Into the dining room comes Tozer, 'Sorry we're late boys and girls…' – hand-in-hand with a gum-chomping teenager who is wearing a dress that barely covers her backside or her chest. Tozer is carrying a small cactus in a plastic pot. Behind the ill-assorted pair strides Daphne in her high heels looking as if she's about to boil over. Jinxie Wicks catches my eye and jiggles her eyebrows meaningfully.

'Wonderful waft of cooking, Daphne,' lilts Tozer. 'Evening all! Meet Holly, my latest muse – *she walks in beauty, like the night / of cloudless climes and starry skies…*'

Holly smiles, wiggles her fingers in a flirty wave and asks, 'Where can I put my gum, Daphne?' Think Princess Diana meeting Camilla Parker-Bowles, and that's the expression on Daphne's face.

Off to the kitchen I go – to help. Sort out an extra chair, extra plate, extra serviette. Daphne won't catch my eye. Her lips are set in a straight line. Looks like she's been hitting the sherry bottle. There's one almost empty on the draining board.

We all sit round the table. Now that the elephant in the room is in the room we've all fallen silent. Daphne comes in with the smoked salmon and celeriac roulade.

'I'm a vegetarian,' pipes up Holly.

'Well, you can eat the roulade and leave the smoked salmon can't you?' snaps Daphne, teeth gritted.

'Is it made with vegetarian mayonnaise?' queries Holly.

'Drink up, everyone,' shouts Tozer. 'To Daphne! The world's best cook, and, if I may say so, wonderful at knitting. A great catch for any unattached, salt of the earth, mature type with a few sponduliks in the bank… my advice to you Daphne, is, in the words of Herrick, *Gather ye rosebuds while ye may / Old time is still a flying…*'

When Daphne brings in the beef in puff pastry everyone applauds. Everyone, that is, except Holly who reminds us again that she's a vegetarian.

'Then you'll have to eat the vegetables only, won't you?' snaps Daphne.

'I don't mind nipping into the kitchen to fry myself an omelette,' says Holly.

'Come on, girl. Don't be picky. Tuck in. Eat. Enjoy…' urges Tozer.

Jinxie Wicks tries to smooth things over with a joke: 'There was this old man goes into the butchers wearing a tracksuit and trainers, jumps up and down on the spot, does two knee-bends and asks all the other customers: "Guess how old I am? Go on, go on, have a guess…"'

'Or I could do myself a slice of toast and marmite,' burbles Holly.

'And everyone in the butchers says, "Can't guess, tell us." "89," replies the old man. "Amazing," says everyone… Then he jogs into the bakers, jumps up and down on the spot, does two knee-bends and asks, "Guess how old I am? Go on, go on. Have a guess…"'

'Just enjoy your vegetables, girl,' roars Tozer. 'Honest to goodness, Shelley only ate vegetables, the immortal Percy Bysshe. Daphne, your gravy is like nectar from the gods. Your baby Brussel sprouts are a melt-in-the-mouth marvel. This is all a bit of a change from boil-in-the-bag kippers, eh?'

'"I'm 89," replies the old man. "Amazing," says everyone… Then he goes up to a woman waiting at the bus stop, jumps up and down on the spot, does a cartwheel and a handstand and says, "Guess how old I am? Go on, go on, have a guess…"'

'Did you know that one Brussels sprout contains a day's supply of folic acid,' chips in Andy – another observation that would interest my mum.

'She puts her shopping bag down, reaches out and squeezes his balls through his tracksuit trousers and says," I'd say you're 89."'

'Another top-up of Chardonnay, Andy? Winston?' says Daphne.

'Bloody Hell," says the old man. "Amazing. How did you know I'm 89?"'

'Yes, please, Daphne. Fantastic food!' enthuse Andy and Winston, speaking in unison.

'"I'll tell you how – I was in the butchers!"'

'Ha-ha-ha. Ho-ho-ho,' we all go except for Holly, who hisses into Tozer's ear:

'Feck's sake, Tex, it's not my idea of a fun Saturday night to be stuck in a room with a bunch of geriatrics telling jokes and two po-faced poofs.'

Tozer downs two glasses of red wine in rapid succession, polishes off the rest of the beef in puff pastry (getting puff pastry crumbs down the front of his bobbly black jumper) belches loudly, stands up and says he'll recite a verse.

'Ooh! Culture! Mad, bad and dangerous to know, that's Tex. Like Wordsworth, Or Keats. Or was it the other one with the club foot? The one who collected his lady-friends' pubic hair? Wouldn't be able to do that today, what with waxing and that,' says Holly, who is slurring her words.

'Right, here goes:

There was a young maid from Madras
Who had a magnificent ass
Not rounded and pink, as you probably think
It was grey, had long ears and ate grass

We don't know whether to laugh or cry. Andy and Winston cough. Then they fiddle with their serviettes.

Holly goes: 'Wah-ha-ha! Wah-ha-ha! And here's a little riddle from me. Why is sex like rain? You never know when it's coming, or how many inches you'll get. Wah-ha-ha! Wah-ha-ha!'

'Not funny, Holly,' says Andy.

Holly is out of control. 'Or what about this one -- Why is a wife like a hurricane? She's wet and moaning when she comes and when she goes, she takes the house.'

'Seriously out of order, Holly,' says Andy.

At this point in the proceedings Daphne, hatchet-faced, fists clenched, leaves the table. Jinxie Wicks and Yours Truly round up the plates (Holly's food untouched) and take them through to the kitchen. Daphne carries in the bowl of Eton Mess.

We all go, 'Ooh! Aaah! This looks amazing, Daphne!'

Holly says, 'Your Eton Mess looks like what Tex's cat sick's up, Daphne.'

Andy says, 'I think we should all drink a toast to the lovely Daphne for providing us with this delicious meal.'

'Hear, hear,' says Winston.

Jinxie Wicks stands up. She helps herself to a large bowl of Eton Mess. She walks to Tozer's end of the table and tips it over his head. 'Take that, you whopping, great lummox!' she shouts. Bits of cream, meringue, pink slop, strawberries and raspberries slither down his face. It drips onto his bobbly black jumper. Clots of cream cling to his eyebrows.

Andy and Winston are holding their hands over their eyes, mouths agape.

Holly shrieks, 'C'mon Tex. Some people don't know how to behave. Let's blow, babe, leave them to stuff their faces with dead animals.'

Daphne hurls the cactus in the plastic pot at their backs as they skedaddle. Tozer skids on a patch of Eton Mess and declaims, '*Oops! I should have been a pair of ragged claws scuttling across the floors of silent seas, as the legendary pen-pushing bank clerk, T.S. Eliot wrote... cheerio, all...*'

Daphne puts her head in her hands and howls.

The upshot is that Daphne's do, in honour of Tozer, and her hopes of love have turned into a disaster. As I leave, having helped clear the table and load the dishwasher, Daphne (a bit the worse for wear, no two ways) is still sitting with her head in her hands. She bangs her fist on the table, making all the empty bottles jump and howls, 'How could I have been so WRONG? He's a Welsh git, a fat, freaking, fake. How *dare* he? How *dare* he? The bastard!' et cetera, et cetera.

I pick up my ukulele (which makes a mournful twang) and discreetly leave Daphne to her contemplations. There's a trail of Eton Mess between the dining room and the front door, intermingled with a scattering of cactus and potting compost. 'Sleep on it, Daphne, sleep on it,' I murmur. Sleep on this evening's debacle, I mean, not the trail of Eton Mess, cactus and compost. Yes, Daphne. Sleep on it... *The sedge has withered from the lake, and no birds* sing as a poet, not Tozer, once put it. Talk about cry me a river.

The phone rings. It's Gladys begging me to pop along and cheer up Cyril. He has suffered a minor setback.

'He was getting out of bed and accidentally dropped his overnight pee bag,' explains Gladys, causing me to push aside the glass of golden-hued Scrumpy Jack I was about to drink. 'It was full, unfortunately and the contents squirted out all over the floor, ran down the cracks between the floor boards and on to the light fittings in the ceiling below, then dripped onto the downstairs floor creating a bit of a puddle.'

'Sorry to hear that, Gladys.'

'It blew all the electrics in the house and the TV set exploded. When I put a new bulb in the light, it made a humming noise and popped.'

'My goodness... Oh dear. Have you managed to – err – mop it up?'

'I've mopped and sprayed disinfectant on it, all is spick and span again, apart from the stain on the ceiling.'

So, on with my power-walking trainers and a speedy power-walk to Brainy Cyril's house, where an electrician is banging and tinkering about upstairs. Cyril is propped up on the downstairs daybed, as usual, his copy of *Lady Chatterley's Lover* at the ready. Gladys pours me a sherry, which I sip, carefully averting my eyes from the wet patch on the ceiling directly above my head.

'Hello there, Tonks, good of you to come. Make yourself comfortable and then we'll continue with the masterpiece written by the man who blasted a hole in English fiction—'

'Eh? Is that the same phallocentric little creep who had an unhealthy preoccupation with the male organ?' snorts Gladys.

'I'll ask you to kindly desist, Gladys, from denigrating a literary giant. Now, where were we Tonks? Chapter 12 I think—'

'You know what King George V said?' quips Gladys, as she flounces out. 'He said, "People who write books ought to be shut up." And in the case of D.H.L. I agree with him.'

Cyril said D.H.L. had to fight an uphill battle to get Lady C published. English publishers thought it was too controversial. So he had to get it published in Italy. Upstairs the electrician is tapping and banging. The light comes on, hums and goes 'pop'.

'D.H.L. had to fight prudish prejudice all the way. Poor sod, no wonder he became mortally ill and died years before his time,' splutters Cyril.

I turn to Chapter 12 and begin:

'*And she felt him like a flame of desire, yet tender, and she felt herself melting in the flame. She let herself go. She felt his penis risen against her with silent amazing force and assertion and—*'

'Mr Tonks! Cyril! Do you fancy a slice of banana cake?' calls Gladys from the kitchen.

And so we while away a pleasant afternoon in quiet literary cogitation. Well, not so quiet because just before I'm leaving I go and stick my foot in it by repeating what the great poetess Edith Sitwell had to say about *Lady Chatterley's Lover*.

'Edith Sitwell?' barks Cyril, his nose suddenly turning purple. 'The woman was barking mad. BARKING. Well, spit it out, Tonks, what *did* the Sitwell lunatic say?'

'In her autobiography, she said that *Lady Chatterley's Lover* is a very dirty and completely worthless book of no literary importance.'

'Hmm. Lunatic woman. What else?'

'She objected to what she refers to as "Mr Lawrence's enthusiastic descriptions of Mr Mellor's sexual equipment."'

'Hmm. That doesn't surprise me seeing that she was a lifelong self-confessed virgin.'

'She also said that she likes to apply a five-letter word to the novel, a word that is used by cricketers, golfers and tennis players in connection with their games, not in connection with the game that interested D.H.Lawrence.'

'*BALLS!* Good old Edith,' hoots Gladys, who has been listening at the door, 'Edith hit the nail on the head.'

At this point our discourse is interrupted by the electrician, who wanders in to fiddle with the ceiling light and TV set. The yellow stain is still spreading.

'I think we've heard quite enough about the activities of Mr Mellors' sexual organ for one day, Mr Tonks,' says Gladys.

It seems a good moment to bid Cyril and Gladys a fond farewell and to head homeward, to do my ukulele practice and sit down for a good old natter with Terry.

In fact, I was able to have a little Bible Bash by referring him to a passage in *The First Circle* by Alexander Solzhenitzyn (Oxfam, 50p, and rather heavy going). According to the Bible, Moses led the Jews through the wilderness for 40 years until they reached the Promised Land. But a character in Solzhenitzyn's book points out that the distance from the Nile, where the Jews set off on their 40-year trek, to Jerusalem was 300 miles at most. So, even if they rested on the Sabbath they could easily have covered the distance in three weeks! You could argue that for the rest of the 40 years, Moses didn't so much lead them through the wilderness as mislead them.

'And another thing, Terry, who wants a God who demands that a bloke has to get the end of his manhood lopped off to get into his good books? If that's God you can keep him. Sadistic sod.'

'Language, Dad,' says Terry.

'So put that in your pipe and smoke it,' I tell him, whereupon he offers me a glass of his homemade beer. 'It tastes like the sulphurous urination of some aged horse,' I tell him, remembering my D.H.L.

Talk about excitement. Jinxie Wicks managed to get me a ticket to see – wait for it – Leonard Cohen in concert! At a venue called The Hop Farm. Somewhere near Tunbridge Wells. LEONARD COHEN live in Kent! My hero in the flesh! Whoo-hoo! Much to my initial disappointment all tickets had sold out as soon as they went on sale back in

March. That's the Internet for you… but Jinxie Wicks knows a man who knows another man, and after some nail-biting negotiations, I had my ticket. Yay! My ticket for the gig of the year! The fact that it cost me three weeks pension money is neither here nor there when it comes to a chance of seeing Leonard Cohen live in concert.

'What with your eyesight and late-life hearing loss, let's hope your seat is near the stage,' said Terry when he discovered that The Hop Farm seats 40,000. Good grief. 40,000! I began to have worries that I might get trampled by hundreds of stampeding fans eager to get Leonard Cohen's autograph after the gig. Or that Leonard Cohen himself might get crushed in the rampage.

For two weeks before the event I was so keyed up with anticipation that I had hardly a wink of sleep. And I was worrying about transport to the venue, The Hop Farm being 45 miles from Saltmarsh. Too far to go by bike. No buses. Too complicated to go by train which involves three changes, a lot of hanging about on platforms and take about four hours. Taxi? You must by joking – £120 return plus waiting time. Then Mr Harry Podger (of It's Your Funeral Funerals) comes to the rescue. Turns out he's also a Leonard Cohen fan! He has a ticket! He said he'd be only too glad to give me a lift to The Hop Farm if I wouldn't mind chipping in with the petrol. So, sorted!

Brilliant. I am so pent-up on the actual day that I have to take a couple of Quiet Life herbal tablets to calm myself.

Mr Podger suggests that I meet him outside It's Your Funeral. I must admit that I haven't bargained for him turning up in one of his hearses. Fortunately he is just parking it, in readiness for the next day's business, round the back. He unlocks his shiny black limo, and off we glide smoothly and silently along the High Street.

What a drive. Mr Podger turns out to be as much of a Leonard Cohen fan as Yours Truly. He plays Leonard Cohen CDs all the way, non-stop, with the two of us singing along at the top of our voices. So what if we get some strange looks from other drivers? So what if Mr Podger turns up the volume and opens the windows when we get stuck in a tailback for nearly an hour, due to a lorry shedding its load somewhere near Paddock Wood? Out comes my can of Scrumpy Jack. Out comes Mr Podger's flask of tea. Then it's pickled eggs and pork pies all round, and a jam tart to finish off.

'Like-a-bird-on-a-wire,' drones the Canadian genius as we slurp and chomp, his gravelly vocals drowning out the Arctic Monkeys blaring from the bloke in the van stuck beside us. 'Lennie always starts his gigs with *Bird on a Wire*…' says Mr Podger, producing a pack of HobNobs from his haversack, 'he started writing the song in Greece and finished it years later in a Hollywood hotel in 1969. He has said that it's still not finished. One of his rock star friends, whose name I forget, is having the first two lines carved on his tombstone.' Blimey! Mr Podger knows more about Leonard Cohen than I do. Who would ever have guessed?

'I saw him at the Albert Hall years back, only 58 he was then, and his voice already sounded like HAL the computer when it gradually grinds to a halt in the film *2001*,' said Mr Podger, tucking into a pickled egg, 'and at the end of the concert he said, '*My friends, you've been writing your kind letters, sending messages of hope to me for 25 years and you know what? They didn't help… life is still bleak.*' What a character…'

As we tuck into the HobNobs I say, 'Did you know that a Burberry raincoat that Leonard Cohen bought in London in 1959, and later made famous in his Famous Blue Raincoat song was later stolen from a New York loft where he was living in the 1970s?'

Mr Podger replies, 'Yes I do know that, the raincoat must have been falling apart after all that time, don't you think?'

Then the traffic starts moving again. Up goes the volume on Mr Podger's stereo and he is off: '*Lover-lover-lover-lover-lover-lover-lover-come-back-to-me...*' tapping in time on the steering wheel. 'Did you know that in 1987 he destroyed his Mexican 12-string guitar by jumping on it in a fit of anger?' shouts Mr Podger.

What a great drive. What a great day, so far. Mr Podger says that getting to see Leonard Cohen live is a dream come true. I reply that it's one of my dreams come true, too. Mr Podger says, 'At the Albert Hall the concert finished at 10 p.m. and the encore ended at 11.30 p.m. Talk about value for money!'

We start passing signs that say 'TO THE HOP FARM'. I am at fever pitch. Somewhere not far away now, Leonard Cohen himself is doing his sound checks, sorting out the microphones, putting his backing singers through their paces. Is he feeling nervous, I wonder to myself? Is he anxious about performing in front of thousands of fans? Speaking of which, where are they all?

'You'd think there would be a right old traffic snarl-up what with all the fans arriving,' says Mr Podger, as the limo cruises smoothly along the strangely deserted road to The Hop Farm.

'I'm getting bad vibes,' says Mr Podger.

I am getting bad vibes too. In fact I'm chewing my fingers, and the water works are starting to play up.

Ahead is The Hop Farm. Oh no! A large notice on the entrance says, 'LEONARD COHEN CANCELLED'.

There is nothing for it. Mr Podger does a U-turn and starts the drive back to Saltmarsh. We are very subdued on the return journey. Mr Podger doesn't play his Leonard Cohen CDs. I nearly doze off. Talk about an anti-climax. Maybe Leonard Cohen had got the last minute collywobbles? Or been taken ill? Or had suddenly legged it to some Tibetan monastery retreat as he frequently does in times of trouble and stress.

Mr Podger starts up a little conversation.

'May I tell you something, Ronald, that I've never told anyone else?'

'Sure go ahead, Harry.'

'You know Leonard Cohen's song, *Who by Fire*, which has the refrain, '*Who shall I say is calling?* from his Greatest Hits album?'

'I do, indeed, great song…'

'Well for years and years I thought that the refrain line was 'Who shall I say is Colin?''

'Ha, ha. Easy mistake. Who shall I say is Colin? Thanks for sharing that with me, Harry. Matter of fact SO DID I!'

Falling silent, we drive onwards. We are both feeling seriously crestfallen by the time Mr Podger drops me off in the High street. He slips me one of his cards and says, 'Business is booming, you never know when…' before gliding towards his parking bay at the back of It's Your Funeral.

Worse is to follow. When I send my ticket back for a refund I am informed by the box office that it is a forgery. Jinxie Wicks had been swindled by dodgy dealers. Oh well, worse things happen at sea!

Here is the letter I wrote to Leonard Cohen:

NOT FAR FROM DREAMLAND

The Shack, Spratling Sea Road, Saltmarsh, Kent

Dear Poet,
Sir,
Greetings from a fan. How is your health? What a sad
disappointment it was to me and my friend, Mr Podger
(of It's Your Funeral Funerals) when we turned up at the
Hop Farm only to find that your gig had been cancelled.
Mr Podger reckoned you had hot footed it back to Mount
Baldy Buddhist Colony where you often go to Meditate
when things are getting on top of you. To be honest I
sometimes wish I was at Mount Baldy myself, what with
my lower-lumbar problems, waterworks trouble, bald dog,
wheezy chest and gin-swilling, nonagenarian mum.

Having read in the papers how your manager made off
with your life-savings leaving you skint, Mr Podger and
Yours Truly wondered whether you'd like us to start an on-
line appeal for funds to keep you going in your old age?
The Saltmarsh ukulele group would be only too glad to do
a benefit gig to set the ball rolling. You once said, in an
interview, 'All I need is a table, chair and bed,' but if Mount
Baldy gets a bit too spartan you have an open invitation to
stay at The Shack. What a privilege it would be to pop open
a couple of cans of Scrumpy Jack and have a little meditate
together. Or we could sing along to your Best Of album
in front of my two-bar coal effect and discuss the meaning
of life and the slightly obscure meaning of some of your
inspirational songs. Terry (my son) could stick one of his
sardine hot-pots in the microwave.

My favourite lines by you (in Paper Thin Hotel) are: 'You
are the naked woman in my heart / You are the angel with
her legs apart.' Lines, incidentally, that Mr Podger tells me
were recently chosen by a client who wanted them carved
on his late girlfriend's memorial stone. However he was
refused permission by the Graveyard Authorities. To quote
another of your great lines: 'There is a crack in everything'

(particularly in the windows, ceiling and walls of The Shack
- be warned!) a profound observation, and all too true. So,
sir, hit the road back to the Hop Farm soon. We fans await.

Ever your humble servant and Yours Truly,
Ronald Tonks
PS I enclose Mr Podger's card - it might come in useful, you
never know when.

SEPTEMBER 2012

Prepare yourself for bad news. Are you sitting down? Box of tissues handy? Sorrow has come knocking on the Tonks' front door. It was the poet, Percy B Shelley, who after he'd experienced some tragic event wrote, 'I fall upon the thorn of life, I bleed'. And so does Yours Truly. I can hardly bring myself to break the bad news. But here goes – My dear old friend has shuffled off his canine coil –

BINGO IS DEAD.

Bingo has passed into the Great Beyond. Just writing the words 'Bingo is dead' had me rushing along the passage to the bathroom for some tissues to mop up my tears. Here's what happened. I was out walking my beloved dog across the marshes, enjoying the sunset, watching the chattering starlings lining up on the telegraph wires, when he became excited, dragging on the lead after some scent (dachshunds being scent hounds and bred originally for hunting rabbits and badgers) and suddenly slipped his collar. He was off like a greyhound let out of the starting traps. I kept calling him, 'Here, boy, Bingo! Good dog. Come and get a biccy…' and so on, repeatedly, but to no avail. I began to worry that he might get stuck in a boggy patch or fall into a drainage ditch. Or *I* might get stuck in a boggy patch or fall into a drainage ditch myself. Or I might end up on the mud flats. It got dark. It started to rain. A stinging wind was howling through the reeds. 'Here, boy, Bingo! Good dog!' No sign of the little devil. My throat was sore with shouting. A flock of sheep suddenly loomed out of the mist. Their spooky baa-ing and coughing gave me the willies. Conditions were getting treacherous under foot. My so-called water resistant, thermal lined, easy entry, zip fronted, easy to pull on, weatherproof boots (mail order £15) were leaking. Fat lot of good they are after a spot or two of rain.

I had to turn back to The Shack. Yes. Back to The Shack without Bingo! By the time I arrived home, where Terry was rustling up one of his vegetarian specials (what I wouldn't give for a lamb chop, running pink), I was in a right old anxiety state. Couldn't eat. Couldn't do anything except worry. Kept thinking of Bingo, alone on the marsh, frightened by the sheep, hungry, his bald patches getting chilled. Terry went outside and stood shouting, 'Bingo! Bingo! Good dog. Come to Terry!' (Some hopes! Bingo hates Terry…) I did the same, 'Bingo! Good boy. Come and get your Chappie. And some nice Pizzle Stix.' But no sign of him.

'Stop worrying, Dad, Bingo will find his way home,' said Terry, handing me a can of Scrumpy Jack and some microwaved chips in curry sauce. 'His canine homing instinct will kick in, and he'll be home in two ticks.' Ticks? Don't mention them. Bingo was due to visit the vet for some tick remover the following day.

The phone rang. It was my mum.

'Mum, can't talk now. Bingo has gone missing—'

'Missing? That's bad. But don't get your knickers in a twist, son. There was a story in last week's paper about a cocker spaniel that went missing during a family holiday in Skegness—'

'Not now, Mum, I've got to phone the police and report –'

'—and four months later he found his way home having walked 300 miles, dragged himself up the front path and through the back door, tail wagging, panting, ribs poking through his coat, but none the worse for his ordeal after a couple of tins of tripe mix.'

But still Bingo didn't come home. We notified the Missing Dogs department. We put up 'Dog Missing' notices in the shops. We taped a photo of Bingo to the front gate and offered a £20 reward for his return. Terry even fired off a few prayers hoping that the Lord might intervene. Anything was worth a try to get Bingo back. I kept roaming across the marshes calling, hoping and moping. Felt like Kathy's ghost must have felt roaming the moors and calling out for Heathcliff.

Then on day nine there came the dreaded knock on the door. A big burly plod was on the doorstep. The same one that cautioned me and Jinxie Wicks for drinking by the creek in an alcohol-free zone.

'Mr Tonks? Bad news I'm afraid, sir. We've found your dog…'

He drove us to the vet's. I was in shock. I felt like blubbing. My final glimpse of dear old Bingo was at the vet's. Bingo – good old Bingo -- was wrapped in a blanket – just the top of his little fluffy head visible. I'd know the top of that little fluffy head anywhere. 'Oh what a noble dog is here o'er thrown' I was thinking to myself, a teardrop trickling off my nose. Goodbye my faithful friend. Bingo was much more than a dog. He was a sort of human being in dog form. He was my pal, my companion, my comfort in times of trouble. The following words came into my head, as the plod stood by in silence.

Time like an ever rolling stream, bears all our dogs away,
They fly forgotten as a dream, flies at the opening day.

The plod said that Bingo had been hit by a car. He had been found mangled at the side of a road that crosses the marshes. What remained of my pet (and I could *not* bring myself to open the blanket and view his battered remains, no way) was put back in the freezer. The vet said that he would await my further instructions. I had tears running down my cheeks. Terry had tears running down HIS cheeks, and he couldn't stand Bingo. Used to call him 'the mangey four-legged flea bag'. We stood there welling up like a couple of lawn sprinklers. Terry sobbed, 'Bingo is at rest, Dad, having walked through the valley of the shadow of death.' Which didn't do much to cheer me up. There are times when I wish Terry would walk through that same valley himself.

Back to The Shack.

So what do you do with a dead dog?

'Get him stuffed!' quipped Terry, which I thought was most uncalled for. I gave him a very black look. Sheepishly he apologised, 'Sorry, Dad, thought it might bring a smile to your face' and handed me another can of Scrumpy Jack.

He then went on the Internet and came up trumps with a company called 'Treasured Pets' which offers 'same day collection'. I phoned up Treasured Pets and spoke to a bloke called Clive, who could not have been more helpful.

'Please accept my sincere condolences, Mr Tonks. At Treasured Pets we offer cremations or burials for much-loved pets, and clients can feel secure in the knowledge that your wishes will be carried out correctly and with dignity. Should you choose to go down the cremation route at our tasteful, purpose-built crematorium, we promise that the ashes returned will be exclusively those of your pet.'

In other words, Bingo's ashes would not be all jumbled up with loads of other unknown pets' ashes. That was some sort of consolation, I suppose. When my time comes I don't fancy having my ashes mingled with those belonging to a bunch of strangers.

As Terry remarked, it's a relief to know that people like Clive are out there doing such a good job. Clive even offered to send a bereavement leaflet to help me out at this difficult time, and informed me about some 'optional extras' such as a personalised hand-carved wooden dog casket. Or a scheme to have Bingo's ashes put into a special 'scatter tube' which, Clive explained is a practical way to scatter. The personalised, hand-carved wooden dog casket and the scatter tube were very enticing – no two ways – but as Terry pointed out, the whole pet funeral shebang could cost almost as much as a human send-off. And Terry knows what he's talking about being in the funeral business himself.

Meanwhile Bingo (may he rest in peace) was still in the vet's fridge. Terry arranged for him to be cremated via our own local vet at the end of the week, no frills, no fancy hand-carved wooden casket. No having to take out a bank loan to pay for it. This was a huge relief as I'm still paying off the loan to cover my replacement partial bridge. Bingo's ashes were returned to The Shack in a small ornamental plastic urn with a slot where we inserted a recent photo of Bingo chewing one of Terry's novelty slippers.

The urn has pride of place on the kitchen shelf. Terry said, 'It's my opinion, Dad, that all animals, especially dogs, pass into the great beyond where they wait to be reunited with their owners.'

I said that I hope Bingo is scampering happily about in the Great Beyond, his tail wagging, his bald patches a thing of the past. Perhaps he is barking joyfully, a member of a heavenly chorus with all the other dogs. And I hope he is not feeling inferior to the posh dogs who arrive in the hereafter via Clive's purpose-built crematorium or the scatter-tubes. Who knows, Bingo may have already bumped into Charles

Dickens and all his dogs – Mrs Bouncer, Turk, Linda, Don, Bumble, Sultan – all whooping it up with the angels.

Bev-the-Rev called round and offered to say a prayer for Bingo and one for Yours Truly in my grieving state. Terry hid all my Leonard Cohen CDs in case they made me suicidal. He also gave me a bronze-effect memorial with 'TO A GOOD DOG, NEVER FORGOTTEN' printed in silver. Daphne who, following the dinner party debacle, was away visiting her grandchildren, sent me a circular cardboard plaque with a picture of a dachshund with wings and the words 'RUN FREE NOW TO PLAY WITH THE ANGELS'. This was narrowly beaten by Jinxie Wicks' small imitation stone-effect book printed with the verse,

'If tears could build a stairway
And memories a lane
I'd walk right up to heaven
And bring Bingo home again'

The word 'Bingo' being printed in gold.

But I remained very low. Great waves of grief kept overwhelming me when I caught sight of Bingo's empty basket. His rubber bone. His stripy knitted coat. His feeding bowl. Terry's novelty slippers all chewed up. One evening I was standing outside, gazing at the sunset and I spotted Bingo's abandoned ball, and it set me off. Tears. Sniffles. I missed his funny little ways. I kept imagining I could hear his little paws padding around The Shack. His little claws clicking on the lino. Twice I went to see Doc Ng, all my worries back again. Would she prescribe some happy pills? No such luck.

'Bingo was a DOG, Mr Tonks,' she said, hard-nosed harridan that she is. 'Only a DOG. You must get over it, and you will get over it if you stop moping. Go home. Do your ukulele practice. Sign up for the SPAM Keep Fit. Go on a little holiday… Or I could fix you an appointment with a grief counsellor.'

Stone the crows! I was out of there faster than you can say 'Shrink Alert'. ONLY A DOG? ONLY? How hard and unfeeling can the woman be? But you can't expect sympathy from Doc Ng. They EAT dogs where she comes from.

On the way home my spirits lifted a bit when I came across a brilliant book *Palaces for Pigs* by Lucinda Lambton (Cancer Research, 75p). It reassured me that I am not ALONE in my prolonged mourning for a beloved pet. Would you believe it, Matthew Arnold – the same Matthew Arnold who wrote *Dover Beach* – was so upset by the death of his dog, Geist, aged four years (a dachshund) in 1881 that he wrote a 20-verse poem to him called *Geist's Grave*. Here are two sample verses:

> *Only four years those winning ways,*
> *Which make me for thy presence yearn*
> *Call'd to us to pet thee or to praise*
> *Dear little friend at every turn*
>
> *We stroke they dear broad paws again*
> *We bid thee to thy vacant chair,*
> *We greet thee by the window pain*
> *We hear thy scuffle on the stair.*

Now that's what I call a heart felt bit of poetic writing. Several up on Tex Tozer's outpourings, eh? 'We hear thy scuffle on the stair' moistens the old tear ducts, not that I ever heard a scuffle on the stair at The Shack of course, seeing as how it's a bungalow, but I'm always imagining that I can hear Bingo's scuffle in the kitchen, first thing.

From *Palaces for Pigs* I discovered that many bereft (but rich) pet owners have erected memorials to their four-legged friends. Lord Byron, who reckoned that his dog – Boatswain – was his only friend, had a lengthy ode carved on a huge memorial in the grounds of his country estate, a memorial which is more impressive, bigger and ornate, than Lord Byron's own tomb. The lines, '*To mark a friend's remains these stones arise / I never know but one / and here he lies*' bring a lump to my throat.

In Eltham Palace, a Kent tourist attraction with a medieval hall and moat, a ring-tailed lemur called Mah-Jongg ('Jongy'), the pet of Virginia Courtauld, was buried in the palace grounds in 1938 under a black and white striped obelisk to match Jongy's tail. Jongy's remains and the obelisk were transported to Africa in 1950 when the mega wealthy Courtauld's moved there.

In Gloucester, a man called James Neidpath had an ornate memorial built for his golden Labrador, Old Smelly, in 1984. On either side are carvings of Old Smelly, who died aged 16, above which is a carved tin of P.A.D. ('Prolongs Active Death') held on high by an angel's wings. Mr Neidpath included a long inscription, carved onto the memorial in Latin.

Compared to the extravagant tributes of these wealthy owners I feel that Bingo has got 'the rough end of the pineapple' as the Nutcracker might say. Jinxie Wicks' imitation stone-effect book is certainly not in the same league. Nevertheless Bingo might be gone, but he is certainly not forgotten… Yes, it's been a sad September for Yours Truly. Many a tear have I shed. Not that I'm ashamed to admit it. As the great Dickens put it in *Great Expectations*, '*Heaven knows we need never be ashamed of our tears, for they are rain upon the blinding dust of earth, overlaying our hard hearts.'* Too true. Any day now I will force myself to round up Bingo's empty basket, rubber bone, Pizzle Stix, little knitted coat and take them to the Dog Rehoming Centre. Then I shall dust myself down, pick myself up and try to get back into the swing of things. Meanwhile I still can't help worrying that compared to all those temples, obelisks, Corinthian columns, scatter tubes and hand-carved caskets, Bingo's plastic urn looks a bit cheapskate. No two ways.

The rest of September is a hazy blank. To quote a line from Leonard Cohen's poem, Destiny, '*Come back here, little warm body / it's time for another day...*' Only he wasn't referring to his dog. Ah Bingo, what is life to be without you?

OCTOBER 2012

Tragedy or no tragedy life goes on. Tried to perk myself up by going along to the ukulele group. I twanged and strummed and managed to get all the way through 'Knees Up Mother Brown' without a wrong note, but my heart wasn't in it. During the bring-your-own-booze break Diesel told us that learning to play the ukulele – or any musical instrument – boosts a person's IQ.

'Listen up, dudes... these university geezers have scientifically proven that practicing chords and learning to finger complicated notes – changes the shape of the brain. They've even scientifically proven that some bits get bigger!'

Big Babs rattled her maracas and shouted, 'Bring it on! Tah-dah!'

Diesel said, 'So, dudes, you'll soon have brain boxes the size of Einstein's.'

To be honest I'd question whether this 'scientifically proven' fact has worked on Diesel. Brainbox the size of Einstein's? Pull the other one.

Then we all tuned up and twanged away at a spunky-sounding version of Puttin' on the Style with a few extra twiddly bits, following which Diesel outlined his plan for us to form a group and do a gig. A GIG! We've been booked to play at the Old Folk's home up the posh end of town. We will be Saltmarsh's first old-boy band. Diesel has chosen the group's name – we're the SPUGS – Saltmarsh Pensioners Uke Group. Bring it on! 'The SPUGS are gonna grab music by the lapels and shake it to within an inch of its life,' Diesel promised. 'Get grooving, guys, *a-wop-bop-a-loo-wop-bop a-loo-bom-bam!* Kick ass!'

Talking of twiddly-bits, learning to play the ukulele has made me appreciate the amazing guitar skills of Rolling Stone, Keith Richards. What a man! What a legendary son of Kent! I found a copy of his autobiography 'Life' (£1 from the R.N.L.I. coffee morning). Bloomin' hell! Keith, or Keef as he is known to his billions of fans worldwide, has certainly lived life in the fast lane. No two ways. In his book he looks back at the gigs, groupies, drug busts, fatalities, feuds, car crashes, orgies, mattresses set alight, guitars smashed, hotels trashed, TV sets hurled out of hotel windows, guns, knives, cold turkey cures, and the death-defying lifestyle that has transformed him into a universal folk hero. Am I, a humble, novice SPUG jealous? You bet.

The biggest shock about his five decades of dissipation and hectic rock 'n' roll is that he can actually remember it all in such lurid detail. What a survivor!

Keef once did a gig during a monsoon when he couldn't see the fret board, and rain bounced off it, splashing into his lungs like a water-boarding torture. He was once electrocuted and thrown across the stage by a faulty amp connection. A near fatal fall from a coconut tree, and emergency surgery, has left him with six titanium pins holding together a chunk of his fractured skull. Many times he's been knocked unconscious and had his clothes ripped off by rampaging female fans. He was badly burnt at the start of a concert when a lump of white-hot phosphorus from an exploding firework landed on his finger, searing it to the bone, yet he CARRIED ON PLAYING. Some time later he punctured a lung falling off a ladder.

He punctured the other one when he slipped on some sun tan oil and broke three ribs. He sliced off half a finger on a broken guitar string. His relationship with the love-of-his-life, Anita Pallenberg (mother of three of his children) fizzled out in squalor and drug-fuelled acrimony. As Keef puts in in his book, 'Things went beyond any point of return with Anita when her young boyfriend blew his brains out in our house, on the bed.'

Keef has definitely never been one to let the grass grow under his feet. You wouldn't catch Keef lying awake at night worrying about his prostate. Or how to cut his toenails. Or, if he had a dog, worrying about it going bald. Keef probably wouldn't *notice* if it went bald all over. Good old Keef. One remark he makes in his book sticks in my mind.

When you've got 3,000 chicks in front of you ripping off their panties and throwing them at you, you realise what an awesome power you have unleashed.

Blimey. Ripping off their panties?

Chance would be a fine thing. Can't see the 'chicks' doing that when the SPUGS get cracking.

To further get my mind off sad thoughts I made my regular visit to my housebound, widow friend, Gita Chandury, to trim her hedge.

There she was walking frame at the ready, sitting on the patio, surrounded by overgrown shrubs, leafing through her cruise brochures. Turning to a page advertising a three-month luxury cruise she said, 'Imagine it, Mr Tonks, Spain, Italy, Egypt... Dubai, Abu Dhabi, Colombo, Penang, Kuala Lumpar, Singapore, Cambodia, Ho Chi Minh, Hong Kong... Australia, South Africa...What I wouldn't give!'

Looking over Gita's shoulder, I read 'Unleash your mojo today... for £18,000 you can enjoy the holiday of your dreams'. I pointed out that us old crocks on the rocks had better dream on. And by the way, what is a mojo? Neither of us knew. Gita thought it might be a hamster-like rodent. As I was putting the hedge clippings in the garden-waste recycling bin she remarked that China is the one destination that she doesn't fancy. She's read in the paper that in Hutou, a village in Eastern China, the residents are fattening 10,000 dogs to eat at their annual 3-day dog meat festival. This festival is to celebrate the day that a Ming emperor once saved their town which was being overrun by dogs, killing them all.

The very word 'dog' started up my sad thoughts about Bingo, thoughts which were interrupted by Gita asking, 'And how are your chickens, Mr Tonks? Doing well I hope? No chicken-bottom rot? Gizzard worms? Avian egg drop syndrome? Beak damage? I always say there is nothing as tasty as a fresh, soft-boiled egg.' At this point I walked into an R.S.P.B. fat ball that was dangling from a tree, nearly knocking myself out.

What I needed was a little snifter. Cheerio Gita! And off I toddle, into the buzzing ambiance of the Friendly Winkle – damn great bump on my bonce where the fat ball hit me. Walk in and the barman says, 'Evenin' Ronald, where's that dirty, filthy, stinking old flea bag of yours?' Silence falls. A dozen faces turn towards me with faces screwed into expressions of exaggerated sympathy. A hollow voice from over by the window mutters, 'Croaked.'

'Oops,' says the barman, and offers me a beer on the house. The buzz begins again and Tex Tozer pipes up, 'Met this guy who said to me, 'Every day, my dog and I, we go for a tramp in the woods. And she just loves it. Mind you, the tramp is getting a bit pissed off.' Boom, boom. Come on, boyo, have a drink on me…'

Half an hour later I'm back at The Shack, nose stuck in a book about Leonard Cohen, 'I'm Your Man' by Sylvie

Simmons (Girl Guides jumble sale, 40p). Leonard Cohen's second name is Norman. He taught himself to play the ukulele – THE UKULELE! – from a 1928 instruction booklet written by someone called Roy Smeck known as the 'Wizard of the Strings'. Must remember to tell that to Diesel. And – get this – Leonard Cohen once had a dog called Tinkie!

At the start of a sell out concert at the Albert Hall in 2008 when he was 74 he told the fans, *'Last time I did this I was 60 years old, just a kid with a crazy dream.'* What a guy. What wit. He's still up there, performing around the globe, even though – as he says – his fingernails are crumbling due to damage from his guitar strings. His throat is going. As for sex, he says that he is *'no longer terribly active in that realm!'* Ah, tell me about it Leonard, you and me both.

I'm suddenly brought back to the real world by Terry blundering in (followed by a great gust of howling wind as he opens the front door), back from one of his funerals. He tells me that he saw a chap make the sign of the cross with his mobile phone in the chapel of rest, 'You see, Dad, God is in the modern world.'

Oh right Terry. He'll be on You Tube next. Or Facebook, moving in His mysterious ways his wonders to perform.

Then he tells me that Mr Podger is about to become the first funeral director in Kent to start installing bar-codes on gravestones. Cor blimey, whatever next! The bereaved can now scan gravestone bar-codes with their smartphones and get through to their loved one's life history, maybe even hear their favourite hymn or prayer. They can even update details – 'if Albert was still alive he would be celebrating the birth of his sixteenth great grandchild' sort of thing. 'It's the way forward, Dad,' says Terry, 'grave bar-codes are catching on fast. Like I said, God is in the modern world…'

'Oh belt up, you Bible-bashing berk,' I feel like shouting, but you can't say that to your own flesh and blood. Instead I turn to Terry and quote Leonard Cohen, *'Let me be, for a moment in this miserable, bewildering wretchedness, a happy animal.'*

'Okay, Dad, fancy a cup of cocoa?' says Terry.

Is Terry getting too big for his boots? Ever since he became 'Good Egg of the Week' in the *Saltmarsh Gazette* he has been bombarded by the media. Broadcasters and journos have been beating a path to Podger's 'It's Your Funeral' Funerals. It's my opinion that all the fuss has gone to his head. Last week he was on the local TV news rabitting on about his job as the nation's only professional mourner. Two days later he was on Radio Four and the national TV news. The *Saltmarsh Gazette* reports that Harry Podger is 'over the moon' at all the free publicity and is so overwhelmed with demand for Terry's services that he has advertised for a back up professional mourner to share the workload. The *Saltmarsh Gazette* also reports that two rival services, 'Grave New World' and 'Coffins 'R' Us' have tried to poach Terry, offering him double money. On the day Terry appeared in the *Daily Mail* my old mum had to be prescribed pills to bring down her blood pressure.

Phone rings.

'Ronald? RONALD! Guess what? Terry's hit the headlines! There's a big photo of him on page seven. All togged up in his funeral get-up. The headline is GRAVE FUTURE FOR TERRY. At last! Fame for the Tonks. Ooh! I always said that boy would go places. A little word of warning though. Don't let his meteoric rise to fame drive him to drugs and debauchery... I don't want him winding up drowning in a swimming pool like that bloke in the Rolling Rocks, or choking on his vomit like that Jimmy Appendix.'

Fame apart, for several weeks now Terry has been hinting at having something he wants to get off his chest. He's been humming and haa-ing and sloping off to his room to read his Bible or whatever it is he gets up to in there. Anyway, his secret worry is out in the open. Returning from a SPAM session (on how to get the most from your buss pass) I arrived back at The Shack. The front gate was wide open. Sitting on the doorstep was a woman. Young-looking. Frisky. A small child was throwing pebbles at my spattered bird-bath. Little vandal.

'I am looking for Terry Tonks,' said the woman in a stroppy voice.

'Tewwy Tonks,' echoed the vandal.

Oh no! I was thinking she must be one of Terry's mad fans. She must be stalking him. She's managed to track him down following his meteoric rise to fame. She's a funeral groupie! At this moment Terry arrived home, strolling up the front path in his funeral get-up.

The woman gave a shriek.

'I know this is a bit out of the blue, Terry Tonks, but my name is Natalie Tonks and you are my FATHER.'

Well stripe me pink!

Terry shouted, 'Wh-a-a-a-t' and fainted. The Vandal wet her knickers. I nearly wet my own knickers with shock. Natalie started sobbing. You could have knocked me down with a feather.

Into The Shack we all trooped. On with the kettle. Out with the Jammie Dodgers. Talk about drop a bombshell. Turns out Natalie is the result of a brief amorous skirmish enjoyed by Terry and Natalie's mother during their summer stint with the 'Seaside God Squad' – an evangelical youth group – which evangelised on Margate beach for one week in 1995. Natalie's mother, about whom Terry has no recollection whatsoever, was also a Seaside God Squad activist. For 20 years she has kept Natalie's paternity a closely guarded secret. But Natalie, being of an enquiring nature, decided to find her biological father. Then she saw Terry in the paper and on the telly, and put two and two together and contacted the Child Services.

And now here she was, large as life, at The Shack. Terry was flat out on the settee, shallow breathing, white as a sheet. A hot cup of sweet tea was called for. Later he told me that he had NO IDEA, not an inkling, about Natalie's existence until a few weeks before when he received word from a Missing Person's set-up. As I poured the tea it suddenly hit me – I AM A GRANDFATHER! Whew! In fact I am a GREAT GRANDFATHER. The Vandal – Kylie, age three – who had polished off half the packet of Jammie Dodgers and was wiping her sticky fingers on the settee, is my great granddaughter.

'Say 'hi to Terry, Kylie,' said Natalie.

'Hi Tewwy,' said the Vandal.

Turning to me, Natalie said, 'Hi there, Pops, nice to meet you!'

'POPS? POPS! All of a sudden I've become 'POPS'.'

'Kylie wants a dwink, Pops,' piped up the Vandal.

'If it's not a rude question, Natalie, where is Kylie's father?' bleated Terry from the settee where the Vandal was jumping up and down on his chest and grinding Jammie Dodgers into his black suit.

'That scum bag? Who knows? Don't ask,' replied Natalie.

Good grief! It was like being in a Thomas Hardy novel.

'But let's put it this way, Terry Tonks – er Dad,' said Natalie with a dangerous twinkle in her eye and mischievous curl of the upper lip, 'When I tried to sign on with the Child Support Agency I was asked to list as many details as possible that I had about my baby's absentee father. So I wrote, 'I do not know the identity of the father of my child but he drives a red BMW that now has a hole made by my stiletto heel in one of the door panels."

Terry didn't laugh. His eyes were closed. The Vandal was dripping orange squash on his hair. Maybe he was communing silently with the Lord?

Natalie continued, 'Mind you a friend of mine went one better. She wrote, 'I can't name the father of my child who was conceived after unprotected sex at a rock festival. I do remember that it was so good that I fainted. So if you track him down give him my phone number.'

You have to hand it to Natalie for lightening up a tense situation with her lively sense of humour. I couldn't stifle a wry chuckle.

'Good old Pops, at least he appreciates a little joke,' chortled Natalie.

'I'm glad he finds it funny,' said Terry.

'Oh come on, son, lighten up. Be a bit open-minded –'

'You're so *open-minded* that your blinkin' brains are falling out,' said Terry.

'Kylie want 'nuvver drink Tewwy,' screamed the Vandal.

'Now, now, Son, we all make mistakes – I married your mother—'

'So, Natalie, your child will never know her own father,' said killjoy Terry ignoring his own father.

'Whoa, son! This is not the right moment—' I began, trying to pour oil on troubled waters.

Pulling his hangdog face Terry said, ' Seems like it's a Tonks' tradition, absentee fathers, love children crawling out the woodwork. What about YOUR father, Dad?'

'Now, now, Terry, that's hitting below the belt. Very sore point…'

Fact is – as Terry well knows – the identity of my own paternal parent is a murky mystery. But let's get things into perspective. There was a war on. Three quarters of the kids in my class at infant school had fathers who 'had been killed in the war'. It wasn't until the local municipal big-wigs got the war memorial erected that we noticed our own particular surnames were not carved upon the expensive granite obelisk and we put two and two together and kept our traps shut. As did our mums. That's war for you.

What I needed was some fresh air. And not to be in the same room as the Vandal. I decided to leave Terry, Natalie and the Vandal (the latter, pulling my books off the shelves and hurling them across the floor) to bond. To sort things out. On my bike and off to The Frying Squad for some eat-in fish and chips. And here's something I didn't know. According to the *Daily Mail*, 1.6 million tonnes of spuds are made into chips every year in the UK 1.6 million tonnes are the same as 14,000 blue whales or 4,000 jumbo jets. That's a lot of spuds. My mum related these facts to me last week. The Frying Squad produces a fair proportion of the 1.6 million tonnes here in Saltmarsh. Very tasty they are too. Also enjoying his fish and chip supper was the whiskery-faced, posh, yacht-club type who wears the jersey with OLD SAILORS NEVER DIE THEY JUST GET A LITTLE DINGHY across the chest. He was regaling the Frying Squad's diners with one of his 'chav' jokes.

'It's Saturday night and there's this chav lying in a puddle of blood outside the pub. 'Where are you bleeding from?' asks the anxious ambulance man, his emergency kit at the ready. 'I'm from bleedin' Margate, what about you?' says the chav.'

But the yacht-club type hadn't reckoned with Edna Higggins whose hairy legs were blocking The Frying Squad's door.

'You are a blinkin' snob and a trouble-maker,' roared Edna, all heads at the tables turning with one accord in her direction. 'The term 'chav' is insulting and totally unacceptable, TOTALLY, and don't make snide jokes about Margate either.'

That was telling him!

'Right on, you give him a piece of your mind,' shouted a diner through a mouthful of chips. 'No where in the country can rival Margate for sunsets and Elvis tribute acts.'

And I bet not many people know that one of the 20th centuries biggest selling, highest earning authors lived on and off in Margate between the 1920s and 1960s. Dennis Wheatley, who sold 50 million books worldwide and was nicknamed *the public's number one thriller writer* spent his formative years in Margate. His school in Dalby Square up the road from Dreamland is still there, though it's been converted into flats. His occult bestsellers such as *The Devil Rides Out*, which Brainy Cyril refers to as 'all that Satanist claptrap', may not be everyone's cup-of-tea but they enabled old Dennis to enjoy a pleasure-loving, playboy lifestyle and to become the inspiration for Ian Fleming's James Bond character.

Anyway, knowing Jinxie Wicks' weakness for fish 'n' chips I ordered her a take-out (with curry sauce) and biked along to her static. There she was huddled over her paraffin heater, hair in curlers, sinuses playing up and informing someone on the receiving end of her mobile that big bums are back in fashion. I was obliged to listen to the conversation – very much girly-talk and mostly incomprehensible to someone who doesn't care one way or another whether big bums are in or out.

'If you log on to www.betterbuttocks.com you'll see that buttock augmentation is all the rage,' Jinxie Wicks was saying. 'A Harley Street cosmetic surgeon has announced that the flat bottom is out and the fat one is in. Women are paying a fortune to plump up their rump! Three cheers! 4,000 American women had bottom enlargements last year at £10,000 a go. Even when they were warned that they wouldn't be able to sit down for a fortnight they still went ahead...'

Phone off and unwrapping her chips, Jinxie Wicks continued with the topic.

'Ronald, if some woman out there wants a fuller, rounded bum then she is very welcome to have a chunk of mine. I wonder if they do transplants? Is there a demand for donors? Is there a buttock bank?' On the newspaper that had been wrapped around her chips was the headline SHOCKED WOMAN WAKES TO FIND A STRANGE MAN IN HER BED. Jinxie Wicks guffawed, 'So what? I had to put up with that for 30 years...'

And then I broke the news about Natalie and the Vandal.

''Pops'? What a lark. Who'd have thought it, Ronald, Terry breaking his ten commandments! Must have been a bit of a shock finding out he's a dad and a granddad on the same day! That's life for you – a few moments of mad delirium, the bloke goes on his way and the girl has to bear the brunt. Tell me about it. The world is full of absentee fathers.

Out came the bottle of Prosecco Jinxie Wicks has been saving for a rainy day. And a box of crispy caramel truffles left over from her Hire-a-Hubby interlude. 'Of course, I blame it on the Nutcracker. Going off like that, leaving poor little Terry motherless, a forlorn little latchkey kid—'

'He was 27 for crying out loud—'

'Okay, keep your hair on. Where will they live?'

'Not at The Shack. Over my dead body.'

We sipped the Prosecco, shaking our heads. We crunched the crispy caramel truffles.

'What about your dad, Jinx? In all the years I've known you, you've never mentioned him.'

'My dad was killed in the war,' replied Jinxie Wicks.

Say no more.

Life moves on. Or, at least, Natalie and the Vandal have moved on. Natalie, the minx, said she'd rather stick pins in her eyes than live at The Shack. Terry found her a flat in Margate. Not far from Dreamland. Not far from the Great, Great, Grandmother.

Phone goes. It's herself:

'That child! Spawn of the devil! She comes in here and smashes three of my china dogs, spills milk all over my carpet... and that mimsy-pimsy mother of hers – spitting image of Terry, mind you, I'd have recognised her anywhere – she threatens to make her sit on the 'naughty stair'. What's that when it's at home? I haven't got any stairs. What that child needs is a right good clip around the ear...'

Back to the old routine. Off I go, on my solitary Bingo-less walk to Brainy Cyril's. Gladys takes the bag of groceries – 'Ah, Mr Tonks, are we to be entertained with some more of the adventures of Mr Mellors' over-active sexual equipment?' We go through the usual sherry and digestive biscuits routine. Gladys hangs my coat and furtrapper's hat on a rhino horn wall hook. Cyril is wheezing and hacking away – cough, cough, cough.

'It's not the cough, that carries you off / It's the coffin they carry you off in,' quips Gladys, handing Cyril a bottle of herbal linctus. Her remark strikes Yours Truly as very out of order, bad form to mention coffins to a man in Cyril's condition.

'Now, Tonks, my good man, hand me the great masterpiece, second shelf, three along…'

Gladys plumps up Cyril's cushions, re-adjusts his oxygen cylinder and says, 'Before you get the bit between your teeth, Mr Tonks, I want you to guess which 'Great Masterpiece' is being referred to in this little excerpt I am about to read aloud from the magazine John Bull 1929. It is headed 'FAMOUS NOVELIST'S SHAMEFUL BOOK – A LANDMARK OF EVIL'. Here goes – are you paying attention Cyril? And I quote, ' Lawrence's book is the most evil outpouring that has ever besmirched the literature of our country. The sewers of French pornography would be dragged in vain to find a parallel in beastliness.'

Gladys cackles triumphantly. She adds 'And by the way, your 'famous novelist' is referred to as 'sex-sodden'.'

Cyril is grinding his tarnished dentures and his large tufty ears have turned very red. Yours Truly is munching a digestive biscuit and appreciating Gladys' nimble-witted contributions to our reading session.

'I'll thank you to leave us men to our literary pursuits, Gladys,' rasps Cyril.

The book falls open on my lap. I glance down and see a paragraph that begins, '*Th'art good c***, though, aren't ter? Best bit o'c*** left on earth…*' Good grief. Not wanting Gladys to catch sight of it I flip over the pages at random and see '*her knees begin to quiver. Far down in her she felt a new stirring, a new nakedness emerging…*' To tell the truth my own knees were beginning to quiver what with all the tension in the room and Cyril's red ears. I flipped over another page. '*Shally 'ave a cup of tea? T'Kettles on t'boil.*' This was more like it, the gamekeepers showing his domestic side.

'Let us begin, Tonks, and allow Gladys to return to her kitchen duties?'

So I begin to read, with Cyril's chest making whistling and clicking noises in the background. It's the episode when Lady C and Mellors, having capered about the woods with bare bums et cetera, return to the gamekeeper's hut and throw themselves onto the bed: '*Connie was threading in the hair at the root of his belly a few forget-me-nots that she had gathered on the way to the hut. Outside the world had gone still and a little icy...*'

A loud snort of laughter from behind the closed door interrupts my flow.

As Cyril bellows, 'Bugger off, Gladys' I have a vivid image of myself frolicking naked in a woodland glade... what's more – frolicking with Daphne. Would Daphne be the sort to thread forget-me-nots in the hair at the root of the belly belonging to Yours Truly? And if she did would I panic? Or pass out? Or get one of my lower lumbar spasms? Best not to dwell... And mention of the world turning 'a little icy', makes me wonder whether I'll be out of order if I ask Gladys to turn up the paraffin heater. Can't feel my feet, I'm so cold.

When I reach the end of the chapter and close the great masterpiece, Cyril remarks, 'Nicely read, Tonks, but you need to brush up a bit on your North Country accent.' Fair comment. Gladys reappears carrying a linseed poultice to put on Cyril's chest. She wants to know whether I have any literary gossip to impart. I tell them that I heard an entertaining radio interview with Dame Barbara Cartland who died in 2000 aged 99:

'She sold over a billion of her romantic books worldwide. She said, '*I always stop at the bedroom door in my books, and leave the amorous activity to my dear readers' imaginations.*'

'Hmm,' snorts Gladys, 'D.H.L. could have taken a leaf out of her book.'

'Dame Barbara dictated her copy to her secretary at the rate of 3,000 words an hour. She could finish a book in two weeks and was fuelled by 29 different vitamin pills and bee pollen.'

'Vitamin pills and bee pollen? Maybe that's what I need,' croaks Cyril.

'What you need is a linseed poultice, my boy, and some Vick in your croup kettle.'

'Ah, Gladys, the sands of time... as the great Javier Marias said, *'We all at some time grow unutterably weary of who we are and who we were.'*'

'Never heard of him,' snaps Gladys.

At this point I chip in. 'And when a BBC interviewer asked Dame Barbara whether she thought social and class barriers had been broken down during her long lifetime she said in her lah-di-dah voice, *'Of course, why else would I be talking to you?'*'

Cyril pulls his tubes out of his nose and roars, 'Women like that ought to be shot, Tonks, toffee-nosed cretins. D.H.L. would have sorted her out. Contrary to Gladys' low opinion of D.H.L.'s great masterpiece, it is absolutely *not* about sex but about the breaking down of social and class barriers...'

Cyril then tells this joke:

'An Eton boy – and take note, Tonks, an ETON boy, like all the poncy toffs who are currently running our country – an Eton boy is asked to write an essay on poverty. He writes, 'There was once a very poor family. The father was poor. The mother was poor. The children were poor. Even the butler was poor.''

He grins, flashing the tarnished dentures. Gladys chortles. I smirk. And then it is time for me to depart, leaving Cyril to his thoughts. To his linseed poultice. His croup kettle. And to Gladys.

Wandered back home by way of Daphne's upmarket end of town. Images of hairy-ness and entwined forget-me-nots flashed again onto my mental plasma screen. Face up to it, Ronald, I said to myself, You and Daphne will never happen. But, alarm bells! Parked outside Daphne's bungalow was the Hire-a-Hubby van. Good grief! That man never stops working. Then I bumped into Len who regaled me with details of a newspaper cutting he had in his wallet headed 'Nude Flier's Startling Take-Off'. Apparently a male passenger caused uproar on a flight from Hamburg after stripping off in the in-flight WC and prancing down the length of the plane stark naked. He remained naked for the entire journey even though the flight attendants tried desperately to persuade him to get dressed. When the plane landed at Gatwick, police rushed on board to detain the man who was Scottish. A fellow passenger said that the naked Scot was persuaded to keep his tray table down during the flight to cover his manhood. Len said that it's that sort of out of control caper that increases his fear of flying.

But the big news this month is the return of Tex Tozer's wife! She's back! She walked in to '2b (or not 2b)' bold as brass, no warning, discovered the Muse dressed only in a shortie bathrobe and eating a boil-in-the-bag kipper. The wife – Myfanwy – chased the Muse out of the cottage into the garden where she stood shrieking that Tozer is a 'sad, old bastard who thinks he's God's gift to poetry, and good riddance'. She then threw a brick through the creeper-throttled window. At this point the neighbours called the police. All these details I obtained from Terry who happened to be walking past. He phoned Bev-the-Rev, on his mobile, to get her round pronto to help defuse the situation.

Bev-the-Rev roared up on her bike wearing short shorts and a fluorescent bomber jacket. Not a good look for a vicar in my opinion. When the police arrived, the Muse was cautioned and sent packing, and Tozer's wife explained that being made Good Egg of the Week and being in sole charge of looking after the cat had tipped Tozer over the edge. Unfortunately when the wife – Myfanwy – told Tozer that she'd been living on the proceeds of selling his first editions, he had a bit of a brainstorm and ran round the garden wearing only his underpants (Welsh-flag patterned) spouting lines from The Grating Roar of Pebbles until he fell into a patch of nettles and Bev-the-Rev managed to restrain him. At some point Edna Higgins arrived and Myfanwy who was wearing a t-shirt with BIGAMY IS HAVING ONE HUSBAND TOO MANY. MONOGAMY IS THE SAME. across the chest, started screaming, 'Minda dy fusness yr hen gnawes' (We don't want you poking your nose in, you old bag). Let's hope that Edna didn't take the opportunity to give Tozer a Save-A-Flush for his toilet. It would have been the straw that broke the camel's back.

Back home again I was sorting out my bits and bobs and came across a newspaper item written by another of my literary heroes. Booker Prize winner, Howard Jacobson. What an intellect! He could give Brainy Cyril a good run for his money! What a way he has with words! Just a humble Manchester lad who got to Cambridge and thanks to his erudition and formidable brain-box, soon hit the literary big time. No doubt Cambridge gives a bloke a bit more of a leg up the ladder than the Snodland Tech! Turns out that Jacobson is a Leonard Cohen fan. In his article he mentions reading Leonard Cohen's 1960's novel 'Beautiful Losers' (a bit over the head of Yours Truly, to be honest) which was dismissed by one critic as being 'the most revolting novel written in Canada'. Jacobson describes going to see Leonard Cohen perform in London recently

– he and 50,000 other fans – all whooping and waving each time the troubled troubadour started singing a song they recognised. They were there *'for the words, the music and a dollop of nostalgia'*. Bliss it must have been! Did he sing 'Bird on a Wire'? 'Suzanne'? 'Famous Blue Raincoat'? I would have been there – even it had meant two hours each way on a train packed with lager louts – but I couldn't afford the ticket. Or the rail fare. Jacobson, spellbound, saw Leonard Cohen crouching over his microphone into which he whispered his hoarse lyrics, wearing his fedora and flanked by feisty female backing singers belting out their nitty-gritty contrapuntual harmonies. *'Some men do old age better than they do youth. Especially melancholy, sensual men who can't decide whether they are happy or not,'* observes Jacobson, with his characteristic wit. He goes on to say that his motto (borrowed from a Leonard Cohen song) is *'Ring the bells that still can ring'*. A motto, I might add, that all of us SPAM members would do well to adopt. Killjoy Terry insisted that Jacobson's article was entirely ironic. 'He's being sarcastic, Dad, sending Cohen up...' Wrong! Jacobson always hits the nail on the head. He is a man who knows his apples from his onions, no two ways. Ah me. When Jacobson was in Canterbury for the day, last year, to sign his Booker Prize winner, 'The Finkler Question' (which I'll admit, is almost as much above my head as Leonard Cohen's 'Beautiful Losers') I was laid low with waterworks trouble. Another missed opportunity to meet a literary giant. But not to worry. *Ring the bells that still can ring,* that's my philosophy too, and I hope it will see me through what's left of this vale of tears.

Later I dashed off a fan letter to Howard Jacobson:

The Shack, Spratling Sea Road, Saltmarsh, Kent

Dear Howard Jacobson,
Greetings from a fellow Leonard Cohen fan! Did you know that our hero once had a dog called Tinkie? Or that he taught himself to play the guitar from an instruction book written by the 'Wizard of the Strings', Roy Smeck? I always enjoy your erudite articles, which are a living testimony to the advantages that a working class boy gets from going to Oxbridge. No such step-up for those of us who went to the Snodland Tech! Your book *Coming From Behind*, made me laugh so much I nearly burst a blood vessel. And I found your book *Peeping Tom*, the one on Thomas Hardy screamingly funny, but a bit near-the-knuckle to be honest, what with all that sex and sadism and poking fun at *Tess of the Durbervilles*. I often wonder why Tess didn't sell the family diamonds (given to her by Angel on her wedding night) to keep her going when she was cutting mangel-wurzals in the snow. Did you know that Hardy had a dog called Wessex which terrorised Dorchester residents and bit a postman? Keep on keeping on with your prize-winning books and scintillating newspaper columns! Ring the bells that still can ring!
Yours truly,
Ronald Tonks

NOVEMBER 2012

Big drama! Biggest drama of my life! I was sitting in the kitchen eating a sausage sandwich and listening to the cries of a peaky-looking gull perched on the water feature when I heard a loud shout from out the front.

'Hoy there, Ronald, you old bugger, come and see what I've got for you…'

It sounded like Tex Tozer. Good grief! Had the Welsh windbag finally flipped? Could he be armed? Was he wielding a chopper? A machete? Terry, looking alarmed, was heading towards the phone. Another loud shout.

'Hoy, Ronald, open up, I've got a little surprise for you…' Terry picked up the phone, his shaking finger poised above the '9'.

Then we heard loud, frantic barking noises and yelpings and the sound of claws scratching the front door. Talk about the hound of the Baskervilles. I rushed along the passage, clutching my sausage sandwich. I opened the door a chink. And there, with his wet nose poking through the chink was – wait for it – Bingo! Bingo? Yes BINGO!! Large as life and twice as bald as he had been when I last saw him.

'Holy Moly! Bingo has risen from the dead!' I gasped, then passed out. Stone cold.

When I came round, Bingo was licking my face and Tozer was trickling brandy down my throat from his hip flask. I was in a daze. Miracles do happen. Hallelujah! Happiest moment of my life! Turned out that Tozer had found Bingo wandering on the Estuary mudflats. Who knows where he had been for the last six weeks? It also turned out, as we all suddenly realised, that the dog we'd had cremated (£70, no frills) the dog that the vet said had been knocked down and killed by a car, whose little fluffy head had been poking out of the blanket, must have been some other person's wire-haired dachshund. Mistaken identity! THE PLOD HAD BROUGHT IN THE WRONG DOG! An easy error considering that wire-haired dachshunds all look very much alike, especially the fluffy top of their heads.

Meanwhile Bingo was rolling on his back, his legs kicking, making joyful little yelps and gurgles. So was Yours Truly.

Talk about time for a celebration.

'Kill the fatted chickpea!' shouted Terry, making one of his rare jokes.

'Open a bottle – or two,' I shouted, 'Pass round the dip-dab-duck-bites!'

'Our existence is but a brief crack of light between two eternities of darkness,' roared Tozer, my new best friend, so I gave him a hug and possibly a kiss on each cheek in the heat of the moment (not certain about the latter as, due to shock and elation, events are hazy) and told him to make himself at home. I must have become temporarily deranged.

Meanwhile Bingo was polishing off a bowl of Chappie. Then Terry was chasing him round The Shack with one of his new Flopsy Bunny novelty slippers clamped between his teeth. Bingo's teeth, I mean, not Terry's. Good old Bingo, none the worse for his ordeal, apart from weight loss. He jumped up onto to the settee. He ripped open a cushion so that feathers scattered everywhere. He rushed into Terry's room, grabbed a dirty sock and chewed it. What a dog! What a little treasure! By this time word had spread and Jinxie Wicks turned up with a bottle and the man from Hire-a-Hubby. Bev-the-Rev phoned and reminded Yours Truly that the Lord works in mysterious ways his wonders to perform. 'Your prayers have been answered, Ronald, the prodigal dog has returned!' I was about to reply that I don't remember saying any prayers but decide that I didn't want to upset the Lord. You never know… best to be on the safe side in these matters, hedge your bets sort of thing. Bingo snaffled a pack of uncooked sausages that were on the kitchen table – bless his little furry paws. My precious four-legged friend. I fed him a slice of ham. And a pork pie.

The upshot was that the assembled revellers all chipped in for a take-away curry and we danced round the room to my Rolling Stones Greatest Hits album. Well I say 'all' but Terry sloped off to his Morris Dancing group.

So Bingo is back. The urn containing ashes no longer stands on the kitchen shelf. Terry's bronze-effect pet memorial stencilled with TO A GOOD DOG, NEVER FORGOTTEN has been donated to the RSPCA. As has Jinxie Wicks stone-effect book with *If tears could build a stairway…* When the vet was informed of the mistaken identity, he suggested that we return the urn containing ashes, minus Bingo's photo, to him for safe keeping, in the hopes that the right owner might turn up to claim them.

He said, 'A bad business, Mr Tonks, a sad mix-up and one of those strange coincidences that two dogs of the same breed and appearance should go missing at the same time. But then, truth is often stranger than fiction. Please bring Bingo in for a health check, and for me to have another squint at his baldness problem.'

Health check? Forty-five quid? So what. Cheap at the price. Which just goes to show how unbalanced I've become. And, guess what? Bingo went and gobbled up our chicken vindaloo leftovers. This resulted in Yours Truly spending half the night mopping up the kitchen floor. Same old, same old…

Holy Moly! What a blunder! This month Daphne and Jinxie Wicks both have birthdays during the same week. Off to the cardshop... The card I chose for Daphne had a picture of a thatched cottage, roses, hollyhocks et cetera and inside a simple verse that read,

> *'Dream a little dream*
> *Sing a little song*
> *Have a jolly little time*
> *That lasts the whole day long'*

Jinxie Wicks' card had a picture of the sun setting over the Saltmarsh mudflats with a row of lobster pots in the foreground, blank inside, where I penned a cheeky verse not dissimilar to the one I received way back in January from my vintage bookseller friend,

> *'You're seventy-one today*
> *Your follicles in trouble*
> *And what was once a burning bush*
> *Is now a patch of stubble'*

Good old Jinxie Wicks. She enjoys something a bit near-the-knuckle, she'll have a little chuckle, I was thinking to myself, as I posted the cards in the box opposite the bottle bank.

On my walk back along the seafront – in a howling gale – I was surprised to see a fat – oops! OBESE (as we all have to say nowadays, to be politically correct) – woman wearing an orange track suit running on the spot. Knees up, knees up, never get the breeze up... Bingo began barking and the fa— obese woman thundered towards us shouting, 'Oooh, what a darling dog! Oooh good doggy! My favourite breed…' And burst into great racking sobs. Alarm bells! I knew what was coming.

'I have a wire-haired dachshund – or HAD, I should say (howl) – just like your dog, called Tufty – the spitting image (sob, sob, sniffle) apart from the bald patches, if you'll excuse me for mentioning them. My dear little Tufty. He slipped his collar six weeks ago and I've been looking for him ever since.'

Oh no! An image of the urn containing Tufty's ashes flashed into my head. What do I do? Do I tell her the terrible truth? Or would the shock tip her over the edge? At that moment Tex Tozer – wearing a hi-viz storm jacket – came crashing out from behind Fat Willie's Surf Shack where he'd been enjoying a fag away from the wind, and banged me on the back all matey-like.

'Morning ma'am,' he said to the wailing woman, 'I see that you are admiring my friend's companion dog – the dog that came back from the dead!'

'Shaddup Tozer' I hissed from the side of my mouth.

The woman backed away. She started running. I panted after her, Bingo dragging me along.

'Stop! Madam stop!' I shouted, black spots appearing in front of my eyes due to sudden exertion. Must see Doc Ng about it, high blood pressure? Low blood pressure? No blood pressure?

The upshot was that I was able to catch up with the woman and announce somewhat portentously, 'Madam, to cut a long story short I suggest that you call the local vet because I am certain – positive – that he has news of Tufty. But don't raise your hopes too high. Best not to raise them at all. Tell him that Tonks sent you.' Let us hope that she heeded my words.

Duty done, I made my way home via the bank where I am negotiating a loan to pay off my dental expenses and my

Leonard Cohen ticket bill. I had to present my passport as proof of identity. Good grief. It's getting worse than Russia.

'Don't you agree that my passport photo makes me look like the young Bob Dylan?' I asked the youth behind the glass.

'Who's Bob Dylan?' he replied.

No culture, these smart-phone toting youngsters. Their culture ration comes from logging on to Facebook, YouTube, taking 'selfies' and playing Angry Birds every spare moment.

But all hell broke out two days later. The day started like any other – sausage sandwich, tell Terry to turn his Cliff Richard CD down, tell him that it's time he was thinking of finding a place of his own, feed Bingo, let him out, get rid of the stray cat that sneaked in through the back door – and bit my hand, the little devil, ran it under the tap (my hand, not the stray cat)…

Phone goes. Got it in one:

'Son! The brat from hell was here yesterday, our own flesh and blood and she smashed—'

'Not now, Mum. Bad moment. I'm just looking for the Germolene and a plaster, a stray cat bit my hand—'

'Wh-a-a-a-t! Oh my Gawd. Get straight down to Accident and Emergency. You hear me? Cat bites can be fatal. It was in the *Daily Mail* – ONE IN THREE PEOPLE WHO GET BITTEN BY A CAT HAS TO BE HOSPITALISED, and—'

'It's nothing, Mum, no more than a pin prick –'

'That's just the danger! Cat-bite victims think a small pin prick is nothing to worry about but then the flesh-eating bugs start multiplying. Next thing you know the victim has to go UNDER THE KNIFE and have the infected tissue removed. They often have their limbs amputated—'

'No worries, Mum. I've got my Germolene…'

And that was just the start of my day. Shortly afterwards Jinxie Wicks phoned, said she needed cheering up and why didn't I call round for some of her faggots-in-onion-gravy? Bring a bottle. Or two. On with my cycle clips and safety helmet, pretend I'm Wiggo – who is now *Sir* Wiggo, England's knight in shining Lycra – and arrive at the static to find Jinxie Wicks in pensive mood, her birthday cards on display and – oh no! – there bang in the centre of them is the card with the thatched cottage, roses, hollyhocks et cetera. My blood runs cold. Daphne! Daphne must have received the one with the near-the-knuckle verse. Mega blunder!

'Hang about, Jinx,' I squawk, putting my cycle clips back on, 'just thought of something...' and I am out of there and pedalling like fury towards Daphne's bungalow when – collywobbles – there's Daphne coming down her garden path. She takes one look at me. Daggers. Like I'm something the cat dragged in.

'You can go and boil your head, you,' she snaps. 'Your card was crude, vulgar and insulting. Beneath contempt. And, as a matter of fact, I'll have you know I have absolutely no problems in the follicle department, none whatsoever. ANYWHERE, thank you very much...' and she storms off without a backward glance. Major sense of humour failure I'd say.

So back I pedal to Jinxie Wicks who is in a right old lather. She shouts that I have no manners, clearing off like that just as she was about to dish up her faggots-in-onion-gravy.

'I've eaten mine and given your share to the next door's dog,' she snaps, snarls almost, her *Very Best of Buddy Holly* CD playing in the background. 'What's more, I think it's time you knew the truth – those faggots-in-onion-gravy that you wolf down like a pig at the trough are *not* homemade They come from the deep-freezer shop. They take four minutes to microwave.'

No fool like an old fool. Communications between Jinxie Wicks and Yours Truly are temporarily severed.

Pick yourself up, Tonks, brush yourself off…

Hey baby let the good times roll… my winter fuel payment has arrived, so I can treat myself to switching on the second bar of my two-bar coal effect. Or I can buy a second hot water bottle. Speaking of bottles, I reach for mine every time the weather forecasters come on the wireless warning of cold fronts and icy blasts, or prevailing winds and tidal surges blowing in from the North Sea. What with global warming, icy blasts, melting icebergs, prevailing winds, tidal surges and freak floods it is on the cards that the raging sea, being only a few yards from my back door at high tide, will come crashing over The Shack one of these days and me, Terry and Bingo will meet our Maker. It doesn't bear thinking about, the raging sea crashing over The Shack, I mean not meeting our Maker which, I imagine, will be a bit like being sent to the headmaster when I was a schoolboy. That's if our Maker exists. Watch out for His blog. And His YouTube videos.

As for weather forecasting, in my wanderings along the beach I often bump into a whiskery old sea-salt, called Wilf, who is a whizz at predicting the weather.

'Get them geraniums taken indoors tonight, me ol'hearty,' he'll say, his salt-encrusted boots planted firmly in the shingle. 'Mark me words there's an arctic blast and heavy frost a'coming.'

Wilf is always spot on. He licks a gnarled finger and holds it up to the wind and says things like, 'When the cod swim upside down / Yer home-grown spuds are like to drown,' or he whirls a smelly bunch of bladderwrack seaweed around his head and says, 'If the ducks forget to quack / Run indoors and get your mac.'

Bumped into him this week by Fat Willie's Surf Shack with the sea boiling and smashing against the breakwater, frothy bits of spume spraying across the pebbles looking like snow.

'Ah, Ron, me ol'hearty,' he called, holding a shell to his ear, 'listen up – when tossing trawlers make small catches / 'tis time to batten down the hatches – mark me words, Ronnie me lad, we're in for some icy blasts down from the Cairngorms!'

When I asked him to let me into the secret of his accurate weather predictions he took a long drag on his reeking pipe and replied, 'Stands to reason, me ol'hearty, I logs on to weathernews.com, never fails.' Funnily enough it does fail now and then. That very afternoon the weather turned unseasonably mild for November.

But where would we be without the Wilfs of this world? Or the Lens, come to that. Last week Len got knocked down crossing the road. By a bike. Two days in hospital, then home to his solitary bedsit, right arm in plaster, left foot in one of those giant A&E foam boots. He limped into SPAM on crutches with a book – *The Plot to Bring down Britain's Planes* – under one arm. Edna Higgins sorted out his Meals on Wheels. But his accident didn't prevent him from taking part in Andy's SPAM coach outing to the countryside for a walk in the woods and an over-sixties mid-week special lunch at an historic inn. Total cost £10. Call me the last of the big spenders, but I offered to treat Daphne and Jinxie Wicks. 'Time to bury the hatchet,' I said to them both, without actually mentioning the birthday card mix-up. 'Life's too short to bear grudges.'

Daphne said, 'Thanks, but no thanks' and is still giving me the cold shoulder but Jinxie Wicks was game. I am coming round to the idea that a friendship (platonic) with someone who you can a have a laugh with is better in the long run, than all the agony and ups-and-downs of a romantic entanglement.

So, we travel by coach to Elmhill, a village that still looks like every Kent village once looked in my youth. Unfortunately Tex Tozer had a slight mishap on the journey to Elmhill. He goes into the on-board toilet and forgets to lock the door. As the coach speeds round a roundabout the toilet door suddenly swings open and Tozer is pitched forward, knickers round knees and almost lands in Len's lap. We SPAM members, in the seats near the toilet, all avert our eyes (except for Len who can't stop laughing for the rest of the journey) and Tozer after a couple of yells and Welsh curses, picks himself up with as much dignity as he can muster. Otherwise the coach ride is uneventful. Andy tells one of his jokes that we have all heard before: 'Three men, all a little deaf, are standing by the bowling green. One remarks to the other, 'Windy, isn't it?' The second man replies, 'No, it's Thursday.' The third man nods in agreement, 'So am I. Let's have a cup of tea."

Jinxie Wicks has her nose stuck in an article in the *Daily Mail* headed, 'Why Control Pants Can Give You Panic Attacks'.

At first glance Elmhill is your classic chocolate-box English village – with its olde-worlde inn (circa 1350), village green, ancient church, lichen-spattered gravestones and a sparse scattering of picturesque thatched cottages. Elmhill even boasts a rare 'squeeze stile' along a lane leading to the woods. What's a 'squeeze style', do I hear you ask? There were once all kinds of different English stiles – clapper, stone slab, ladder, stepping stone, plank – a fact that I learned as a boy from the cigarette cards I collected. Useless information nowadays and I can't see today's kids (and I'm thinking of the Vandal) showing any interest in Kentish stiles. Mind you, most of today's population, including the Vandal and all the other fat kids you see everywhere, would find it impossible to squeeze through a 'squeeze stile' what with the national obesity epidemic.

Yes, at first sight Elmhill is classic chocolate box. Without doubt the Eton boys who don't know the price of a sliced white loaf who run our country would say that a place like Elmhill represents the unchanging, timeless, Hovis ad, English way of life. Yours Truly can soon set them straight on that score. Elmhill is certainly no rustic idyll. The ploughman no longer homeward plods his weary way. For a start those picturesque thatched cottages are all second homes owned by people who work and live in London. The big house that once belonged to the head honcho of the village is now used as a conference centre and wedding reception venue. As we wander round the grounds hoping to enjoy the last of the autumn colours, we keep coming across blokes in suits shouting into their mobile phones or sitting on the ancient mossy stonework benches punching their laptops. Silly ringtones disturb the tranquillity. Having seen the last of the autumn colours and the duck pond and a flock of exotic looking creatures – llamas? alpacas? Whatever. They certainly aren't sheep – in a field, Jinxie Wicks and Yours Truly decide to take a peaceful ramble round the churchyard. Strolling among the graves we find ourselves wondering what all the long gone Percys, Elsies, Mabels, Rubys and Alberts mouldering away beneath their grassy slabs or marble chippings would make of Elmhill today. No shops. One bus a day. The Old Rectory owned by an ex-rock musician. The church falling down. Only one church service a month, and one lady vicar in charge of three local churches. A constant roar of traffic rumbles from the distant motorway. Would Elmhill today be recognisable to the long gone man with 'all I ask is a tall ship and a star to steer me by' carved on his tombstone? Or to the young man, aged 34, whose tombstone tells us he 'died saving his dog'?

A line from Omar Khayyam springs to mind, '*Ah, make the most of what we yet may spend / Before we too into the dust descend*' as Jinxie Wicks and Yours Truly survey the graves, but our peaceful contemplations are shattered by a loud burst of jangling pop music blaring from a radio on the church roof where workmen are doing repairs. At the same moment from the nearby Old Rectory comes the crash and thump of someone doing their drum practice. Every few seconds a Range Rover roars past the church, going way over the 30 mph speed limit. Then a fleet of veteran artists arrive in various clapped out motors. They park haphazardly around the green before settling themselves under the ancient oak tree (which has a plaque explaining that 'the mighty and marvellous oak was planted in 1936') noisily assembling their folding stools and easels and starting to sketch. The artists are followed by a straggling group of ramblers who ramble through the churchyard and across the green talking nineteen to the dozen. From the opposite direction appears a crowd of dog walkers doing a sponsored walk to raise funds for the church roof repairs. Next come a dozen Sir Wiggo worshippers all togged up in their hi-viz Lycra get-ups, parking their bikes round the mighty and marvellous oak. And, of course, all us SPAM members are milling about, taking snaps, dropping litter, churning up the turf on the village green. And then Terry hoves into view. He is plodding slowly and solemnly up the hill towards the church in all his funeral glory followed by Mr Podger driving the hearse at 2 mph with Bev-the-Rev bringing up the rear. Obviously it is one of Terry's 'lonely funeral' days. A bunch of local hooligans start clowning about behind Bev-the-Rev, pulling funny faces and doing silly walks, no doubt bunking off from school.

'Yoo-hoo, Terry,' shouts Jinxie Wicks, but he doesn't bat an eyelid. Takes his work very seriously does Terry. A true pro. And a good thing too. There's a great flashing of mobile phone cameras and then the church clock strikes twelve.

'Opening time!' shout the artists downing their palettes and paint brushes. Everyone - SPAM members, roof repairers, artists, ramblers, dog walkers, cyclists, suits – make a beeline for the Royal Oak inn. Far from the madding crown it is not. In the stampede someone treads on Len's giant A&E foam boot and he has to be revived with a hot toddy. Overhead, above the oak beams on which we keep bumping our heads, is the pounding thump of music, stamping of feet and other indications of celebration.

Turns out it's the Kent Gender Re-alignment Group enjoying another one of their private get-togethers. I can't hear myself think. As for the Royal Oak's 'Over-Sixties Mid-Week Special' – well 'special' is putting it a bit strong. There's not much special about omelette and chips followed by rhubarb and custard in my opinion.

At least I had the SPUGS' first gig to look forward to. Our debut! Whew! But as Diesel made clear at the SPIUGS' rehearsal, we must not expect our first gig to be the sort of raving, knicker-throwing, head-banging occasion to which he had been accustomed, during his wild rock 'n roll past. 'Just go for it, guys, spread the love!' he said, chivvying us up before we went on the road. 'Remember, the SPUGS stare music hard in the eye and never back down.'

The great day dawns. We meet at the Dun Roamin' care home. Thanks to Big Babs, in her role as 'Wardrobe', she has got us all kitted out with Hawaiian shirts, Bermuda shorts and pirate headbands like the one Keef Richards wears. To get into the rock 'n' roll spirit of things Diesel — his illegal substance abuse days being long over – slips us each a herbal KavaKava pill to make us relax (from Boots) and a can of Beaver Buzz energy drink. This has the effect of making us all troop off to the WC Back in the lounge the Dun Roamin' staff have set up a small 'stage' and two microphones. There's one of those silver foil strip curtains as a backdrop, a glitter ball dangling from the ceiling and multi-coloured flashing fairy lights which give our best player a nasty migraine before we've even started so he has to be sent home. 'The show must go on, dudes,' says Diesel whose winkle-picker, Cuban-heeled boots don't really go with the Bermuda shorts. Nor does my titanium knee-brace. What with all the silver foil, glitter ball and flashing lights, all we need are some swirls of dry ice and it would be like a mini Eurovision. Bring it on!

While the SPUGS tune up in the hallway the residents of Dun Roamin' shuffle into the lounge. To add to the gig-like atmosphere they are all holding glo-stix to be waved in the air. After about five minutes some of the Dun Roamers start slow hand-clapping and singing 'Why are we waiting?' Why they are waiting I have no idea because the SPUGS have been raring to go for half an hour. Talk about collywobbles. My ticker is thumping against my ribs. My shanks shaking. The care home manageress steps onto the stage and says, 'Ladies and gents, let's have a big hand for the SPUGS.' And we are off! We strut into the spotlight (yay!) with a mighty twang, and blast off with our opening number – a high speed version of *It's a Long Way to Tipperary*. Fantastic! This must be how Mick Jagger feels when the lights go up and the fans start roaring.

Several of the Dun Roamers are still slow handclapping and singing, 'Why are we waiting' but no matter, the SPUGS are belting it out – only problem being that half of us are playing *Tipperary* and the other half are playing *Pick up your Troubles*. No one seems bothered. The glo-stix are waving.

But then one of the sound speakers explodes and our sound is drowned out by the earsplitting shriek of the reverb from one of the faulty microphones. We pluck on regardless. Most of the Dun Roamers are getting well into the spirit of things, singing along, waving their glo-stix. Admittedly two in the front row have nodded off but the rest are going wild in a muted OAP sort of way. If the Nutcracker could see me now! She'd see a cool dude who never says never. She'd be kicking herself. After half a dozen numbers a bloke, with a head as bald as a ping-pong ball, calls out, 'Let's have *Jumpin' Jack Flash*!' Big Babs – Wardrobe – leans towards him, rattles her tambourine and tells him to belt up. After six numbers we have a little break which results in all the SPUGS trooping off to the WC again. Ping-Pong Head shouts out, 'Has anyone heard the ancient Kentish proverb that goes "God save me from a bad neighbour and a beginner on the ukulele"? Wa-ha-ha…' The Pluckers ignore him. Like all live bands we are learning how to cope with the odd heckle. And so the show goes on – another five songs including '*Roll me over in the clover, roll me over lay me down and do it again*' and '*She'll be coming round the mountain when she comes*'. Is it just me or are these lyrics distinctly vulgar?

We end up with *Knees-up Mother Brown* and with Ping-Pong Head knees-upping all around the room until he keels over. Another Dun Roamer looks as if she has conked out in her armchair and has to be carried off by Dun Roamin' staff. Diesel invites a lively female Dun Roamer up to the stage – it takes her some time to travel the distance from her armchair, but once she's arrived she starts singing *The Birdie Song* with everyone joining in and flapping their arms – except for the band who don't know the chords. As we are leaving the stage, to tumultuous applause, in a shower of well-aimed glo-stix, my feet get tangled up in my music stand and I take a tumble, bringing down the silver foil backdrop. No harm done, apart from twisting my bad knee. As they say there's no biz like showbiz. Way to go!

DECEMBER 2012

Ding-dong merrily on high and all that.... When it comes to Christmas my attitude is more 'humbug' than 'Herald Angels', but there's no escaping the festive frenzy. I blame it on Charles Dickens and all his punch-swilling, merry-making Christmas characters. Even the nation's most famous atheist, Richard Dawkins, has admitted that he enjoys warbling along to the occasional Christmas carol. Terry has hung an inflatable reindeer's head in the hallway and stuck plastic holly round the mirror. I've been tucking in to the local butcher's 'Rudolph's Revenge' seasonal sausages, and the High Street cafés are all doing Turkey and Tinsel pensioners specials for £5. Jinxie Wicks and Yours Truly have enjoyed taking advantage – along with almost the entire SPAM membership – everyday at noon. December is a busy time for Terry at It's Your Funeral, what with flu and bronchitis. And he's been busy helping Bev-the-Rev with the nativity play. As I write I can hear Cliff Richard's *Mistletoe and Wine* blaring from Terry's stereo.

Another great triumph this month for the SPUGS at our Christmas Special gig! Diesel had us practising a merry medley of seasonal favourites – 'Rudolph the Red Nosed Reindeer', 'When Santa Got Stuck Up the Chimney' et cetera, which went down a treat when the band once more took to the boards at the Dun Roamin' Care Home. 'Okay guys – we're cooking up the groove,' rasped Diesel, nudging us onto the stage. The SPUGS wore red rubber reindeer antlers on our heads. Diesel wore a novelty hat of a chimney pot with Santa's big boots poking out as if he's got stuck down the chimney head first. Big Babs wore a satin Santa suit and high-heeled boots, and kept clinking her finger-bells. Yay! *Ring the bells that still can ring* as the bedsit bard might say. The Dun Roamers wore paper hats and went wild, singing along and tooting their feather blowers. The stroppy bald-as-a-ping-pong-ball resident was skipping about with a rubber turkey on his head and toot-tooting a kazoo. Halfway through the SPUGS' upbeat arrangement of 'Jingle Bells' he climbed onto a chair and started singing the rude version and was escorted from the room. You'd be amazed at what goes on in these places. In his book *Rogues, Villains and Eccentrics* (St Mildred's Hospice, 75p) William Donaldson, describes the scandalous goings-on at the Hazelmere Home for the Elderly in Great Yarmouth where a male inmate died of a heart attack and five more were treated for shock after an 81 year old female inmate danced a raunchy striptease. The following year there were three more deaths from shock after an 87 year old male inmate dressed up as the Grim Reaper for a laugh, went out into the garden and peered through the windows at the other inmates, brandishing a realistic looking scythe. Shortly afterwards the home was closed down. It makes you realise how carefully you should vet these OAP havens before checking in.

Anyway, December has got off to a chilly start. '*The winter is tuning up*,' to quote Leonard Cohen. It felt even chillier when the first thing I saw when I got up and made my way to the bathroom was a leaflet on the doormat headed, 'HOW TO AVOID RISING FUNERAL COSTS – why not order your FREE no-obligation information pack now?' Next to it, on the doormat, was another leaflet headed, 'HEART DISEASE AND STROKE – are you at risk?' with a gory full-colour photo of a heart with an arrow pointing to a blobby maroon bit telling me that the maroon bit was, in fact, 'pooling blood containing fatal clots'. Good grief! There was also a small package from my vintage book-seller friend containing a card with an illustration of a turkey wearing a Santa hat. Inside my friend had scrawled,

'Your eyeballs are red
Your nose is bright blue
Is mistletoe snogging all over for you?
If so, open the envelope...'

Inside the envelope were items called Horny Goat's Weed Capsules and blurb informing me that Horny Goat's Weed is a potent natural aphrodisiac which increases sexual urges and which has been a best kept secret for hundreds of years. To be honest I'm beginning to have my doubts about my vintage book-seller friend's mental state. Think I'll pass on the capsules – maybe give them to someone who can benefit from them – the Hire-a-Hubby bloke perhaps? Oh yes, also on the mat was a Christmas card from the Nutcracker! Post marked London! Oh no! She's back, almost within spitting distance. I'll be looking over my shoulder every time I leave the house.

Terry comes padding into the kitchen barefoot, humming 'Mistletoe and Wine' and grumbling that Bingo has chewed up his latest pair of novelty slippers. He then informs me that he has invited Natalie, the Vandal and my mum to a slap-up dinner at The Shack on Christmas Day. Nightmare.

Heart sinks. Then the phone goes. Heart sinks further.

'Bet that's Grandma,' says Terry, stirring the porridge. It is. The UKIP theme tune, *I'm Dreaming of a White Christmas* sung by Bing Crosby is crooning in Mum's background.

'Son? Are you there? Did you know that more people commit suicide at Christmas than at any other time of the year?'

'What are you trying to tell me, Mum?'

'What do you mean 'What am I trying to tell you'? I'm trying to tell you that more people commit suicide at Christmas than at any other time of year—'

'Right. Well. You've been reading your *Daily Mail*, haven't you?'

'Too right I have. A person has to keep up with world events. And it's not only suicide that claims lives at Christmas, there are more accidents in the home—'

'Aw, Mum, that's because more people – most people – are at home during the—'

'—Last week a housewife fractured every last bone in her right foot after dropping a frozen turkey on it. Then there's dozens of people who break their necks falling off ladders putting up paper-chains, or they get fatal food poisoning from not defrosting the turkey enough, or they spill boiling hot gravy over themselves or choke on the lucky charms hidden in their Christmas pud—'

'Get a grip, Mum! You're making it sound like the nation takes life in its hands at this time of the—'

'Mock not, Ronald! In Cornwall a vicar leaned forward to blow out one of those big altar candles and, you know what? Boiling hot wax splashed into his eyes and made him permanently blind. And don't, whatever you do, heat up one of those therapeutic wheat bags in the microwave—'

'What's a *therapeutic wheat bag* when it's at home?'

Terry chips in at this point having heard my side of the conversation, to say that he has a therapeutic, lavender-scented wheat bag that he holds against the fibrositis he suffers from.

'Did you hear that, Mum? Terry has a lavender-scented wheat bag for his stiff neck—'

'Wha-a-a-t? His stiff what? Not that his stiff whatsit's any of my business but you warn him about the hazards. It was in the paper, this woman from Skegness heated up her wheat bag in the microwave, took it to bed, the wheat bag I mean, not the microwave, it exploded and she went up in flames...'

Give me strength! What a start to the day. While Terry is getting himself togged up for his funeral duties I decide to look back over the year and check out how my January horoscope predictions for 2012 panned out. Here they are with my end-of-the-year responses:

LIBRA

Still sitting in the same room? (Yes, and it's even more ruddy damp and freezing than it was in January).

Still thinking about the same situation? (Yes, *Well my friends are gone and my hair is grey. I ache in the places where I used to play* to quote Leonard Cohen)

Still eating the same kind of food? (Yes, mostly sausage sandwiches. But there's a seismic shift now that Terry sometimes dishes up his vegetarian hotpots to ring the changes.)

Still wrestling with the same problems? (Yes, no money, the meaning of life, the increasing sorry-ness of my earthly tabernacle, spasms in the lower lumbar area and waterworks trouble.)

Still up against the same challenges? (Yes. Can't make ends meet, dog still bald, prostate hanging over my head, long-reach toe nail trimmer no longer works, specs fall off. PS Challenges have got worse since Terry moved in.)

Well enjoy all that consistency and familiarity while it lasts. 2012 has just begun. You will soon have to start getting used to a lot of positive changes. Things really are going to get significantly different.

(Positive changes? Does that mean SPAM? The Pluckers? The Vandal? Terry moving in? My dental bridge? All I can say is, if things are going to get seriously 'significantly different' they had better get a move on. Not much time left… I live in hope!)

Next stop – I meet Jinxie Wicks for a Turkey and Tinsel pensioners' special. Daphne comes too. Hey ho! Not a single twitch in the magic flute department. When a lovely flame dies, you must realise, smoke gets in your eyes. Fact is, the magic has faded. Vanished. Len turns up, so the four of us share a table. Len, his foot still encased in a giant A&E foam boot, immediately starts banging on about a Malaysian airlines suicide crash which occurred in 1997 aboard a Silk Air 737 flight. The Captain killed his first officer with an axe, disabled the planes flight systems and deliberately nose-dived the plane into the ground.

'Did you know that more people commit suicide at Christmas than at any other time of the year?' says Daphne. Good grief. She's sounding just like my mum. Then she starts moaning about her neighbours who want planning permission to build a granny flat which will block out her sun. Len tells anyone who wants to listen that Daphne should be thankful that she hasn't got a nun like Sister Mary Michael from Lincolnshire living next door. It was in the papers. Sister

Mary Michael is planning to erect a 24ft high neon crucifix (which flashes) in the garden of her bungalow.

'People have been trying to block her planning application for what she calls her "cross of love",' explains Len, who is having a bit of trouble with his teeth, as we all get stuck into our turkey and roast spuds. 'She says she wants it to be a symbol of hope which will offer spiritual protection to the neighbourhood, but the woman living next door says that a flashing neon cross is not in keeping with a residential area and that it will shine into her bedroom and disturb her sleep.'

'Mad religious maniac!' says Jinxie Wicks, raising her voice to be heard above Bing Crosby crooning from the ceiling speakers. 'Pass the gravy, Ronald. And the bread sauce.'

We pull our crackers. We don our paper hats. We read our jokes.

'What happens to men who get too big for their pants? They get exposed in the end.' Boom boom.

'What do you call a three-legged donkey. A wonky.' Boom boom.'

'Did you hear about the chap whose whole left side was cut off? He's all right now.' Boom boom.

Daphne says that at Christmas 432 million Brussels sprouts are eaten in Britain. I tell you, it's like listening to my mum.

Len, who has been taking furtive little nips from his hip flask starts to tell a joke in a very loud voice and everyone goes quiet. And quieter. We all start busying ourselves with our stuffing balls and parsnips.

'This bloke goes to the doctor about his constipation. The doc gives him some pills and says "put one of these in your back passage twice a day…"'

Daphne puts down her knife and fork. She looks daggers.

Len continues regardless: '...bloke comes back the following week and says to the doctor, "For all the good your ruddy pills have done I might just as well been sticking them up me arse!"'

Boom boom.

'Schoolboy smut,' hisses Daphne and flounces out. Jinxie Wicks is roaring. Everyone else in the café has started talking in loud voices. Len's jokes are no laughing matter. I'm thinking that there's a time and place, Len, but not during the Turkey and Tinsel Pensioners' Special.

My good turn for the month was accompanying my new best friend, Tex Tozer – the hero who found my lost dog – to the hospital outpatients for 'tests'. Poor old Tex, griping stomach pains and a wife who says he's making a lot of fuss about nothing. He has been instructed to undergo a 'fasting' test which means he's had no food or fluids since the previous day. We enter the waiting room, packed full of apprehensive-looking outpatients. 'Bear with,' says a shouty, cross-looking receptionist woman with a wide-angle mouth and eyes like a shot pigeon. Tex discovers that he's lost his paperwork. After a lot of tut-tutting and angry punching of computer keys the shouty, cross-looking woman hands Tex a pack of suppositories and tells him to take a seat. Above her head is a notice that says, 'Please stand behind the line and wait to be called.' 'Called what, I wonder?' quips Tex. On the pack of suppositories it says, 'Before use first remove the silver foil wrapping'. Talk about the nanny state in over-drive. Have we become a nation of idiots? Tex sits down and starts coughing. He coughs and coughs. He's coughing his head off. He can't soothe it with a sip of water because he's meant to be 'fasting'. Another explosive cough. Cough. Cough.

The cross-looking woman with the wide-angle mouth shouts at the top of her voice, 'Look. You can help yourself to some water. We're only doing it up your back passage today.'

All eyes turn towards Tex who shouts, 'Why don't you tell the whole of Kent, you old battle axe. What happened to patient dignity and confidentiality…'

'Are you insulting me, Mr Tozer? Any more threatening language from you and I'll call security.'

A lady in a wheelchair turns to Tex and says, 'Calm down, ducks, it's the NHS, what can you expect? Have one of these,' and offers him a grape. It gets stuck. He starts to choke. I bang him on the back.

His coughing and spluttering gets so bad that the cross-looking woman shrieks, 'And if you don't stop that coughing I'll have to call an ambulance.'

The lady in the wheelchair says, 'Now I've heard everything. The lunatics have taken over the asylum…'

Tex can't take any more. 'Get me out of here, Ronald, take me to the nearest pub…' On the way out he hands back the pack of suppositories to the cross-looking, shouty woman saying, 'Don't eat them all at once, babe.'

It's no joke being bullied and pushed around when you're feeling fragile. I bet the Duke of Edinburgh wasn't treated like that when he had his recent dodgy down-below problems.

As we waited for the Saltmarsh bus, Tex observed gloomily, 'I'm young at heart, Ronald, but a bit older in other places.' The headline on a nearby newsagent's billboard caught my eye. It announced SKINT GRAN GREW DRUGS IN HER LOFT. Good grief! Thank the Lord that my mum lives on one floor. A headline like that could put ideas in her head.

Then Tex Tozer bought a copy of the *Saltmarsh Gazette* with the headline TRIUMPHANT RETURN TO DREAMLAND and the fantastic good news that Dreamland is to be restored to its former glory BY POPULAR DEMAND! The famous Big Dipper and rides are being done up and Margate's legendary, now derelict, site is to be transformed once again into a day-trippers' heaven! Must tell my mum who can watch it all happening from her tower block.

Back home I'm just settling down to a good read – *The Selected Letters of Edith Sitwell* (St Mildred's Hospice, £1) – with a can of Scrumpy Jack when the phone rings. No peace for the wicked.

'Help me, Son, I'm in a panic—'

'What's up now, Mum?'

'I saw in the paper that this famous footballer, whose name I forget, has been arrested for making a homophobic gesture during a big match—'

'So what's your worry?'

'I need to know what a homophobic gesture is. I'm worried that I might make one by mistake and get arrested—'

'You've got me scuppered there, Mum. I don't know what a homophobic gesture is either. Leave it with me and I'll get Terry to look it up on the Internet.'

Stone the crows. Yet one more thing to worry about. For all I know I could have been making homophobic gestures for years without knowing I'm doing it.

It's time for my regular date with Brainy Cyril. Leaving Terry at home decorating a Christmas tree and singing along to Cliff's version of *The Lord's Prayer* sung to the tune of *Auld Lang Syne*, I set off along the Spratling Sea Road. I'm wearing my fur-trapper's hat and ankle length, ex-army great coat (Help the Aged, £3). A howling gale makes my eyes water and Bingo's ears flap out horizontally like two windsocks. Knock on the front door and in I go. Gladys has a hot water bottle tied round her waist, dangling down like a sporran.

'He's in his bedroom, Mr Tonks, easier to keep him warm,' says Gladys, leading me past the hand carved giraffe, the ukhamba basket collection, the lions' tooth necklaces and the Masai art works decorating the walls up the stairs. Bingo pads along, too, wearing his stripy knitted jacket.

'Yoo-hoo, Cyril, here's Mr Tonks arrived to entertain you with a further instalment of D.H.L.'s filthy book…'

Cyril, looking brighter than usual, greets Yours Truly with one of his low-pitched bronchial chuckles and has Gladys flitting about and sorting out the sherry. Bingo jumps onto Cyril's bed, turns round a few times, curls up and starts snoring. Gladys squawks. She sprays Bingo with air freshener. Cyril's tubes pop out of his nose, he quickly pops them back.

'Stop fretting, Gladys, let him be… I've always liked dogs. Even sausage dogs, although they're German. Ruddy Huns. Here's a question to keep you on your toes, Tonks, what is the name of Mellor's, the gamekeeper's dog?'

'Flossie,' I reply, quick as a flash.

'And here's a historical fact you can have for nothing… Not many people are aware that King George I made a law stating that "the severest penalty will be suffered by any commoner who doth permit his animal to have carnal knowledge of a pet of the Royal House." As far as I know the law still stands, so make certain that you never let Bingo get near the Royal corgis.'

Cyril's wheezy chortle has Gladys spooning out the herbal cough linctus and handing him his sputum dish before leaving us with the words, 'I'll be downstairs if you need me. I'll leave you lads to salivate over the man who wrote a short story with the title *The Escaped Cock* – on which topic Mellors the gamekeeper seems to have been an expert.'

Cyril snorts and ripostes hoarsely, 'I'll thank you Gladys to leave the literary discourse to Tonks and myself, and I'll remind you that the famous story by D.H.L. to which you allude, is about Jesus who comes back from the dead only to abandon his mission of saving mankind.'

Cyril is certainly on top form (for him), knocking back a second sherry after a spoonful of his herbal linctus, patting Bingo, asking me to open THE book which is on his bedside table. I pick it up. It falls open at a page that begins:

She was gone in her own soft rapture, like a forest soughing with the dim, glad moan of spring, moving into bud. She could feel in the same world with her man, moving on beautiful feet, beautiful in the phallic mystery...

To my way of thinking passages like that could very well have been written by the much derided, by intellectual types, Dame Barbara Cartland, but I keep my opinion to myself. When Cyril gets the Lady Chatterley bit between his teeth he champs at it, raring to go:

'Lady Chatterley's Lover is an attack on the English class system, Tonks. It's a novel about upper-class sense of entitlement, scorn and fear of the working class. Sir Clifford Chatterley is a land-owning toff. The seducer who has set fire to Lady C's haystack is a member of the lower orders. It's not so much Lady C's adultery that upsets the applecart, it's the fact that she's getting her jollies from one of his servants. Turn to chapter 19—'

I turn to chapter 19. This is the big showdown bit, when Lady C tells Sir Clifford that she's up the duff by the gamekeeper. Sir Clifford then goes for Lady C hammer and tongs. Very dramatic it is, and I throw myself into it to the best of my ability.

If he could have sprung out of his chair, he would have done so. His face was yellow, and his eyes bulged...

Cyril is doing his wheezy chuckle. Glancing across at him I notice that his face is rather yellow, his eyes a bit bulgy. I continue to read in a posh, raging toff sort of voice:

My God, you ought to be wiped off the face of the earth. That scum! That bumptious lout! That miserable cad! One of my servants! My God, my god, is there any end to the beastly lowness of woman!

My God! Sir Clifford C's fury is getting to Yours Truly. I'm feeling quite het up. I pause. I could give the late, great Sir Alec Guinness a run for his money. I blow my nose. Cyril tops up our glasses saying, 'By Jove, that's a great scene, Tonks. The toff reveals his true colours...'

We both take a sip or two of sherry.

Gladys sticks her head round the door and reminds Cyril it's time for his pills. He knocks them back, relaxes against his pillows and says, 'You know what, Tonks, I'm in the mood to fill my head with a few lines of D.H.L.'s more lyrical prose passages. Be a good man and turn to chapter 15. Read to me the naked romp in the rain sequence—'

I turn to chapter 15 and begin: *She opened the door and looked at the straight heavy rain, like a steel curtain, and had a sudden desire to rush out into it. She got up, and began swiftly pulling off her stockings, then her dress and underclothing, and he held his breath—*

'Anyone fancy a mug of Bovril?' shouts Gladys from downstairs.

— her pointed animal breasts tipped and stirred as she moved. She was ivory-coloured in the greenish light, she ran out with a wild little laugh, holding up her breasts to the heavy rain –

'Or a chocolate HobNob?' shouts Gladys.

—lifting and falling, bending so the rain beat and glistened on the full haunches

Pausing for breath I glance at Cyril. He has a look of rapture on his face. His bleary eyes are staring into the distance. His mouth is hanging open. His clicking and wheezing sounds have stopped. In fact he doesn't seem to be breathing. In fact – oh no! Nightmare! It looks as if he's – well – dead. DEAD! Dead? Good grief! Holy Moly – Bingo makes a little howling noise and jumps off the bed. My knees start to quiver (like Lady C's in Chapter 10). Will the shock be too much for Gladys? I can hear her stomping up the stairs with the Bovril and HobNobs. She opens the door. She sees. She takes in the situation at a glance. No dramatics. No wailing or breast beating. What a woman! She closes Cyril's eyes. 'He's still warm, bless him. Let's give it a few minutes, Mr Tonks, before I phone for the doctor. We don't want a pesky emergency CPR crew dashing in here, thumping his chest with electric shocks to bring him back, brain-damaged and in a vegetative state. Absolutely not. No point. He went without a murmur. Lucky chap.'

So we sit silently sipping our Bovril and munching the HobNobs.

What a way to go when you think about it. Good old Cyril, speeded on his way by D.H.L., full of beans to the very end.

Gladys stoops to pick up the book which – in the shock of the moment – I had dropped, mid-sentence. On the words 'full haunches' as it happens.

'Mr Tonks, I would like you to have this book to keep. You have been more than kind to Cyril. Take it. It's yours. It's probably worth a few bob. All Cyril's books are. It's a little memento of Cyril, he would have wanted you to have it—'

'Oh but I couldn't, Gladys, really—'

'Oh yes, you *could*. If you won't take it I will only chuck it in the bin. Frankly I can't bear to have the disgusting item in the house. To my way of thinking it's porn masquerading as art – so take it, please *do*.'

So take it I do. Thanks very much Gladys. We wrap it in newspaper to protect it from the elements. Once the ambulance has arrived and a careworker to help Gladys, I make my way back to The Shack, battling my way through violent blasts of sleet, much subdued. Bingo's tail is between his legs. Time like an ever-rolling stream et cetera… Some lines by the poet Algernon Swinburne flash into my mind as I walk buffeted by the storm:

From too much love of living
From hope and fear set free
We thank with brief thanksgiving
Whatever gods may be

That no man lives for ever
That dead men rise up never
That even the weariest river
Winds somewhere safe to sea.

A cup of hot tea was called for. And both bars of my coal effect. And, definitely, Leonard Cohen's *Like a Bird on a Wire* to chime with my mood.

So outside the wind is whipping up the waves which are crashing against the breakwater, then receding with a rattle and hiss of shingle. The grating roar of pebbles, no less.

This is what happens next:

I unwrap Cyril's copy – now mine – of *Lady Chatterley's Lover*. It has an attractive dust jacket. You'd think that the book was new. Good old Cyril – RIP – certainly looked after his books. Now let me see, I'm thinking to myself… it looks like a fairly early edition. Hmm. Hang about! Stone the crows! It's actually inscribed! INSCRIBED! It's blinkin' well signed by – Holy Moly! It's signed by the great man himself! It reads, in spidery handwriting:

'D.H.Lawrence – Forte dei Marmi. June 1929'.

Blimey! It's unbelievable! It's beyond my wildest imaginings! I'm pinching myself to make sure I'm really awake!

I'm in shock – second time today.

I'm reaching for the phone.

I'm dialling my vintage bookseller friend's number.

My knees are knocking. My fingers in my fagins are trembling so much I can hardly dial.

I'm holding the phone to my ear.

He's there. He answers. He's listening.

He's shouting, roaring, gasping... 'Mint condition? 1929? Signed? Florence, Italy?' Ye Gods! Soddin' hell, Ronald! Jackpot!'

He's saying he needs a chair to sit down on before he passes out.

I need a chair to sit down on. I need –

Oh my goodness, what a blinkin' turn-up.

Amazing, miraculous! Good old Cyril! A dream come true! Hurrah, my horoscope has come up trumps in the nick of time!

Richard Dawkins is wrong. This proves that He does exist. He is up there planning his wonders to perform – (God, I mean, not Dawkins.)!

Oh my goodness!

Where are the cruise brochures? Where's my passport? This is where the lights go on for Ronald Tonks! *Ring the bells that still can ring*! Bloody hell—

FEBRUARY 2013

Selfie-Postcard from Ronald Tonks to
Doris Tonks and Bingo,

Greetings from Honolulu Mum!
Hotter here than Saltmarsh no two ways!! Place crawling
with ukulele players! The tanned dude in the photo wearing
the razzle-dazzles, Hawaiian shirt and parrot-patterned
Bermudas is YOURS TRULY! The game old girl in the grass
skirt with the garlands of hibiscus blossoms round her neck
is Jinxie Wicks. STRICTLY PLATONIC Mum, by the way,
don't panic… Bet Terry hasn't stopped moaning about me
upping stumps and cruising off into the sunshine without
warning. Remind him to give Bingo his worming pills.
Hope his baldness is improving (Bingo's, not Terry's). Can't
get long-reach toe-nail clippers on board for love or money.
Will explain all when I get back.
If I ever get back. Next stop Waikiki.
Your loving son,

Ronald

RONALD TONKS'S
READING LIST, 2012

Beautiful Losers	Leonard Cohen
The Old Devils	Kingsley Amis
The Sun King	Nancy Mitford
Silly Verse for Kids	Spike Milligan
D. H. Lawrence	Keith Sagar
Journals	Alice James
It Never Rains	Roger McGough
Dickens	Frank Kaplan
Iris Murdoch	A. N. Wilson
The God Delusion	Richard Dawkins
Liber Amoris	William Hazlitt
Lady Chatterley's Lover	D. H. Lawrence
Thomas Hardy	Claire Tomalin
Experience	Martin Amis
Taken Care Of	Edith Sitwell
The Works: The Classic Collection	Pam Ayres
George Formby	John Fisher
Dickens	Peter Ackroyd
Inside of a Dog	Alexandra Horovitz
Tess of the d'Urbervilles	Thomas Hardy
The Austerity Olympics	Janie Hampton
Dubliners	James Joyce
The First Circle	Alexander Solzhenitsyn
Palaces for Pigs	Lucinda Lambton
I'm Your Man	Sylvie Simmons
Peeping Tom	Howard Jacobson
Life	Keith Richards
Rogues, Villains and Eccentrics	William Donaldson
Selected Letters of Edith Sitwell	Richard Greene
Dubliners	James Joyce
The Penguin Book of English Verse	

ACKNOWLEDGEMENTS

My thanks to Naim Attallah and David Elliott, two unsung giants of independent publishing. To *Saga Magazine* in whose irresistible pages the seeds of Saltmarsh and Tonks-like mishaps were sown. To Sarah Horner for her computer wizardry and for deciphering my longhand. To Joanna Labon, Anna Fewings, Patsy Clarke, Sadie Hennessy and Brian Patten for urging me to keep on keeping on. To Liz Lukes Howe for her life-long friendship, Trevor Grundy for many hilarious emails, and Gordon Etheridge, whose Herne Bay City Ukers group takes music by the scruff of its neck and shakes it to within an inch of its life.

Thanks to all of you.

Val Hennessy